THE PARROT'S BEAK

A Viet Nam War Novel

By

1SG David Allin, USA, Ret.

Text copyright © 2016 David L Allin
All Rights Reserved

The Parrot's Beak is a work of fiction. Names, characters, and incidents are either the product of the author's imagination or are used fictitiously. Any resemblance to actual persons, living or dead, is entirely coincidental.

Cover photo by the author

Table of Contents

PROLOGUE 1
ONE 6
TWO 16
THREE 28
FOUR 38
FIVE 54
SIX 63
SEVEN 72
EIGHT 79
NINE 91
TEN 113
ELEVEN 123
TWELVE 134
THIRTEEN 144
FOURTEEN 152
FIFTEEN 166
SIXTEEN 176
SEVENTEEN 186
EIGHTEEN 195
NINETEEN 204
TWENTY 217
TWENTY-ONE 226
TWENTY-TWO 236
EPILOGUE 243

PROLOGUE

The two officers sat in flimsy metal folding chairs, gazing thoughtfully at the map mounted on an easel in front of them. Although the sides of the tent had been rolled halfway up, there was no breeze, and the heat and humidity were oppressive. The floor, made of PSP, the pierced steel planking normally used to make hasty airplane runways, still had water standing in the channels from last night's rain. Flies from the nearby shitter buzzed annoyingly around their ears, prompting repeated swats that accomplished nothing.

Lieutenant Colonel Rance Thompson, the battalion commander, had on neatly pressed jungle fatigues and polished boots only slightly blemished by splashed mud. His wavy black hair was neatly combed, and his blue eyes squinted as he studied the map. In his left hand was a yellow legal pad with hastily scribbled notes, and in his right was a pencil which he repetitively tapped with the West Point ring he wore.

In the other chair Major Elliott Howard, the battalion S-3 operations officer, patiently waited for Thompson to make a decision. Howard was medium height, medium build, and totally unremarkable in appearance. He was the perfect assistant—unobtrusive, agreeable, and willing to do whatever his superior proposed.

The map was of the battalion's AO—Area of Operations—with the EOB overlay. The Enemy Order of Battle consisted of various symbols marked on the clear plastic overlay with different colors of grease pencil, and purported to show all the enemy units in the area, along with their size and designators. It was all bullshit, of course, and everyone knew it. The S-2 Intelligence Officer updated it weekly, based mostly on years-old reports, wild-ass guesses, and dubious information from the South Vietnamese. A copy would be sent to Brigade, who would combine it with the other battalions and send it up to Division. Division would combine all three brigades and send a nice clean copy to Saigon, where the USARV generals would create a Theatre EOB map that would be sent to Washington to justify increased troop levels and additional equipment. It was all part of the game, but it had to be played with serious attention to detail. Officer promotions depended on it.

At the entrance to the tent, First Lieutenant Daniel Lewis cleared his throat and said, "Sir?"

Thompson and Howard turned to look at him, and Howard waved him in. Lewis was the battalion S-1 personnel and administration officer, and currently he also served as the Headquarters and Headquarters Company commander. Blonde, slender, and slightly effeminate, he was nonetheless a competent administrator. He carried a file folder in his left hand, and offered it to the colonel as he stepped forward. Thompson made no move to take it from him. Lewis pulled the file back and held it against his chest.

"Good news, bad news, sir," Lewis said.

"What?" Thompson said, a little impatiently.

"We just got in a new lieutenant, sir, First Lieutenant John Jones." Major Howard started to say something, then shut his mouth, suppressing a smile.

"About damn time," the colonel remarked testily. The battalion was short four junior officers, due to combat casualties and normal rotations. "Infantry?"

"Yes, sir. ROTC."

"Better than OCS," Howard interjected. The Reserve Officer Training Corps officers were college graduates who had just come on active duty, while the Officer Candidate School men were former enlisted who had spent six months at Fort Benning learning to be officers. The ROTC officers were more malleable than the OCS guys, who thought they already knew everything. The OCS officers also tended to try too hard to show they were officers and gentlemen, and no longer enlisted scum. Neither, of course, was as competent, professional, and suitably revered as West Point graduates, the wearers of the ring.

"So what's the bad news?" Thompson asked, sighing with resignation.

"He's black," Lewis said flatly.

"What?" Thompson's eyebrows rose in consternation.

"He's, uh, a soul brother, sir. A Negro."

"Oh, fuck me!" Thompson moaned. He laid his pad and pencil in his lap and covered his face with both hands, breathing deeply through the gap between them. Although the Army had been integrated for years, there had been very few black officers, especially in the infantry. The Viet Nam war, however, had increased the need for junior officers, and school integration in the civilian world had increased the number of blacks graduating from college. The inevitable result was now upon them.

"That's all I need," Thompson complained, lowering his hands. "The troops don't want to fight, they're smoking dope, and the soul brothers are the worst. A black officer will just encourage them."

"Maybe he'll improve their attitude," Howard offered optimistically.

"The Great Black Hope?" Thompson countered sarcastically. "I don't think so."

"So," Lewis said politely, "where should we assign him?"

"Third platoon, A Company?" Howard suggested. "They haven't had a platoon leader for a couple months."

"And Sergeant Helton is doing a fine job filling in," Thompson said. "I can't have a black officer upsetting that unit."

Other positions were suggested, and Thompson shot them all down. There was a long pause in the discussion as each man mulled over the possibilities. Finally Major Howard raised his index finger as a thought occurred to him.

"Jackson is about the DEROS anyway. Why don't we put this new guy in the CRIP platoon?" A couple years earlier each infantry battalion had been ordered to create a Combined Reconnaissance and Intelligence Platoon. Originally the platoon was to include South Vietnamese soldiers, and the concept was that they would make low-key patrols into the hamlets and villages, schmooze with the locals, and gather intelligence while winning the hearts and minds of the populace. Cultural differences between Americans and Vietnamese led to many issues and general disgruntlement, so the combined nature of the platoons slowly diminished until the only Vietnamese in most such platoons was a single Kit Carson scout, a former VC or NVA soldier who had surrendered and volunteered to work for the Americans.

The colonel gave Lewis a calculating look. As HHC commander, Lewis nominally controlled the platoon, but in reality it was under the operational command of the S-3. Thompson raised one eyebrow as he spoke: "In other words, put him in with the rest of the fuck-ups?"

Lewis had often complained that CRIP had become a dumping ground for problem soldiers, and that idea was not without basis. Soldiers who couldn't seem to get along with their officers or NCOs, or with the other members of their platoon, were sometimes transferred to CRIP just to avoid a lot of paperwork.

"Actually," Major Howard said thoughtfully, "that's not such a bad idea. That way he wouldn't disrupt any of the line units, and he'd be here where we can keep an eye on him. And you never know, maybe those guys would respond to him better than they do to our regular officers." It was understood that by "regular" officers, Howard meant "white" officers.

Thompson scratched his ear while he considered the proposal. "Okay," he finally said, "that'll work. For now, at least."

"Do you want to meet with him now?" Lewis asked. It was standard operating procedure for new officers to have a meeting with the battalion commander so he could brief them on their mission and impress upon them his command philosophy. Basically it was a combination of rah-rah encouragement and a dire warning of what might happen if they screwed up.

"No," the colonel replied quickly. "I've got to go to Division. Maybe when I get back. Or maybe not."

Lewis nodded in understanding. He turned and left. Thompson and Howard resumed staring at the EOB map.

ONE

Specialist Fourth Class Thomas Daley was bored. It was after 2:00 a.m., and he was sitting on top of a bunker on the perimeter of the base camp, staring across the rice paddies to the far distant tree line, just trying to stay awake. Scattered high clouds muted or covered the myriad stars overhead, and a quarter moon was setting behind him. His butt was wet from the sand bags still soaked by the rain in the afternoon, and despite the actual temperature, he was starting to feel a little chilled. After you had been in Nam for a while, any time the temperature dropped below eighty it felt cool. A few weeks ago there had been a cold snap that lowered temps into the sixties, and Daley had seen Vietnamese huddled in blankets and bundled up in field jackets. He had heard that in Saigon an old man had died of exposure. He supposed it all depended on what you were used to.

Another hour to go before he could wake his relief—Tankersly?—who was sleeping in the bunker below him. Daley didn't really know the other guys who manned this bunker on the base camp berm; it was a rotating duty assigned to all of the base camp warriors, and Daley's name had come up on the roster. He wouldn't have the duty again for a couple weeks, or at least he hoped so. This was too much like being a real soldier, he thought. Daley was in military intelligence, an interrogator/translator, and spent his days questioning captured or surrendered Vietnamese and writing up reports, all in the relative comfort of wooden buildings not far from the mess hall and the PX. Sure, he was in Viet Nam, but he was better off than those poor bastards that had to hump the boonies every day. So an occasional night standing guard on the berm wasn't really a major hardship. It was just boring, and interfered with his sleep.

If only he had made better choices. For instance, if he had taken ROTC in college, he'd be an officer now. And if he had majored in something better than geology, he might have been able to dodge the draft longer, or been able to get a direct commission. He still wasn't sure he had made the right decision when he enlisted rather than wait to be drafted. Yes, it kept him out of the infantry, but it meant a four-year commitment instead of two. Of course, it hadn't helped that the recruiters had lied to him when he joined up. When he took the Defense Language Aptitude Test, he found it fairly easy due to his having taken Latin in high school and German in college, and he had scored very highly. The recruiter said Daley qualified for the Defense Language Institute in Monterey, California, and had painted a picture of a paradise on the beach.

It sounded like a good deal, and language school would delay his being permanently assigned anywhere for almost a year, perhaps time enough for the war to be over. The recruiter even said he could request to take whatever language he wanted, and Daley wanted to learn more German. And what the recruiter told him was mostly true—he could request any language, but that didn't mean he would get it. It turned out that the "needs of the Army" outweighed any request or promise made by the recruiters. After Basic Training Daley was sent to Monterey to learn German, only to be told when he arrived that his orders were incorrect. He was put on casual duty for three months while they straightened things out, and then he was sent to Biggs Air Force Base, Texas, near El Paso, to take Vietnamese. Eight months of grueling classwork had given him just enough Vietnamese fluency to get by. Eight weeks of interrogator training at Ft. Huachuca, Arizona, followed, and then off to the war zone.

Out of the corner of his eye Daley caught a flicker of light in the distant trees, like someone had lit a cigarette or briefly turned on a flashlight. His first thought was to mentally chastise whoever it was for violating the rules of light discipline, imagining some infantry patrol out there wandering around in the dark. Then he saw the shower of sparks climbing into the air and arcing toward the base camp, leaving a trail of smoke illuminated by the fiery discharge. Although he had never seen one before, Daley knew what it was—a rocket.

"Incoming!" he yelled as he grabbed his rifle and jumped off the roof of the bunker, seeking the entrance. He fell through the narrow opening and sprawled on the muddy floor of the bunker, yelling "Rockets!" The whoosh of the missile was now audible, growing in intensity as the rocket neared their location. An explosion somewhere outside the bunker shook sand from the roof and lit the interior of the bunker for an instant.

"Did you call it in?" one of the other guys in the bunker asked. Daley felt a twinge of guilt, but it quickly passed. There had been no time for that, and the explosion was self-explanatory.

"No," Daley said sarcastically, sitting up, "but I'll go back up top and do that in just a minute. In case nobody else heard anything." The bunkers along the berm were connected to a central command post by landline, and the field telephone was left on top of the bunker so the person on guard could call in regular situation reports.

A couple of the guys had stood up and were looking out the gun ports near the roof the bunker. "There's more coming," one of them said conversationally. They all heard the whistling sound of the rockets and ducked down to await the detonations. These were not as close, sounding like they were farther inside the base camp.

"You gotta go call it in," one of the guys told Daley. From the sound of his voice, Daley was pretty sure it was the sergeant, an infantry guy on light duty while he recovered from his wounds.

"Why me?"

"Because," the man said calmly and reasonably, "you saw the first one launch, and can tell them where it came from."

Daley reluctantly accepted the logic, and cautiously stepped out of the bunker.

"Just bring the phone in here," one of the other guys suggested, and Daley silently thanked him for offering a safer alternative. He scrambled up the side of the bunker, keeping a wary eye out toward the horizon for more rocket trails, grabbed the canvas-covered field phone and headed back down. He had gone only a few feet when the phone wire went taut and nearly jerked the phone out of his hand. Daley tugged at the wire, and finally realized it was caught under a sandbag. A flash from the tree line caught his attention just as he climbed back up on top to free the wire, and he was torn with indecision—duck inside or free the line? Cursing his own stupidity, he crawled across the roof and pulled the wire free, watching the trail of the rocket at the same time, hoping it was headed somewhere else. With relief he noted that the rocket passed way overhead and impacted several hundred yards inside the base camp.

With the phone line no longer tangled, he climbed back down and reentered the bunker. Leaning his rifle against the side of the bunker, he lifted the handset and cradled it between his shoulder and his cheek while he spun the ringer on the side of the base.

"What?" yelled a tinny voice on the phone.

"This is bunker. . ." Daley couldn't remember the designator for this bunker. The sergeant told him it was Echo Seven. ". . . Echo Seven. We have rockets being fired from our front."

"No shit," the voice on the phone said angrily. "Tell me something I don't know."

"Just reporting," Daley stammered. "No one is hurt here. I saw where they're coming from."

"Yeah, yeah, we know. Just watch for a ground attack. Out."

Daley returned the handset to the cradle and set the phone down on a sandbag ledge. "He says to watch for a ground attack," Daley told the others.

He heard distant explosions, and one of the guys at the gun ports said, "Counter-battery fire. They're plastering the little bastards now." Daley moved to an unoccupied port and looked out to see flashes as artillery rounds blasted the tree line. They were nowhere near the area where Daley had seen the rockets launch from. He wondered if he should call back in and try to redirect the fire, but decided it would be a wasted effort. No one would listen to him anyway.

About ten minutes after the last incoming rocket had been heard, and as the arty fire on the tree line began to diminish, the sergeant told Daley to go back up top and resume his watch. Dragging the phone with him, Daley reluctantly complied. Some mortar battery was periodically launching parachute flares that illuminated the paddies and trees outside the perimeter. The slowly descending flares made shadows move, as if there were gooks approaching stealthily. Daley took up a prone position and watched the area to his front carefully, trying to ensure that the moving shadows were just that, and not an assault. The fact that other soldiers were depending on him to detect an attack weighed heavily on his conscience, but at least it kept him awake and attentive.

From the south he heard the approach of a large propeller-driven aircraft, and guessed that it must be a Spooky, the cargo plane converted to a gunship that often patrolled the night sky. Although it was invisible in the dark, Daley could tell from the sound that it had begun circling overhead. Then its minigun opened up, and Daley was overcome with awe. The Gatling-style gun roared with an angry growl and sent a glowing red stream of tracers toward the ground. Six thousand rounds a minute, Daley had heard. Like bright crimson water from a powerful fire hose, the bullets poured down at a terrible rate, and Daley could only imagine what it was like on the ground beneath that onslaught. The attack lasted only a minute or two, and then the Spooky flew back south, probably out of ammo. It was an amazing show of American technological superiority. Daley felt a little safer now.

After berm guard was over in the morning, Daley dumped his gear at the barracks hooch and went to breakfast at the mess hall. When he returned to his bunk, he was surprised to see Major Wheeler, his commander, waiting for him just outside the entrance. The barracks was a long low wooden building with a corrugated tin roof and a two-foot high wall of sandbags around the base. The lower half of the walls were wooden planks attached at an angle that matched the eaves of the roof, and the upper half was screen wire to keep out the bugs. There were open doorways at both ends, with no actual doors mounted in them. The major was sitting on the sandbags next to the doorway.

"Rough night, Tom?" Major Wheeler greeted him, standing up to meet him.

"Got rocketed," Daley said as if it happened every day.

"I heard. Look, why don't you take the morning off and catch up on your sleep? There's not much going on, and the other guys can handle it." The major was a pudgy red-head, and he was smiling in what Daley guessed was supposed to be an avuncular way. Hardly a hard-core officer, Wheeler went out of his way to be liked by his subordinates, but as a result they didn't respect him and took advantage of his generosity. Despite that, Daley liked him, and didn't talk bad about him like the others. In this case, however, he was going to accept what was offered.

"Thanks, sir. I'm really bushed."

"No problem, Tom. You can report to work after lunch. Take it easy." Wheeler patted Daley on the shoulder and walked away.

Daley entered the hooch and sat down on his bunk, which was near the middle of the hooch. Like most of the other residents, he had created the illusion of privacy by hanging plastic strip curtains purchased from the Vietnamese around his cot. The dividers were basically flowered shower curtains that had been sliced into three-inch strips and hung from thin stalks of bamboo. The rest of the occupants of the hooch were gone, presumably to work. Daley stripped to his boxers, slipped his feet into his flip-flops, grabbed his shaving gear, a towel, and a bar of soap, and headed for the crude shower area behind the barracks area.

After showering, he shaved at the make-shift sinks and mirrors just outside the wooden shower stalls. Someone had made a shelf that held three old helmets, minus their liners and camo covers, and put small metal mirrors above them. After setting down his glasses, towel and soap, Daley filled one with water, lathered up, and began drawing the safety razor across his face. His mousy brown hair was kept fairly short, but his new moustache was filling in nicely. When the Army had finally allowed moustaches, Daley had started growing his immediately. It had taken a couple months to get the way he wanted it; he had grown it mostly so he could look more mature. He was twenty-two, but still looked sixteen. He was thin—

Daley liked to think he was wiry—and he had no discernible muscles. Yet he was strong enough for his size, he felt, and had plenty of stamina.

Back in the barracks Daley lay down on his cot wearing just his boxers and closed the mosquito net. He tried to sleep, but the morning heat and the constant noise from the normal base camp activities made that impossible. And truth be told, he was still a little buzzed by the rocket attack in the night. It was the most excitement he had experienced since arriving in Nam three months earlier. His normal daily duties involved asking a set list of questions to every prisoner and Chieu Hoi that came through, writing up the results, and occasionally translating captured documents. It was basically a nine-to-five job, leaving plenty of time to go the PX or EM club, or just hang around the barracks hooch. There had been rocket and mortar attacks on the base camp before, but never when Daley was on the perimeter, and usually on some other part of the base camp, causing only a brief interruption in his sleep. Last night had been different—he had seen the rockets launched, heard them fly overhead, and seen the flash when they hit. It had been scary, but thrilling. Now he had a war story to tell.

While there were hundreds of thousands of GIs in Viet Nam—soldiers, sailors, airmen, marines—only about ten or fifteen percent were actually engaging the enemy in combat. The rest, like Daley, were support personnel. The more polite designation was base camp warriors, but Daley had heard that the guys in the field referred to them scathingly as remfs—rear echelon mother-fuckers. Although he was mildly insulted, Daley rationalized that everyone had their own part to play in the war, and each job was essential to achieving victory. On the other hand, he couldn't help thinking about how he would answer his potential children when they asked, "What did you do in the war, Daddy?" He wanted to be proud of his service, even if it was part of a war that increasingly seemed pointless.

After tossing and turning on the cot for an hour, he tried reading one of the paperback novels from the SP packs, but couldn't get into it. Finally he gave up and got dressed, then sat on his cot and wrote letters home. He was just sealing the envelopes when a couple guys entered the hooch and plopped down on folding chairs around the small table that comprised the hooch's "day room." It was Montgomery and Meyer, who were collectively referred to as "the M&Ms" by the other guys in the unit, since they were always together. Daley pushed through the curtains around his cot, letters in hand, and started down the center aisle toward the door.

"Hey, Daley," Meyer called out, "what are you doing here?"

"The major gave me the morning off, since I was on berm guard last night." Daley stopped by the table and nodded at the two young men.

"No shit?" Montgomery said. "That was pretty white of him."

"Yeah, he's a candy ass," Meyer remarked dismissively. "You didn't miss nothin' anyway. Only three gooks today. We took off for lunch early."

Montgomery pulled a box of Marlboros out of his shirt pocket, flipped the lid, and drew out a cigarette. The end was twisted shut, so Daley knew that meant it was filled with marijuana, not tobacco. He had seen the M&Ms and other guys carefully remove the shredded tobacco from filter cigarettes and repack the paper tubes with grass. Some had been offered to Daley, but so far he had resisted. Montgomery lit up and took a deep drag, holding it in his lungs while he passed the joint to Meyer.

"You guys are gonna get caught one of these days," Daley warned them.

Montgomery finally exhaled a cloud of smoke and smiled. "Fuck 'em if they can't take a joke," he said caustically.

Meyer passed the joint back to Montgomery and let smoke trickle from his lips. "Yeah, what are they gonna do, send us to Viet Nam?"

"They could put you in LBJ," Daley suggested. LBJ was Long Binh Jail, the main prison for American military criminals.

"So what?" Montgomery said. "It's still three hots and cot, just like here."

"Ain't gonna happen anyway," Meyer retorted. "Wheeler don't give a shit. He's just serving his time here like us."

Daley had to admit Meyer was probably right. Major Wheeler had skillfully avoided noticing the rampant drug use in the unit, despite ample evidence. He decided his preaching was a waste of time.

"I got to mail these letters," he told them, holding the envelopes up for them to see. "I'll see you at the compound after lunch." He started for the door, but stopped when Montgomery waved at him. He waited for Montgomery to let the smoke out of his lungs before he could speak.

"Kowalski wants to see you today," he said. "At his trailer."

"Kowalski? What for?" Mr. Kowalski was a civilian who worked with the intel unit, a tall thin, gray-haired man who always wore black slacks and white short-sleeved shirts. Supposedly he was with the State Department, but everyone suspected he was really CIA. He had a small house trailer that served as his office and sleeping area.

"Fuck if we know," Meyer answered. "Maybe he needs a blow job."

Montgomery chuckled at this witticism and passed the joint to Meyer. Daley just shook his head and left.

Kowalski's trailer was about 30 feet long, with a three-foot wall of sandbags around it. When Daley knocked on the door, the civilian opened the door with a sandwich in his hand, saw who it was, held up an index finger to wait because his mouth was full, and closed the door. A minute later he opened the door and stepped out, this time with a file folder in his hand instead of a sandwich. As far as Daley knew, no one had ever been inside the trailer but Kowalski.

"Specialist Daley," Kowalski said, guiding him away from the trailer to the shade of a small tree. "Good to see you. Are you really busy right now?"

Daley shrugged. "Just the usual, sir."

"Good. Good. I've got a little project I'd like you to help me with."

"Okay. I'd have to check with Major Wheeler."

"No need, I've already done that. He approves." Kowalski opened the file folder and took out a typed list of names. "You know that questionnaire you use to interrogate the prisoners?"

"Sure," Daley said, wondering where this was going.

"Well, as you know, it's kind of limited in scope, and doesn't allow for much follow-up. The major and I believe there might be more information available if we ask the right questions, and we think you're just the man for the job."

Daley didn't like the sound of that, despite the implied praise. He was pretty sure he was being volunteered for something, and that was never good. He decided to temporize. "What sort of information, sir?"

"There are a lot of GIs and airmen that are listed as missing in action, and the presumption is that at least some of them might be prisoners of war, held by the VC or NVA. Now, the questionnaire doesn't address that issue, but we've been reviewing the completed questionnaires we have and believe that some of the prisoners, based on their function or location, may have seen or heard something that would help us find those men."

"Okay," Daley hedged.

Kowalski hand the typed page to Daley. "Here's the list. We'd like you to re-interview these men, specifically asking them about American POWs."

"When?" Daley knew he was trapped.

"Starting this afternoon. I've already cleared it with Major Wheeler, and spoken to the MPs at the prisoner compound. It's all arranged."

"Yes, sir," Daley said glumly, and turned to go.

"Of course, I'll need a full written report if you find anything," Kowalski said. Daley just nodded.

TWO

By the next afternoon Daley had interrogated more than a dozen POWs and Chieu Hois, all of whom had the same answer to his question: "I don't know." It wasn't surprising from the POWs, most of whom had been wounded in battle, but Daley had hoped that the Chieu Hois would be more helpful. Chieu Hoi—Vietnamese for Open Arms—was a program the Americans had forced on the South Vietnamese government in yet another of the less-than-totally-successful attempts to win the hearts and minds of the people. Through a leafletting campaign the Viet Cong and NVA were informed that if they voluntarily surrendered they would be greeted with "open arms" and given various benefits, including vocational assistance. While Chieu Hois could volunteer to serve in the Army of the Republic of Viet Nam or work as Kit Carson scouts for the Americans, they were exempt from the South Vietnamese draft, a key feature for many young men. It was common for South Vietnamese teenagers who were about to be drafted to suddenly disappear into the jungle, only to reappear a short time later claiming to have been VC but now wanting to participate in the Chieu Hoi program. It was a racket that everyone turned a blind eye to.

Daley finished interviewing a North Vietnamese Army soldier with one leg missing below the knee. The man, who claimed to be an officer, refused to tell Daley anything useful, barking out "I don't know" repetitively. Daley had him escorted back to the prisoner compound and filled in his notes on a pad of paper that was devoid of anything worthy of reporting. A few minutes later the MP Daley had been assigned with brought in the next one on the list. Like almost all the others, he was young, about five-two, slender, with brown hair and brown eyes. The homogeneity of the Vietnamese people made written descriptions mostly a waste of time, unless the individual had some obvious distinguishing mark. Daley told the young man to sit.

They were in a small room furnished only with two chairs and a small wooden table. Barred windows provided the only light. Daley turned to a clean page on his pad of paper, noted the date and time at the top, and then asked the man his name.

"Nguyen Van Ky," he answered readily. He smiled as Daley wrote it down.

Daley knew his command of the Vietnamese language wasn't that great, but he could generally make himself understood. He sorted through a stack of questionnaires and found the one for Ky. From the name, he knew the man was from a South Vietnamese family. North Vietnamese used different naming conventions, although for all Vietnamese the first name was their family name, equivalent to an American's last name. South Vietnamese men usually had the middle name Van, and the last element of their name was their given name. Nguyen was by far the most common surname for those in the south. Daley reviewed the questionnaire that had been filled out the first time Ky was interrogated; it had been done by Montgomery, and was typically sparse in detail.

"So, Ky," Daley began, "I see that you operated in the area near the Cambodian border."

"Yes," Ky said, nodding and smiling.

"And you were in the Viet Cong there?"

"Yes," Ky replied, frowning. "They were bad people."

All the Chieu Hois said that, Daley knew. But what would you expect? They had just defected, and wanted to please their new masters.

"Did you ever work with the North Vietnamese Army?"

"Oh, yes, many times. They are very bad people, too."

"Of course. And why were they bad? Did they mistreat you?"

Ky pursed his lips and looked down. After a moment he replied, still looking at his hands which were handcuffed in his lap. "Not really. They didn't feed us as well as they fed their own soldiers, and made jokes about us, but that's all."

Daley made some notes, then looked up and asked, "Why did you decide to defect?"

Ky raised both hands so he could scratch his head with one of them. "They gave us classes every day about Communism and the workers' state. I didn't believe them. The Northerners just want to take over our land and steal our rice."

Daley wrote this down, surprised at the young man's political awareness. He seemed to truly understand the motives and aims of the communists, and wasn't just parroting slogans. Despite the propaganda on both sides about the ideological struggle between communism and democracy, Daley had concluded that the real issues were economic. North Viet Nam was an industrialized nation, while South Viet Nam was primarily agricultural. The North needed the produce that the South grew in order to support its growing population. South Viet Nam was one of the greatest rice-growing areas in the world, and even China wanted access to this bounty. The South Vietnamese realized that under a communist regime imposed from Hanoi, their land and rice harvests would become the property of the state, depriving them of their just profits.

"Before you joined the Viet Cong," Daley asked, "did you grow rice?"

"Of course," Ky replied, confused by the question. In South Viet Nam, almost everyone grew rice. "The Northerners don't know how to do it right. I saw some of their paddies in Cambodia, and they were doing it all wrong."

"Cambodia?" Daley was suddenly very interested. All the intelligence agencies wanted to know about what was going on in Cambodia with the NVA. Cambodia was a neutral county, and the American soldiers had been warned about the political complications that could ensue if they violated the Cambodians' neutrality. The NVA, however, had no such compunctions, and it was common knowledge that they had sanctuaries there from which they infiltrated into South Viet Nam. "When were you in Cambodia?"

"Several months ago," Ky answered. "My unit was delivering American rice to the Northerners there."

"Was there an NVA base there? With many soldiers?"

"Oh, yes. It was hidden in the trees, so I don't know how many soldiers, but from the amount of rice we brought them, I guess there were several hundred."

"And it was American rice? How do you know? Where did it come from?" Daley was jotting down notes as fast as he could write.

"The bags all said 'Product of USA' on them. I was told they came from a South Vietnamese District Chief who is corrupt."

That wasn't so surprising. Corruption was rampant among local officials. The District Chief had probably made a profit of it somehow.

"How many bags did you deliver?" Daley asked.

"Two hundred and seventeen," Ky replied. "I had to count them when we picked them up and again when we delivered them, to make sure none were stolen along the way."

"Where in Cambodia was this?"

Ky shook his head dolefully. "I do not know, sergeant. I am not very good with maps or directions. I could find it, though, I think." Although Daley was only a specialist, he decided to let Ky call him sergeant if it helped him talk.

"What sort of base was it? What were they doing there?"

"I think maybe it was a hospital camp. I saw many men with bandages and crutches."

Daley wrote this down and tried to think what other questions he had.

"We went by the French fort to get there," Ky offered.

"To get where?"

"To that base in Cambodia. The fort is in Viet Nam, I think."

Daley knew there were several old French forts in the area, left over from colonial days. Some were just blockhouses along roads or bridges, and others were fairly large enclosures with stone walls and revetments. "Where is the French fort?" Daley asked, hoping to be able to triangulate from the fort to the base in Cambodia.

Ky winced and lowered his head. "I do not know, sergeant. It is across the river, in some jungle. I could find it, I think."

"The Vam Co Dong River?"

Ky nodded. "We had to cross the river in small boats at night. Your big patrol boats kept coming by, making us hide in the reeds." The US Navy had a fleet of river patrol boats and landing craft that tried to interdict any communist infiltration across the rivers, but obviously they weren't one hundred percent successful. Despite Ky's earlier comments, Daley pulled a map from his messenger bag, one showing the area between Tay Ninh and the Cambodian border. The map showed the location of a few of the larger French forts, and Daley pointed them out to Ky, while tracing his finger along the blue line that represented the river. Ky just shook his head and shrugged. Maps were Greek to him. Daley tried to narrow it down.

"Was the fort near the river?" he asked.

"I think it was about ten or fifteen kilometers from the river. It took us all night to get there." Ky was smiling again, apparently glad that he could help at least a little.

"What did it look like? How big is it?"

Ky looked up at the ceiling and closed his eyes, obviously trying to recover a visual image. After a moment he said, "It is about the size of four rice paddies. There is one big cement building in the corner, a smaller building in the other corner, and cement walls connecting them. The big building is two stories high, with a round metal box on top."

"Is it in the open, or is it in the jungle?" While Ky answered, Daley began drawing a rough schematic of the fort on a sheet of paper.

"It is in a small patch of jungle. There are open plains and reeds around the jungle."

Daley showed Ky his drawing, but Ky shook his head and took the pencil, modifying the drawing with quick strokes that demonstrated a fair amount of artistic talent. Daley took it back and studied it for a moment while he gathered his thoughts.

"It's abandoned, correct?" Daley asked.

"Yes, the French left many years ago," Ky said. "Now the Northerners are there."

"The North Vietnamese Army is occupying the fort?" Daley was a little surprised. The NVA normally shunned fixed locations and buildings.

"Oh, yes. There are many soldiers there, with guns and rockets and mortars. We stopped there to rest one day on our trip to Cambodia. It is hard to see the fort because of the trees, so American planes and helicopters do not attack it."

"How many men are there?"

"Perhaps fifty, or more. There were many officers, and radio antennas."

"Could it be a command and control center?" Daley asked, scribbling away on his pad.

"I am not sure what that is," Ky replied.

"A place where the senior officers plan operations and tell units where to go and when to attack," Daley explained.

"It could be that," Ky agreed without conviction.

Daley remembered what the purpose of this interview was, and finally asked, "Have you ever seen any Americans being held prisoner by the NVA or Viet Cong?"

"No Americans, sergeant. Just the foreigners at the fort."

"Foreigners?" Daley was now truly intrigued. Ky's story was getting more and more interesting. He had to remind himself that it all might be a fantasy that Ky was making up as he went along, just to impress Daley, but Ky seemed sincere.

"Just before we left in the evening, I saw two foreigners walking with an officer into the big building. One was Chinese, and the other was white, but not American."

"How do you know he wasn't American?"

"His uniform was different. He wore his rank on his shoulders, on small boards. He had three symbols on each board."

Daley was now very excited. This was tremendous intelligence. It was accepted that there were Chinese and Russian advisers in North Viet Nam, but there had been no reports or even hints that these advisers had ventured south of the DMZ.

"What kind of symbols?" Daley asked, hoping they would be stars that indicated a senior officer.

"I couldn't see them well enough to say for sure. They looked kind of like flowers. The Chinese man had no rank at all that I could see."

"What color were these boards on the white man's uniform?" Daley asked. He seemed to remember that Russian officers had red shoulder boards.

"It was already dark," Ky explained. "I couldn't tell what color for sure. Maybe red, maybe brown."

Now Daley felt his level of interest growing exponentially. The presence of Chinese and Russian advisers in South Viet Nam would be a major intelligence break, giving the U.S. a significant revelation to trumpet on the international stage and justify the continuation of the war. Such advisers would prove that the communist effort was not a national uprising of the Vietnamese struggling to be independent, as Ho Chi Minh claimed, but instead was a nefarious plot by the communist bloc to keep pushing over the dominoes.

"What were these foreigners doing?" Daley asked. Ky gave him a look that indicated he saw the increased interest on Daley's face.

"They were walking into the building with an NVA officer and two soldiers. I just saw them for a few seconds." Ky's expression was earnest. Daley mulled over this statement and decided the advisers—he was now convinced that was what they were—were meeting with the fort's commander to discuss plans for upcoming operations. It made perfect sense. He seemed to remember reading that the Chinese People's Army didn't have ranks, as such, so the lack of badges on the Chinese man's uniform was actually confirmation of his identity.

"And you just saw them once," Daley asked, "just before your unit left the fort?"

"Yes, sergeant."

"Did you stop at the fort on the way back from Cambodia?"

"No. We traveled a different route back. Since we no longer had the rice to carry, we were able to move more quickly."

"Okay. Okay." Daley kept making notes, already composing the report he would write for Mr. Kowalski. "Here. Look at this map. See if you can figure out where that fort is." He pushed the map across the table again, and placed his finger on it. "This is where we are now. And here is the Vam Co Dong River." Daley slid his finger along the blue line of the river, and then jumped to a wide red line. "And here is the Cambodian border."

Ky leaned over to study the map, but his posture and expression made it clear he had no idea what he was looking at. He sat back and shrugged. "I don't understand maps," he explained apologetically. "But I could take you there. I remember the way."

That, Daley knew, wasn't likely to happen. He asked Ky more questions, but it became evident that Ky had told him all he could. Anxious to write up the report, he finally turned Ky over to the MP for return to the prisoner compound. He told the MP he would not be doing any more interrogations that day, then gathered up his notes and hurried back to the hooch that served as the interrogators' office. He couldn't wait to get it all down on paper.

Using a portable typewriter he had bought at the PX, Daley typed up his report, pausing often to search for the right word or phrase that would fully convey the significance of the information. Although he knew he should limit the report to actual facts, he couldn't help interpreting, extrapolating, and inferring what Ky had told him. He then took his first draft out of the typewriter and marked it up with a red pencil when he spotted errors or places he wanted to expand. Then he put two fresh sheets of paper, with carbon paper in between, into the little machine and carefully typed up his final version of the report. At the top was the title: "Interrogation of Nguyen Van Ky conducted by SP4 Thomas Daley", and the date. He wanted to make sure he got credit for the work.

By late afternoon he was ready. After filing the carbon copy in the team's filing cabinet, he placed the original in a manila folder and rushed over to Mr. Kowalski's trailer. Daley rapped twice on the aluminum door and stepped back from the short staircase. After a moment the door opened a few inches and Kowalski stuck just his head out. "Yes?" the older man said, raising an eyebrow.

"Sir," Daley told him earnestly, "I just interrogated a Chieu Hoi named Nguyen Van Ky, and he gave me some information that I'm sure you'll want to see immediately." Kowalski furrowed his brow, apparently not remembering the assignment he had given Daley. Then his face cleared.

"Right. You've been re-interviewing about possible American POWs. Has he seen some?" Kowalski opened the door just a little wider, but his body blocked Daley's view of the interior.

"Not exactly, sir," Daley said, holding out the folder. "But he may have seen Chinese and Russian advisors here in Viet Nam."

"Surely not," Kowalski demurred, shaking his head. "But, here, let me see that." He took the folder, opened it so he could read the report. Daley watched Kowalski's bushy gray eyebrows slowly rise as he read through the report. He closed the folder and told Daley, "Wait right there." With that he disappeared back inside the trailer and closed the door firmly. Daley stood there in the hot sun, wondering what Kowalski was doing inside. Perhaps calling someone else to relay the news? Daley looked around for some relief from the afternoon sun, but the only nearby shade was right up next to the trailer, and it would like he was eavesdropping if he moved there. So he just baked.

Finally the trailer's door opened, and Kowalski motioned him inside. "Sorry you had to wait out there," Kowalski told him as he climbed the steps, "but I had to straighten up a little." Daley almost stumbled on the top step; the interior of the trailer was very dark coming in out of the bright sun. The blinds were drawn and curtains were mostly closed over them. As his eyes adjusted to the dimness, Daley saw that he was in a small living area, with a very basic couch covered in dark green fabric, a small matching easy chair, and a built-in desk with a stool. Behind the couch, at the front end of the trailer, was a wide window just visible through the curtains. Opposite the couch, just beyond the desk, was a short bar that separated the living room from a tiny kitchenette.

"Take a seat," Kowalski told him, waving at the couch. Daley carefully lowered himself onto the cheap-looking piece of furniture, afraid it might collapse under him. While Kowalski sat down in the easy chair and began re-reading the report, which he had pulled from the breakfast bar, Daley stared with curiosity at the interior of the trailer. Despite its obvious cheapness, it seemed far more luxurious that the hooches and tents Daley was used to in Viet Nam, almost like a touch of home. The interior was immaculate, making Daley wonder what had taken Kowalski so long to straighten up. Then he noticed the total absence of letters, magazines, papers, or any other sign that the area was actually lived in. Only a map of South Viet Nam decorated the walls. Then he noticed that the desktop was draped with a thin black cloth that covered rectangular lumps. Security of classified materials, Daley realized. That's why Kowalski made him wait—he had to put away or cover anything that might be classified or reveal what he was working on. Daley felt a little flash of pride for having figured this out.

"So this Ky fellow believed these men were advisors?" Kowalski suddenly asked.

"He didn't know who they were, sir, but what else could they be? A Chinese man and an officer with shoulder boards for rank. Red ones."

"Or brown," Kowalski corrected him, reading from the report. "True, those are usually only used by European armies."

"Right," Daley agreed. "And what other Europeans would be working with the NVA? Ky said he had blond hair. Must have been Russian."

"But why would a Russian and a Chinese advisor be here in South Viet Nam. They know that would be a tremendous risk."

"I know," Daley agreed enthusiastically, leaning forward to put his elbows on his knees. "The publicity alone would be really damaging. And wouldn't that be against international law?"

"Not exactly," Kowalski told him with a brief shake of his head. "But it would pose the risk of an escalation of the war. I mean, we know they're helping the North, but they've denied any direct assistance other than supplying arms and equipment. If we caught them here, it would be a major coup politically." Kowalski stood and walked over to the map pinned to the wall, studying it intently. "Now where would this French fort be?" he mused.

"From the way Ky described it," Daley offered, "it can't be too far across the river. Is there a map that shows all the old French forts?"

Kowalski shook his head. "There may have been at one time, but I've never seen one. The French put up forts and outposts all over Indochina, some of them almost a hundred years ago. So there's no telling when this one was built or abandoned. Presumably it was located along a road or river, but that area hasn't been populated for years, so the road could have been overgrown, or the stream changed course. The fort was probably built before Indochina was subdivided into Viet Nam, Cambodia, and Laos, and was no longer needed afterwards."

"Ky says he could find it again," Daley said encouragingly.

"I'm sure he would say that," Kowalski replied. "But that could just be a ploy."

"For what? He's a Chieu Hoi. He turned himself in voluntarily. And, I don't know, I kind of believe him."

Kowalski turned and gave Daley an appraising look. Then he gave Daley a brief nod. "You may be right," he said. "Let me think about this, discuss it with some others. And thank you, Specialist Daley, this may be a real breakthrough. If this pans out, I'll see that you get a medal."

Daley understood he was being dismissed, and rose to leave. "Thank you, sir, but I'm just doing my job."

"But better than most," Kowalski commented as he politely ushered Daley out of the trailer.

THREE

"Hey, Daley, dickhead wants to see you." Meyer had just stuck his head in the door of the interrogation room where Daley was finishing up a questionnaire. The latest prisoner had already been sent back to the compound, another in an endless stream of fruitless interviews. Daley had finished the Kowalski project the day before, with none of the other subjects admitting to anything, and now he was back doing his normal routine. It had been two days since his conversation in Kowalski's trailer, and Daley had decided that the civilian had essentially dismissed Ky's assertions as bogus. Which meant no medal for Daley, not that it was a big deal, Daley told himself.

"Which dickhead?" he asked Meyer.

"Wheeler. He's at the office."

"Okay, I'm coming."

"Wish I was," Meyer said lasciviously, turning to leave. "I need to go downtown to the whorehouse again."

Daley just rolled his eyes as he gathered up his papers.

When Daley walked into the office hooch, he found Major Wheeler sitting at a desk in the main area reading the latest edition of *The Stars and Stripes* newspaper. As soon as he saw Daley, Wheeler quickly folded the paper and stood up to meet him.

"Tom, good to see you," Wheeler said. "Come on into my office." A small section at the back of the office hooch had been partitioned off with plywood into an eight-by-eight cubicle with a desk and two chairs. It even had a flimsy door that Wheeler closed once they were both inside. "Have a seat," he said, maneuvering around Daley and the desk so he could sit in the chair behind it. Daley sat down, setting his stack of papers on the floor beside him.

"Problem, sir?" Daley asked, wondering what this was all about.

"Definitely not," Wheeler assured him. "I was just talking to Mr. Kowalski, and he told me about your interview with that Chieu Hoi."

Daley realized he hadn't told Wheeler about it, even though Wheeler was technically his boss. He thought that the Major might be pissed at him for going around him. "I meant to tell you about that, sir," Daley sputtered, "but I wasn't sure if it was anything yet."

Wheeler waved his hand dismissively. "That's okay, I understand. Need to know, and all. But Kowalski thinks there might be something there. Thinks we need to investigate."

"You want me to interview Ky again?" Daley guessed.

"Better than that," Wheler said, nodding sagely. "We want to send Ky out with a patrol to locate this French fort and see if there really are advisors there."

"Great!" Daley said enthusiastically. Maybe he would get a medal after all.

"Well," Wheeler hedged, "that's the good news. The bad news is you'll have to go with him."

"Sir?" Daley frowned.

"Since Ky speaks no English, and you've developed a rapport with him, we think it would be best if you go along. You'd also be escorting him as a guard, since technically he is still a prisoner."

"Out in the field, sir?" Daley was almost whining. He had not expected this.

"Well, certainly. Since he can't locate this fort on a map, he'll have to show the patrol how to get there on the ground. Is there a problem with you going to the field?"

Daley took a deep breath. "I'm an interrogator, sir. The last time I was in the field was in Basic Training, and that was over a year ago. I don't even have the necessary equipment."

"They'll issue you what you need," Wheeler assured him. "you'll be going out with a CRIP platoon, and they'll take care of you."

"Crip? Like crippled?"

Wheeler chuckled. "No, Combined Reconnaissance and Intelligence Platoon. They go on patrols to gather intelligence and talk to the locals. They've got a Kit Carson scout, but his English isn't that good, and we're not sure how the two Vietnamese would get along."

"And when is this going to happen?" Daley asked apprehensively.

"They'll fly you out to FSB Haskell tomorrow."

Daley spent that evening obsessing over what he should take with him on this unexpected adventure. The only field equipment he had been issued included an M-16 with three magazines, a pistol belt, a helmet, a canteen, and a poncho. He doubted that would be sufficient. The other interrogators in the hooch, sympathizing with his plight, contributed what they could spare—Daley got a second canteen, an ammo pouch, a field dressing pouch, and a camouflage poncho liner. Stuffing most of it in a laundry bag, Daley added a spare uniform and two pairs of socks, his English-Vietnamese dictionary, a spiral notebook with several ball-point pens, and his little Instamatic camera. Then he lay on his cot and worried.

It just wasn't fair. He wasn't trained for this sort of thing. Sure, every soldier was potentially an infantryman, but base camp warriors like him never expected it to really happen. He hadn't even fired his rifle since his in-country orientation three months ago, and that had only been one magazine for familiarization. They hadn't bothered to zero their weapons, since they never expected to fire them in anger. He was used to sleeping on a cot in a barracks hooch and eating at the mess hall, not sleeping on the ground and eating C rations. And how was he going to carry all this equipment while they were tromping through the jungle and swamps? Amid all this internal grumbling, the one thing he avoided thinking about was the potential danger.

The next morning, after a restless night tormented by worries and mosquitoes, Daley grabbed his gear and went to get Ky. The young Vietnamese, still dressed in the black pajamas and Ho-Chi-Minh sandals typical of Viet Cong, was waiting with a smile of anticipation. The MPs made Daley sign for the prisoner, and offered handcuffs, which Daley declined. Together they trudged over to the helicopter landing pad, Ky insisting on carrying some of Daley's equipment for him. They had to wait an hour before their Huey arrived in a cloud of dust and the crew chief hustled them on board. Neither of them had ever ridden in a helicopter, and both looked all around them at the aluminum walls hung with straps and equipment, deafened by the roar of the engines. Daley noticed that Ky looked both frightened and excited by the experience as the chopper lifted off and slipped sideways through the air as it climbed over the base camp.

The crew chief grasped an M-60 machine gun hanging from the top of the open door, scanning the countryside as it passed below them. Daley was fascinated by how much different things looked from the air; buildings looked lower, the terrain seemed flatter, and paths and streams seemed more prominent. He looked over at Ky, who had a death grip on the edge of his seat, and saw the gleam of pleasure in his eyes as he took in this incredible experience. Ky took one hand off the seat long enough to point out the conical mountain rising from the billiard-table flatness of the rest of the area, and proudly announced, "Nui Ba Den!" Daley nodded in agreement. Nui Ba Den, or the Black Virgin, was an extinct volcano near Tay Ninh that rose high above the plain like a grade school science experiment. It was visible for miles in any direction, and was an easy way to keep track of your location.

A few minutes later they zoomed over the berm of Fire Support Base Haskell and settled quickly onto the bare patch of dirt that served as the landing pad. Daley and Ky were almost pushed out of the aircraft and scrambled to the edge of the pad as the chopper spooled up again and took off. When the dust settled and the roar of the helicopter's blades subsided, the pair was approached by a tall black man in jungle fatigues and boonie hat. "Specialist Daley?" the man called out as he walked up to them. Only then did Daley notice the black bar on the man's hat and lapel.

Daley came to attention and saluted. After a moment's hesitation, Ky did the same. "Yes, sir," Daley replied.

"We don't salute here in the field," the man admonished them. "Makes us officers a prime target for snipers." Chagrined, Daley dropped his hand, which the lieutenant grasped to shake. He then shook Ky's hand as well while he introduced himself. "I'm Lieutenant Jones, platoon leader for CRIP. And this must be Nguyen Van Ky." Ky nodded rapidly like a woodpecker, obviously pleased by the attention he was receiving from the American officer. "Welcome to FSB Haskell, gentlemen. Let's get you over to the platoon area so you can meet the rest of the team."

Motioning for them to follow, Jones strolled off toward some big metal Conex shipping containers. Like a devoted servant, Ky picked up Daley's laundry bag and followed. Daley hurried to catch up, taking his place just in front of Ky. They passed between the Conex's, walked alongside a mess tent, around a small group of trucks and jeeps, and finally came to a cluster of sandbag and ammo crate bunkers around which lounged a group of soldiers, most with no shirts on. Only a few looked up as they approached, and even those that did showed little interest.

"Hey, guys," Lieutenant Jones announced, "this is Specialist Daley and Nguyen Van Ky. They'll be going out with us tomorrow." A few of the men looked up from their magazines or letters with mild curiosity. Daley tried to look friendly.

"This is Carl Tanner, our RTO," Jones said, motioning toward a tall lanky blond who was leaning against the side of the bunker smoking a cigarette. Daley nodded politely at him, but got a scowl back in response. Next to Tanner, sitting on a plastic jerry can, was a guy with dark hair and blue eyes. "And that's Roberto Ortiz, out medic." Ortiz actually stood and stretched out to shake Daley's hand.

"Need any drugs?" Ortiz said with a grin, obviously joking. He didn't look very Hispanic, but he did have a very slight accent. Daley chuckled and shook his head.

"Sergeant Roosevelt Gardner," Jones continued, nodding toward a slim but muscular young man with very dark skin who squatted beside the bunker holding a copy of *Ebony* magazine. He glared up at Daley but didn't say anything.

"Just call him Rosie," Tanner remarked with a sneer. Tanner had a thick southern accent. Gardner shot a nasty look at him, but remained silent.

Jones identified the other five men quickly, and Daley promptly forgot their names. One of them was cleaning a sawed-off shotgun which did not appear to be Army issue. Daley hoped that tomorrow they would all be wearing shirts with name tapes on them. A small dark head popped out the door of the bunker but immediately went back inside.

"Dodie," Jones called. "Come on out here."

A Vietnamese man in a tight tiger-pattern camouflage uniform tucked into shiny combat boots reluctantly stepped into the sun, looking warily at Ky. "This is Do Di Duong, our Kit Carson scout," Jones said. "We call him Dodie. Dodie, this is Specialist Daley and Nguyen Van Ky, a Chieu Hoi who will be going out with us tomorrow."

"VC number ten," Dodie spat out, staring at the ground.

Ky spoke to the other man in Vietnamese, introducing himself and thanking him for helping. In return, Dodie said rude things about Ky's mother and warned him to keep his distance.

Using Vietnamese himself, Daley chided Dodie for his remarks and asked him to welcome Ky as a fellow defector. Dodie looked at Daley with amazement, surprised than any American could speak Vietnamese, even as poorly as Daley did. The rest of the platoon also appeared intrigued by this development.

"You speak gook?" Tanner asked. Daley nodded.

"Where'd you learn that?" Ortiz asked. "College?"

"No, in the Army," Daley replied. "At DLI, in Texas."

"DLI?" Jones inquired.

"Defense Language Institute. It's mostly at the Presidio of Monterey, in California, but the Vietnamese Department is at Biggs Air Force Base, next to Ft. Bliss."

"I'm from Oakland," Jones said, "and I've heard of the Presidio of San Francisco, but I didn't know there was one in Monterey."

"Yeah, it's right next to downtown Monterey. And there's a branch of the school at Presidio of San Francisco."

"Be sure to wear some flowers in your hair," one of the other guys sang off-key. The others laughed.

"Okay," Jones said. "There's some of the guys not here right now, but you'll meet them later." Jones directed the next question Sergeant Gardner. "Where's Sergeant Stagakis?"

"I think he's over at the mess tent, shootin' the shit with the mess sergeant," Gardner grumbled.

"Drinkin' some Kool-Aid, I'll bet," Tanner said snidely. A couple of the other men stifled laughs or gave knowing smirks. Daley wondered what that meant.

"Just as well," Jones said. Turning to Daley, he said, "Let's go over there and discuss what we'll be doing tomorrow. I want to hear what Mr. Ky has to say." Daley started to correct the lieutenant and point out that Ky was the man's given name, and technically he was Mr. Nguyen, but decided that could wait. Together they strolled back to the mess tent, a very large peaked-roof tent with the sides rolled up and long picnic benches lined up inside. The tent was mostly empty, except for a couple scattered guys writing letters, and two older men at the far end sitting down facing each other with paper cups in their hands.

"Sergeant Stagakis," Jones called out to the two older men, "can you join us, please?" One of the men looked up and squinted at the figures silhouetted by the bright sun just outside the tent. He was stocky, with thinning red hair and a prominent red nose. He gulped down the rest of his drink and stood up, revealing that he was fairly short.

"Be right there, sir," he said, crumpling the paper cup. He bent down to whisper something to the other man, and both chuckled. He walked over to the trash can and threw his cup away, then paused to dig a stick of chewing gum from his pocket and slowly unwrap it. Tossing the wrapper in the trash, he shoved the stick in his mouth and began chewing vigorously as he slowly made his way between the tables to where Daley and the others were standing. Daley noticed that Stagakis swayed as he walked. When he reached them, Jones had them all sit at one of the tables, Daley and Ky on one side, and Jones and Stagakis on the other. The sergeant left a lot of space between himself and the lieutenant and kept rubbing his chin with his hand covering his mouth. Although he wore Staff Sergeant pin-on insignia on his collar, his sleeves showed the needle-holes and loose threads where Sergeant First Class insignia had once been sewn, back when the Army had still been using sew-on stripes. It appeared Stagakis had been demoted fairly recently.

Jones introduced Daley and Ky, and told them Stagakis was the platoon sergeant. The sergeant nodded at them, but didn't offer to shake hands. "Mr. Ky is a Chieu Hoi," Jones explained to Stagakis, "and Specialist Daley is his interpreter and escort. Ky says he can lead us to a French fort occupied by senior NVA officers, where there might also be Chinese and Russian advisors."

"Where?" Stagakis asked.

"That's the problem," Daley said. "Ky has been there, but he can't read a map. He's sure he can find it again, though." Beside him Ky heard his name being used, and smiled like he was trying to pay attention.

"That's where we come in," Jones said. "CRIP is going to provide support and protection while they locate this fort, and see if we can confirm the details, especially about the advisors."

Stagakis looked dubious. "So how far away is this, and in which direction?

"It's to the west, across the river," Daley said. "Ky thinks it's about ten or twenty clicks from the river."

Stagakis scratched his head. "That's getting pretty close to the border," he noted. "Can't go into Cambodia."

"Understood," Jones chimed in. "But he believes the fort is this side of the border."

"Hmph. So how are we going to work this?" Stagakis was obviously not enthused about the mission. "It's not gonna be a one-day search, that's for sure."

"You're right," Jones agreed. "We need to plan on being out for at least three days, maybe more."

"The guys will have to dig out their rucks," Stagakis said. "What about these two?"

Jones looked at Daley questioningly. Daley shrugged.

"I've got a pistol belt and a couple canteens, but not much else. They don't issue us guys in the base camp much. Ky hasn't got any gear at all."

Jones turned his head to Stagakis. "Have we got some spares we can give them?"

"I'll find something. Walker's on R&R. We can borrow some of his stuff."

"Good enough. Now the question is when and where do we start. The BC wants us moving out first thing in the morning, but first we have to figure out where. Specialist Daley, can Mr. Ky find where he crossed the river last time?"

Daley asked Ky, and got a long complicated answer that he only understood part of. He tried to clarify, and finally got the gist of it. "He says he can recognize the place from the river, if we have a boat."

"Got to have a boat to cross the river anyway," Stagakis commented.

"Of course," Jones said, nodding. "The Navy has already been contacted and will have a landing craft for us at Go Dau Ha. We can cruise the river until Ky sees where we need to land."

"I hope he can find it." Stagakis didn't sound convinced. "Do we go up the river, or down?"

Daley turned to Ky and asked in Vietnamese, "Did you cross the Vam Co Dong up river from Go Dau Ha, or down river?" He had to repeat the question in a couple different ways, motioning with his hands, until Ky understood.

"He thinks it was down river," Daley told them, sounding more certain than he felt. Between Ky's vagueness and his own limited language skills, he wasn't positive either of them knew what they were talking about.

"That's getting close to the Parrot's Beak," Stagakis warned. The Parrot's Beak referred to a section of the border with Cambodia that jutted into South Viet Nam in the shape of its namesake.

"Yes," Jones said, "we'll have to keep that in mind."

"And what are we gonna do if find this fort?" Stagakis asked. "If there's advisers there, there'll be a bunch of gooks, and they aren't gonna just let us walk in and interview 'em."

"We'll have to play it by ear, Sergeant. Observe from a distance. Call in an air strike if necessary."

"Kind of iffy, if you ask me," Stagakis grumbled.

"Agreed. But that's our mission. Sergeant, get all the men together at fourteen hundred and we'll brief them then. I'm going to the head shed and iron out the details. Specialist Daley, Sergeant Stagakis will take care of you two."

FOUR

The deuce-and-a-half truck roared out of the base camp and headed west, the morning sun behind them mostly obscured by the cloud of dust thrown up by the tires. Some of the CRIP members stood, holding on to the bare roof supports that were intended to support a canvas cover, and others were propped precariously on the edge of the raised tailgate. Up front Lieutenant Jones and Sergeant Stagakis leaned against the back of the truck's cab. Daley sat uncomfortably in the middle of the dirty metal floor of the truck bed, bouncing with every bump in the road while he clutched his rifle in one hand and held his helmet on with the other. Beside him Ky squatted and watched the passing countryside with blissful enjoyment.

"Here," the medic, Ortiz, shouted over the roar of the engine. He was sitting with his back against the side of the truck, and he moved over to make a space. Daley gratefully scooted over beside him, leaning back so the short metal wall at least gave his back some support. Placing the rifle in his lap, he grabbed one of the side braces to hold himself in place. All the equipment he was carrying was both unfamiliar and uncomfortable; he hoped he would either be able to adjust it or get used to it once they started the patrol. He had the pistol belt with two canteens, a backpack half full of C-rations, poncho and liner, and personal items like his dictionary. Around his waist were two bandoliers of filled M-16 magazines. The bandoliers were made of thin cotton, and came in new cans of 5.56mm ammo. Sergeant Stagakis had scrounged extra magazines and shown Daley how to stuff them in the bandoliers, which were then tied around waist. Unlike the other soldiers, he carried no grenades or flares, a choice he made because he wasn't at all sure how to use them. On his head was the steel pot he had been issued back in base camp, the straps of the helmet liner still not properly adjusted so it sat comfortably; the camouflage cover on the helmet was clean and new, and held in place by an elastic band that also held a small bottle of LSA lubricant for his rifle. Daley felt like a kid playing Army, and suspected he looked like it, too.

In front of him Ky seemed perfectly happy to be alone in the middle, swaying with the truck's jolting ride. His sandals kept him steady; they were the typical VC issue, made from the treads of old automobile tires with rubber straps made from inner tubes. Over his shoulders were the straps for two bags: one held a two-quart square bladder canteen, and the other was an old Claymore bag stuffed with C-rations. As a prisoner, of course, he carried no weapon. On his head was a ridiculous dark green cowboy hat. Al Most, one of the platoon members, had given it to Ky. Most had bought it from one of the local vendors, intending to send it home to his little brother, but couldn't figure out how to mail it. Ky had been so happy with the gift he had shaken Most's hand vigorously for two minutes.

"First time in the field, huh?" Ortiz said conversationally, speaking loudly over the noise of the truck.

"Me? Yeah." Daley was glad someone was at least talking to him. He had felt like a pariah since joining the platoon. Jones had been too busy to talk, and Stagakis, while not unfriendly, tended to keep to himself when not giving directions.

"It's no big deal," Ortiz assured him. "We haven't made any contact for a month. It's just a pain with all the walking." Ortiz had a very slight accent, more a lilt than anything.

"Where are you from?" Daley asked him, mainly just to keep the conversation going.

"Las Vegas."

"Nevada?"

"Nah, New Mexico."

"I thought Las Vegas was in Nevada," Daley said.

"That's the other one, the new one," Ortiz explained. "We had the name first."

"Where in New Mexico?"

"Northwest of Santa Fe. Small town. Where are you from?"

"Kansas City," Daley answered proudly.

"Which one?" Ortiz asked jokingly.

"Missouri," Daley chuckled, appreciating the twist on his mistake about Ortiz's home town.

"Think we can trust him?" Ortiz asked nodding his head toward Ky.

"Yeah, I think so," Daley said with conviction. "He's kind of naïve, but very earnest."

"Dodie doesn't like him," Ortiz remarked, looking over at the Kit Carson scout who was huddled in the front corner of the truck bed, glaring at Ky's back. Dodie was wearing an old kepi, like the pill-box hat worn by the French Foreign Legion, once white, but now a dirty grey. The hat was perched rakishly to one side.

"Yeah, what's that about?"

"Beats the shit out of me. What's that they say about Orientals? Inscrutable?"

"It's a different culture, that's for sure," Daley agreed. "You'd think them both being Chieu Hois, they'd really get along. Maybe it's because Dodie's from North Vietnam, and Ky's from around here."

"How do you know Dodie's from the north?"

"His name. South Vietnamese always have 'Van' as their middle name."

"No shit," Ortiz said with little real interest.

There was a lull in the discussion as they crossed a bridge over a canal. Then Daley asked, "What's Lieutenant Jones like?"

Ortiz sniffed. "Not bad, not great, just average. Some of the guys don't like him because he's black. Don't make me no difference, though. Long as he don't get me killed."

"And what's the deal with Sergeant Stagakis? Looks like he used to be an E-7."

"Was. Got busted a few months ago for drunk on duty. Still drinks a lot. But not out in the field." Ortiz turned to look into Daley's eyes, a stern look on his face. "Out in the field he really knows his shit. Whatever he says to do, you do it. He'll keep you alive. This is his third tour in Nam. Got three Purple Hearts." Daley nodded his understanding.

"And he carries a radio, too?" Daley asked. Tanner was the platoon RTO, but Stagakis also had a PRC-25 on his back.

"Yeah, he's our backup. Sarge is tail-end Charlie on patrols, and he can maintain contact with the LT up at the front."

"Makes sense," Daley acknowledged. He looked at Tanner, who was sitting back by the tailgate smoking a cigarette. Ortiz saw the direction of his gaze.

"Tanner's an asshole," Ortiz said calmly. "Hates the lieutenant, hates Dodie, doesn't like much of anybody else either. He's a redneck from Florida with a severe attitude problem. Good RTO, though." Ortiz gave a slight head nod across the truck bed toward Gardner, the black buck sergeant Daley had met the day before. "Rosie's got an attitude, too. Believes everyone hates him because he's a brother. Guys mostly hate him just because he's a jerk and a shake-and-bake."

Daley knew that shake-and-bake was the derogatory term for graduates of the NCO Course at Ft. Benning, where new recruits were given extra training and promoted to sergeant to fill the gaps in the ranks in Viet Nam. Generally having less than a year in the Army, these instant NCO's were not highly regarded by the troops.

"Does he get along with the lieutenant?" Daley asked, assuming that the black men would find common ground.

"Nah. Rosie hates officers, too. I think he thinks LT is being uppity. Doesn't really like Jimmerson either." Jimmerson was a pudgy black kid with glasses who was trying to read a paperback novel as the truck bounced down the road.

"Jeez," Daley said, shaking his head. "Does everybody hate everybody else in this platoon?"

"No, no," Ortiz objected, "don't get me wrong. We all get along out in the field. We all cover each other's asses and do our jobs. But in camp we kind of get on each other's nerves sometimes. Don't worry about it."

Daley nodded, but inside he was indeed worried. His first trip to the field, going into a combat environment, and he was with a platoon that seemed dysfunctional at best. What had he gotten himself into? Maybe he should have written that "last letter" home like they do in the movies. He glanced around at the dozen men in the back of the truck, and all of them seemed unconcerned about the mission, which should have reassured Daley. It didn't, however, because he wondered if they were calm simply because they didn't care anymore; apathetic instead of confident. For Daley, the excitement of a new adventure had been replaced by a dread of the unknown.

Daley noticed a subtle change in the countryside through which they were passing. It seemed a little lusher, with taller trees and more rice paddies. The odors of Viet Nam, which he had mostly learned to ignore, were slightly different, with a more fishy smell dominating. Suddenly the truck swerved to the left and came to a halt, and Daley realized they had reached the river. Immediately all the guys stood up, adjusted their gear, and climbed over the sides or jumped down from the lowered tailgate. Daley, unused to his heavy load, gingerly climbed down off the back and joined the others who were milling around between the truck and the bank. The river was a couple hundred yards wide, with smooth brown water flowing from right to left. A couple sampans were being poled up the river, and small rowboats were being used by fishermen in conical straw hats. The far shore was a thick tangle of trees and bushes, broken up by a narrow inlet that appeared artificial. The smell of dead fish permeated the air.

"Here it comes," someone said laconically. Daley looked downstream and saw nothing unusual, and then upstream he saw the blunt square prow of a US Navy landing craft. It was steaming toward them at a moderate speed, the muddy water spreading to either side. It looked just like the landing craft Daley had seen in movies about World War II, taking soldiers to the beaches at

Normandy and Iwo Jima, but with a few additions. At the back was a raised cabin with a circular pill box on top, and a peaked metal roof shaded the cargo area. A shark's mouth was painted on the front of the landing ramp.

"Are we going to ride in that?" Ky asked Daley excitedly, his eyes flashing.

"Yes," Daley told him. "We'll go down the river until you see the place where you crossed last time. Are you sure you will recognize it?"

"Certainly. I have a very good memory. Can I ride on top so I can see better?"

"We'll see." Daley wasn't sure what the arrangements were with the Navy. As the ship nosed into shore, Daley approached Lieutenant Jones, who was giving the ship unnecessary signals with his hands.

"Sir," Daley said, "Ky will need to ride where he can see."

Jones ignored Daley for a minute as he observed the ship nudge to a halt and begin lowering the ramp. "Of course," he told Daley finally. "I'll speak to the captain."

As soon as the ramp was fully down, two sailors dressed in jungle fatigue pants and no shirts walked out and checked to make sure it was secure. Behind them a young man in full uniform walked out and came up to where Jones and Daley were standing. On his collar was a single gold bar, so Daley assumed he was the equivalent of an Army second lieutenant, although he wasn't sure what rank that was in the Navy. He was a handsome young man with curly black hair peeking out from under his boonie cap.

"Ensign McMichaels," he introduced himself, holding out his hand to Jones.

"Lieutenant Jones." He took McMichaels hand and gave it a brief shake.

"I'll be your captain for this cruise," McMichaels said with a smile, obviously repeating a standard phrase he liked to use. "So what do we have planned for today's activities?"

"Mr. Ky over there," Jones said, pointing to Ky, who had walked down to more closely inspect the landing craft, "believes he can identify the point where a VC patrol crossed the river a couple weeks ago. We need to land there and follow the trail."

McMichaels frowned. "So you don't know where we're supposed to land you yet?"

"No, we'll just have to cruise down the river until Ky tells us where to land." Jones' tone was apologetic, but firm.

The naval officer took off his hat and ran his fingers through his hair. "Does he speak English?"

"No, sir," Daley spoke up. "I'll be translating for him."

McMichaels looked at him curiously, and then shrugged. "Okay, I guess you and the dink will have to be on the bridge with me." He turned to Jones. "Let's get your men on board and get moving. I sure hope this doesn't take too long." Beckoning to Daley to follow him, he turned and walked back to the ship. Daley called out for Ky, and together they followed the officer on board.

By 1100 hours the landing craft, accompanied by a Navy river patrol boat, had gone over 10 miles downriver without Ky recognizing his crossing point, so they turned around and headed back upstream. The Naval officer was clearly pissed by Ky's uncertainty, and Daley tried to defend him by noting that the river was higher than it had been due to the onset of the monsoon season. No sooner had he pointed that out than it began to rain. Pouring down in sheets, the rain obscured the banks, and the drumming on the metal roof drowned out any hope of conversation. Ky, however, his cowboy hat dripping like a rainspout, persisted in peering at the shore slowly slipping by. Just after they passed the overgrown inlet for a canal, Ky yelped.

Shaking his head like a wet dog to clear the water off his hat, Ky pointed and said, "I think it's there. Can we go closer?"

Daley relayed the request to the captain, who reluctantly told the helmsman to slow down and ease closer. The rain began to ease up, and as they neared the bank Daley could see where the grass and reeds were thinner and what could be a narrow trail led up and off to the west.

"So," the ensign said impatiently, "is that it?"

Ky may not have understood the words, but he clearly understood the meaning, and he nodded vigorously. "That's the place," he assured Daley. "I remember that tree." He pointed to a twisted tree trunk at the top of the bank.

"Okay, Stan," the officer said to the helmsman, "put her in there." Stan swung the wheel over to put the ship into a wide circle into the middle of the river so it could head in perpendicular to the shore. The ensign got on the radio to tell the PBR what was going on, and Daley grabbed Ky's arm to lead him down into the hold where the rest of the patrol waited.

"We're going in," Daley told them. "Ky finally found the spot."

"About damn time," Tanner grumbled. "I'm tired of this slow boat to China."

"All right, men, gear up," Lieutenant Jones ordered, pulling on his own backpack. Daley found his own gear where he had left it on the deck, now all wet from the rain, and shrugged into it. As he did so, he noticed the distinctive and acrid smell of vomit. Cassidy, one of the platoon members Daley had not really met, looked green, and avoided Daley's stare. Ky, smiling as always, slung his two bags over his shoulders and stood close to Daley, ignoring the glares from Do Di Duong, the Vietnamese scout.

"Hold on!" one of the sailors called from the bow above them, just as the prow plowed into the bank and brought the ship to a sudden halt. Daley had just enough time to grab a rail and keep himself from being thrown to the deck, while most of the others, more experienced in this mode of transport, just bent their knees and rode it out. Ky, unable to understand the warning, stumbled and fell to his hands and knees, but immediately rose and laughed like he had just been on a ride at Disneyland.

With clanks and creaks the huge ramp at the front of the ship released and slammed down on the shore, allowing some river water to slosh in around the sides and disappear into the scuppers.

"Go!" yelled Sergeant Stagakis, and the men jogged up the ramp and onto the shore, spreading out with weapons at the ready. As he had been briefed beforehand, Daley and Ky followed Lieutenant Jones and Tanner, forming what constituted the command group of the patrol. Once everyone was ashore, Jones turned to wave at the ship, but the ramp was already being pulled up, the sailors anxious to return to the relative safety of the middle of the river. Jones and Tanner each went to one knee in the center of the semi-circle of soldiers all facing out, so Daley and Ky did the same. While Stagakis carefully scouted ahead down the barely visible trail, Tanner handed Jones the radio handset so Jones could call in a situation report.

After that everyone just knelt in place, the soldiers on the perimeter watching warily with their weapons ready. Jones took out a map covered in plastic and marked their location with a grease pencil. Daley saw Ortiz with the others, the only thing distinguishing the medic from the other soldiers was his aid bag. In the old WWII movies, Daley thought, the medics all had red cross armbands and helmets, and never carried weapons, but not so here in Viet Nam. This was a different war, where no one was exempt from being targeted, not even civilians.

"This better be the fuckin' place," Tanner warned quietly, not bothering to look back at Daley and Ky.

"That's enough, Tanner," Jones said gently. He was apparently used to Tanner's grumbling.

A moment later there was a muffled squawk on Tanner's radio, and he pressed the handset to his ear. "Roger," he said into the mouthpiece. "Sarge says it's clear," he told Jones.

Jones stood up and called out, "Let's move out. Benkowski, take point." Like the rest of the men, Daley stood and waited as Jones followed the first man down the trail, followed by Tanner, Daley, and Ky. The rest of the patrol fell in behind them.

Tanner glanced back and told Daley snidely, "Don't bunch up." Daley resented the command from someone who didn't outrank him, but increased the gap between them anyway, recognizing the wisdom of the advice.

Within a hundred yards the group broke out of the heavy brush and trees that lined the river into a flat open space filled with high grass. Daley could barely make out the geometric shapes of long-abandoned rice paddy dikes that subtly altered the height and color of the grass. The trail itself followed the top of one of the dikes, and had been traveled just enough to keep the grass from taking over. Sergeant Stagakis, seemingly unbothered by the weight of the radio and full rucksack on his back, had stepped off the trail and watched the men as they moved by him, giving occasional corrections or words of encouragement. Daley got the impression Stagakis was completely sober and totally aware of his surroundings. Daley was very relieved. From the patrol briefing Jones had given them this morning before boarding the truck, he knew that the sergeant would fall in at the rear of the column, so he could advise the lieutenant of any problems there by radio.

"Sergeant," Ky said to Daley in Vietnamese, "this is the right trail. I remember it very well."

"Good," Daley replied, and then relayed the message to Jones.

"Can he tell us what's ahead?" Jones asked. They were pushing through the tall grass across what seemed to be an endless line of rice paddies, with occasional patches of jungle visible in the distance to each side.

After a short conversation with Ky, Daley told the lieutenant, "He says we'll go through some jungle and then into a plain of reeds."

"How far to the French fort?"

Daley quizzed Ky again. Ky looked up at the sky, which was till cloudy, but brighter where the sun was directly overhead. "Very far," he said. "We will not get there today."

Daley knew that wasn't an answer Lieutenant Jones would like, so he pressed further. "So when will we get to the fort?"

"Will we stop for the night?" Ky asked.

"Probably," Daley said, hoping he was right. He was getting tired already.

"Then we will reach the fort tomorrow afternoon. Maybe sooner."

Daley considered how best to tell the lieutenant, and finally said, "We should get to the fort tomorrow, possibly before noon. That's assuming we stop for the night."

"Hmm," Jones grunted thoughtfully. When he didn't refute the assumption about stopping for the night, Daley sighed with relief. Lugging all this gear on his back was harder work than he had anticipated.

By mid-afternoon Daley was miserable. His calves ached, his shoulders ached, he was dying of thirst despite the heat and humidity, and every flying insect in Viet Nam was buzzing around his ears and face. The endless slog through high grass, small patches of jungle, and occasional swampy areas was not only tiring, it was boring. They had suffered through a heavy but brief rain shower earlier, and his uniform was still damp and chafed his inner thighs. He had given up on keeping his glasses clean, and just ignored the water spots and bug bodies on the lenses. The only thing to see, really, was Tanner's pack and radio about ten feet ahead of him. He knew it was unreasonable, but he was also annoyed at Ky's apparent indifference to the hardships and perpetually happy demeanor.

Looking at the ground, finding the best place to step on the uneven terrain, Daley almost bumped into Tanner when the RTO stopped and raised his fist in the air as a signal. Up ahead he could see Lieutenant Jones peering through a line of bushes that crossed the trail they were on. Benkowski, a blond young man with an athletic build, was kneeling on the trail with his rifle at the ready, keeping an eye out for anyone who might approach from the other direction. Jones turned and pointed at Daley and Ky, saying quietly, "Come here." Tanner knelt down in the middle of the path, forcing Daley to skirt around him in the weeds. When he and Ky reached the lieutenant, Jones pointed through the line of bushes, which Daley could now see bordered a wide but sluggish creek.

"Is it safe to cross?" Jones asked. Daley wasn't sure if the concern was the depth, possible booby-traps, or an ambush, but figured all were indeed things to worry about. He relayed the question to Ky, who was looking at the creek with a furrowed brow.

Ky began looking around himself with an increasingly worried frown, as if searching for familiar landmarks. Daley saw the uncertainty, and began to worry himself. Finally Ky turned to Daley and hung his head. "I am so sorry, Sergeant," Ky apologized. "I fear we have taken a wrong turn somewhere. I am not familiar with this stream."

"Are you sure?" Daley hoped the young Vietnamese was just temporarily disoriented, because he dreaded telling the lieutenant they were apparently lost.

"Very sure," Ky said disconsolately, shaking his head slowly from side to side.

"Shit!" Daley said to himself, and then turned to face Jones, who dark face reflected his concern at the tone of Daley's conversation with Ky despite his inability to understand the words.

"Ky says we must have made a wrong turn somewhere," Daley said, shrugging.

"Where? How could that happen?"

"I don't think he knows."

Ky moved up to their side, and began speaking rapidly. Daley was only able to catch some of it, and finally got Ky to slow down and repeat himself.

"He thinks he knows where we went wrong," Daley told the lieutenant. "Something about a big tree with crooked limbs."

Jones reached inside his shirt and drew out his map. The plastic covering was yellowed and scratched, but the officer smoothed it down and refolded it so only their current area was visible. He studied the map for a minute, tracing his finger across it from an 'X' he had marked with a grease pencil at their last stop.

"Okay, here's this creek, I think," he said, more to himself than to Daley. He pulled his grease pencil out of his shirt pocket and made another X on the map. From what Daley could tell, their route had been curving around toward the north. "How far back was this tree?" Jones asked.

After a brief exchange with Ky, Daley told him, "About an hour or two, he thinks."

"He thinks?" Jones said angrily. "I thought he knew this trail like the back of his hand!"

Daley shrugged again. "He's only traveled it at night, sir," he explained. "It looks different in the daytime."

Jones blew air out of his mouth in exasperation. He beckoned Benkowski and told Tanner to call Sergeant Stagakis. "Tell him we're reversing course, and I'll explain when I get to him."

Daley and Ky fell in behind Tanner as the head of the column snaked past the rest of the men, most of whom had been sitting or kneeling on the path while they rested and took a drink from their canteens. None of them seemed surprised by the change in direction, and just stood up and followed as the chain of soldiers passed. As they passed Dodie, the scout gave Ky a snide smirk but didn't say anything. When Jones reached Stagakis, he briefly clarified what was going on and then continued back along the trail. Stagakis patiently waited for the column to pass him by, so he could once again be the last man.

Even though it wasn't really his fault, Daley felt a little guilty for the snafu, since he was in charge of Ky, and was the only one, other than Dodie, who could understand him. He was sure the other men were grumbling about the wasted time and effort, and, in fact, he himself was disappointed that the arduous journey would be even longer than expected. The short halt at the creek had given Daley a chance to rest, but it had also allowed his muscles to stiffen up, and he was almost hobbling as he struggled to keep up. At least Ky seemed to recognize his own failure, as he no longer smiled continuously. Instead the young man observed his surroundings intently, often squinting through half-closed eyes as if trying to imagine what the area would look like at night.

Due to their recent acquaintance with the trail, the backtracking went more quickly than the initial probe, but it was still over an hour and a half before Ky again spoke up.

"There!" he said excitedly, pointing back toward a small patch of jungle they had just passed. "That tree!" The column halted and Daley followed Ky's outstretched arm. One of the trees had apparently been struck by lightning, or perhaps a cannon shell, in the distant past, and then kept growing. The trunk made a distinctive S-shaped curve, but due to the heavy foliage around it, it was easy to miss. "The trail goes to the other side," Ky said firmly.

Daley translated, and Jones sent Benkowski ahead to see if he could find a trail that forked to the south of the grove. Everyone else knelt down and waited. A minute later there was a whistle from Benkowski, and Daley stood up so he could see the point man waving his forearm to indicate the direction they should have gone. As Jones led the patrol down to the intersection and made a sharp right on the new trail, Daley noticed that the fork occurred just after a large bush that had hidden it from view when they first came this way. He felt a little better about Ky's memory of the route now.

The afternoon wore on. Ky, now sure they were on the right track, was again ebullient, chattering to Daley's back about what they were seeing, despite repeated demands from the other men that he keep quiet. Daley was too wrapped up in his own pain and exhaustion to pay any attention to Ky, or anyone else. He just concentrated on putting one boot in front of another, silently cursing Major Wheeler for 'volunteering' him for this mission. At one of their infrequent pauses for rest, Tanner had looked at Daley rubbing his ankles and said, "Hey, remf, how you like bein' a real soldier for a change?" Daley had simply ignored the remark, knowing anything he said would probably be the wrong thing. Sergeant Stagakis had come up the line and started conferring with Lieutenant Jones, each of them with a map and a grease pencil. Ortiz came up and squatted down next to Daley, who was sitting on his upturned helmet to keep his butt dry.

"You gonna make it?" Ortiz asked sympathetically. He was in his medic mode, Daley decided, but any friendliness was welcome.

"I guess," Daley replied. "I'm really out of shape."

"You'll get used to it. You got clean socks in your ruck?"

"I brought a couple pair," Daley said. "I'll change tonight."

Ortiz handed him a paper packet from his aid bag. "Here's some foot powder to use when you change 'em. It really helps."

"Thanks. Got anything for sore shoulders?" Daley rolled his shoulders and winced.

"Nope," Ortiz said cheerfully. "You'll just have to suffer." Ortiz looked up at Jones and Stagakis. "The Martian's not happy about the detour."

"Martian?" Daley looked at Ortiz quizzically.

Ortiz chuckled. "The LT is John Jones, like in the comic books."

Daley nodded in understanding. In the old Superman comic books, there used to be stories about J'onn J'onnz, Manhunter from Mars. Maybe there still were; Daley hadn't read a comic book for years, feeling they were beneath him. Now he kind of wished he still read them, so he could fit in better with these guys.

"Think we're on the right trail now?" Ortiz asked.

"Ky seems pretty sure we are," Daley told him. "Can't get him to shut up about it, either."

"Seems okay," Ortiz remarked casually. "More friendly than Dodie."

"Yeah, Dodie's been kind of pissy around Ky," Daley noted. "Any idea what that's about?"

Ortiz rubbed his face. "Hard to say. I've never been too sure about him anyway. Disappears for a couple days at a time, every couple weeks or so, says he going to see family. But you said he's North Vietnamese, so how could that be?"

"Maybe his whole family moved south when the country was partitioned," Daley suggested. "Does he pull his weight with the platoon, when's he around?"

Ortiz scoffed. "He don't do shit if he can avoid it. Battalion said we had to take him, since we're supposed to get intel from the local villagers, and nobody else speaks gook."

Daley started to say something, but Stagakis brushed by him and Jones told everyone they were moving out again. Ortiz helped Daley get back on his feet, and then dropped back behind Ky. In no time they were again humping the boonies, pushing on toward the lowering sun.

FIVE

"Specialist Daley, would you and Ky join us, please?" Lieutenant Jones had shed his pack and helmet, and was standing with Sergeant Stagakis at the edge of the copse. Daley, who had dropped all of his gear and was enjoying his lightness of being, grabbed his rifle while tapping Ky on the shoulder and hurrying over to join the two leaders. The sun had just dipped below the horizon, but there was still plenty of light, especially there where the trees and foliage gave way to open fields of grass.

After a long afternoon of hiking across an endless plain of grass and reeds interspersed with small stands of jungle, Daley had been at the end of his physical rope, stumbling along to keep up. The relief he felt when the lieutenant had announced they were going to stop for the night had almost been immeasurable. They had found this small patch of jungle about thirty meters off the trail to the south, and Jones had chosen it for their temporary bivouac. The members of the patrol had all quickly faded into the bushes and established a hasty perimeter, before dumping their rucks and relaxing with a watchful eye on their surroundings.

Daley came up to Jones and stood waiting respectfully as the officer and his NCO peered over their maps in the dying light. Ky stood right behind him, smiling as he looked around at the sea of grass and the distant humps of trees. Jones finally turned to Daley and held his map out for inspection.

"We believe we're here," he said, pointing to a circle he had drawn on the plastic. The map had little in the way of markings in this area: few contour lines, no roads, and no buildings. All it showed were vague indications of swamps, grass, and foliage. Along the far left edge, running at a slight angle, was a heavy dark line marking the Cambodian border. The freshly-drawn circle was bisected by a faint dotted line that presumably represented the trail they had been following. Daley had seen the lieutenant take frequent compass readings during the day, so he assumed the young officer had been keeping track of their progress all along and was thus able to pinpoint their location. The lack of permanent landmarks, however, made such determinations almost magical. Daley hoped Jones was really that good with land navigation.

"Ask Ky if he agrees," Stagakis said to Daley.

"Ky doesn't really understand maps," Daley told him, not for the first time.

"Ask him anyway."

Daley shrugged and took the map from Jones. He handed it to Ky, explaining what was being asked, and told Ky what the various symbols and lines meant. Ky studied the map intently, and then passed it back to Daley.

"I don't know," Ky said sorrowfully. "But we are on the right trail," he assured them, perking up. "I remember these trees." The trees all looked alike to Daley, but he translated Ky's remarks anyway.

"So how much farther to the fort?" Jones asked. Daley repeated the question in Vietnamese.

"Not far," Ky said. "Maybe a half day."

Jones and Stagakis both looked doubtful when Daley translated. "We're getting awful close to the border, sir," Stagakis warned.

"I know," Jones agreed. He turned away from Daley and looked off to the northeast, stretching to his full height. "I wish I could see Nui Ba Den," he complained.

"Nui Ba Den!" Ky said excitedly, finally understanding something that had been said. He pointed toward a distant clump of foliage and repeated, "Nui Ba Den." Daley could not see anything that looked like the extinct volcano east of Tay Ninh, but his glasses were dirty and the air was full of humidity.

"Maybe," Jones said, before taking a compass reading. Reclaiming the map from Daley, he set the compass on the map, held horizontally, and traced an imaginary line. "If that is Nui Ba Den, then we may be where we think we are. Which is good, I guess."

The lack of certainty in Jones' voice made Daley a little nervous. It was bad enough being way out in the boonies where the enemy knows the terrain better than you, but usually you could rely on artillery or air support to supplement your firepower or pull you out of danger. If you weren't sure where you were, though, that support had their hands tied.

Ky jostled against Daley, and he looked around to see why. Ky had stepped closer to Daley while looking toward their left along the tree line. At first all Daley saw were leaves and limbs, but then some movement revealed Dodie lurking in the bushes, his tiger-stripe camouflage helping him blend in. His off-white cap was in his hand, held low behind some leaves. Stagakis also noticed the Kit Carson scout, and called out to him in a low voice.

"Dodie, come here."

Dodie slipped through the bushes and came to a halt a few feet from the group, replacing his kepi. He shot an angry look at Ky, and then nodded with respect toward Lieutenant Jones and Sergeant Stagakis. "Yes?" he said.

"Is this where we are?" Jones asked, holding out the map. Dodie took a step forward and accepted the map, tilting it to catch the remaining light from the west. Daley noticed that Dodie's eyes flickered and his expression hardened as he oriented himself to the map.

"Oh, yes," Dodie finally assured them. "We are here," he added, placing a fingertip on an X from a reading taken earlier in the day.

"No, here," Jones corrected him, pointing out the circle.

"Oh, yes," Dodie agreed. "I make mistake." He nodded vigorously. Ky cleared his throat, and Daley detected in that simple sound a seed of distrust.

"Maybe we ought to call for a marking round," Stagakis suggested.

"I'll see what Battalion says," Jones replied. He started to say something else, but was interrupted when Benkowski ran up to them.

"We found some bunkers," the young man told them.

"New?" Stagakis asked urgently.

"No, pretty old. One's caved in."

"You didn't go in, did you?" Stagakis asked, giving Benkowski a stern look.

"Gee, Sarge, give me some credit. Ain't nobody going into a bunker without checking it out with a grenade first."

"No grenades," Jones interjected. "We don't want to advertise our presence."

"Roger that," Benkowski agreed.

"How long since those bunkers were last used, do you think?" Stagakis inquired.

Benkowski shrugged. "A year, maybe."

"Okay, then just leave them alone. Find Sergeant Gardner, and tell him to set up a guard roster. I want four guys on watch, at the points of the compass. Got that?"

"Got it." Benkowski turned and hurried away.

"Is your radio close by," Jones asked Stagakis.

"I left it with Cassidy," the sergeant said, gesturing vaguely toward the east end of the grove.

"Daley, find Tanner and tell him I need the radio," Jones said. "Then you and Ky find a place to sleep."

Daley started to leave, but Stagakis grabbed his arm. "You'll be standing guard tonight, too," the sergeant told him. "But not him." He nodded toward Ky. "Don't forget, he's still a prisoner."

"Roger," Daley answered. With Ky right behind him, he hurried back into the dark foliage looking for Tanner. He noticed as he left that Dodie had disappeared as well.

In the fading light the clump of jungle seemed both foreboding and protective. It was roughly oval in shape, oriented east to west, and while the foliage was thick around the edges, the interior of the grove was almost open except for all the tree trunks. With Ky tagging along behind him, Daley roamed through the small area looking for Tanner, who he finally found by following the smell of cigarette smoke. His radio propped on the ground beside him, the skinny blond sat on a large mound of earth near the west side of the grove, apparently without a care in the world.

"The lieutenant wants you," Daley told him, pointing toward the northeast where he had last seen the officer.

"Fuck 'im," Tanner said lazily, "I'm takin' a break."

"Hey, man," Daley told him, "he sent me to find you. If you don't go, he'll blame me."

"Tough shit, gook-boy."

"Hey, Tanner," a voice called out, "put that cigarette out!" Daley turned to see Sergeant Gardner striding up, his dark eyes flashing in anger. The slender black man came to a halt directly over Tanner, forcing the southerner to look up at him.

"Been humpin' that damn radio all day," Tanner complained. "Can't even take a smoke break?"

"Gooks can smell that smoke a mile away, you moron," Gardner admonished him.

"Lieutenant wants to see him," Daley told Gardner, hoping the sergeant could get Tanner moving when he couldn't.

"Yeah, yeah, I'm goin'," Tanner said, pinching out the lit end of the cigarette and shoving it into his shirt pocket. Putting his helmet back on, he lifted the radio by one of the pack straps and stood up to retrieve his rifle, which he had left leaning against a tree trunk. In a weak show of defiance, he slowly trudged away.

"Cracker asshole," Gardner commented quietly. He looked at Daley appraisingly. "Where's the rest of your gear?"

Daley looked around, trying to reorient himself. "Over there," he said, pointing.

"Get it," Gardner said. "I'll show you where you're going to be."

Daley jogged over and picked up his rucksack, pistol belt, and ammo bandoliers. Juggling all this equipment, along with his rifle, he hurried back to join Gardner. Ky had imitated him, gathering up his own sack and canteen.

"This way," Gardner said, and led Daley east through the center of the grove. It was only about twenty meters before they reach the eastern point of the tree line, where there was another mound of earth. Only then did Daley notice the opening in the side of the mound, and realized it was actually a bunker. He also realized belatedly that the mound Tanner had been sitting on was also a bunker. The mound, he now noticed, rose only about two feet above ground level, and was roughly rectangular in shape. The top had been smoothed and was now sprouting seedlings and grass. "You can put your gear there," Gardner said, indicating a bare patch of earth to the side of the bunker. Daley gratefully dropped the various items he had been juggling.

On the other side of the bunker sat a radio and a couple rucksacks. A few feet away, standing next to a small tree and watching the sea of grass to the east of the grove, was the other soul brother in the platoon. Daley couldn't remember his name, but Gardner reminded him.

"Jimmerson," Gardner said to the other man, "Daley and the Chieu Hoi will be here with you and Cassidy and Sarge." Jimmerson turned his head, his glasses reflecting the fading sunlight, and gave Daley and Ky a brief look of acknowledgement. Then he resumed his gaze outward. "Where's Cassidy?" Gardner asked, glancing around.

"Taking a shit," Jimmerson said, inclining his helmet toward the southeast where a single bush jutted up above the grass.

"I'll let Sarge make your schedule," Gardner said, addressing both Daley and Jimmerson. To Daley he said, "Come on, I'll show you the rest of the layout." With that he strode off, and Daley hurried to catch up. Angling through the trees to the southwest, they quickly came to a small group of men sitting around a partially collapsed bunker. One of the men was Dodie, who scrambled to his feet immediately and leaned against a tree with his legs crossed, assuming a James Dean pose. The other three men were opening cans of C-rations and only casually acknowledged Gardner's presence.

"Romano, you got first watch," Gardner said, after pulling a small slip of paper from his shirt. "Kessler, you got middle, and Gonzalez you got last."

"What about Dodie?" one of the men asked. Daley saw by his nametag that it was Kessler, a gangly guy with mousy brown hair and big ears. Romano was a short Italian who had apparently been badly afflicted with acne as a teenager. Gonzalez was kind of pudgy, with straight black hair longer than Army regulations allowed, and looked more Native American than Hispanic.

"Dodie doesn't pull watch by himself, you know that. He can be on with one of you."

"Okay," Kessler replied without enthusiasm. The three men on the ground exchanged brief glances, and Daley felt sure that they had their own plans for guard duty.

"And keep a sharp eye out. We're in Indian country here, with no support."

"Indians never had AKs," Kessler commented.

"Or RPGs," Romano added.

"Might have won, if they had," Gonzalez said. All three nodded.

Gardner just rolled his eyes and beckoned Daley to follow him. They made their way on around to the west end of the grove, where Daley had found Tanner smoking a few minutes earlier. Tanner was still somewhere with the lieutenant, but Ortiz and Benkowski were now there. Benkowski sat on the roof of the bunker, staring through the leaves at the darkening plain beyond. Ortiz was spreading out a poncho on a pile of leaves. Ortiz nodded at them as they walked up.

"The lieutenant and Tanner will be here with these guys," Gardner told Daley.

"Ortiz, you'll take first watch, Benkowski second, and Tanner can have last."

"What about LT?" Benkowski asked slyly. "What watch does he pull?"

"Rank has its privileges," Gardner told him.

Moving on around clockwise to the northeast, Gardner, Daley, and Ky came to the last bunker, where one guy was digging into his ruck and the other was sprawled on his poncho against the sloping side of the underground fortification. It was getting too dark to read the nametags, but Daley was pretty sure they were Most and Griffin. Most was tall, with sandy hair, and Griffin was short, with a bushy mustache under a nose that had been broken at some time in the past. In addition to his M-16, Griffin also carried a sawed-off shotgun, which he was now swabbing with a rag. Just outside the foliage that bordered the grove Daley could see Lieutenant Jones and Sergeant Stagakis, comparing maps and discussing the situation, while Tanner stood by talking on the radio.

"I'll be here with Most and Griffin," Gardner said, confirming Daley's guess about their identities. "How much do you know about standing guard?"

"I've been on berm guard at the base camp," Daley said with false confidence. "Got rocketed the other night."

"Well, this is a little different. You have to really maintain light and noise discipline. You'll be monitoring the radio and making sitreps every hour, but do it very quietly. Keep an eye out for any movement, and if you see any, wake up Sarge. Any questions?"

"I guess not," Daley answered, although there were hundreds of questions rattling around in his head. It had just now come to him how dangerous their situation was, and he could feel the fear rising in his gut. They were all alone out here, miles from any support, in an area pretty much controlled by the enemy. Lieutenant Jones wasn't even exactly sure where they were. Daley started thinking of all the things that could go wrong, and it made him dizzy.

Outside, Jones and Stagakis reached some sort of conclusion and pushed through the leaves back into the shelter of the grove that was now getting very dark. Stagakis brushed by Daley and headed toward the eastern end of the grove, so Daley and Ky followed him. At the bunker Jimmerson was still standing guard, and Cassidy was sitting on the edge of the bunker eating something from a C-ration can. Cassidy was an average white guy with a slightly upturned nose and reddish-brown hair. The platoon sergeant went to his gear and shoved his map into his ruck.

Maintaining his watch on the area outside the tree line, Jimmerson said quietly, "Sarge, Rosie said you'd do our guard roster."

Stagakis plopped his butt down on the bunker next to Cassidy, holding a couple C-ration cans he had pulled out of his backpack. "You're on until nine," he told Jimmerson. "I'll take the next shift. Daley, you take midnight to three, and then wake up Cassidy."

"Okay," Daley said hesitantly. "How do I make the sitreps?"

"Let me have dinner," Stagakis said, attacking one of the cans with his P-38 can opener, "and then I'll show you. You probably ought to eat now, too."

Daley nodded, and went digging in his ruck. Ky imitated him. Daley had to show Ky how to operate the P-38, but he caught on quickly. By the time they finished eating, the gloom in the grove was almost absolute.

SIX

Daley was awakened by someone roughly shaking his shoulder. "Time for guard," came a hoarse whisper. Daley untangled himself from the poncho that was wrapped around him and sat up, rubbing his eyes. It was pitch dark, but he could just make out a lighter area beyond the leaves that helped orient him. Patting the ground around him, he found his M-16 and a bandolier of magazines. A few feet away Sergeant Stagakis was muttering into the radio handset. Standing up, Daley tied the bandolier around his waist and stepped over to Stagakis.

"I just called in the sitrep," Stagakis whispered to him, so you're good until one. Don't forget."

"No sweat, Sarge," Daley assured him.

Stagakis handed Daley a heavy tubular object. "Here's the starlight scope," he said. "Just use it if you hear something. Don't want to run the battery down." Earlier in the evening Stagakis had shown Daley how to switch the scope on, since this was his first experience with the device. "Wake up Cassidy at three. You know where he is?"

"Yeah. Right over there."

"Okay, I'm gonna catch some Z's." Stagakis found his own poncho and lay down. Daley, rifle in one hand and starlight scope in the other, walked over closer to the edge of the grove where he could see more of their surroundings. There was pale moonlight casting vague shadows over the expanse of grass, occasionally darkening as scattered clouds passed over head. Daley sensed someone come up behind him, and tensed with dread.

"It is a nice night, Sergeant," Ky whispered pleasantly. Daley released the breath he had been holding.

"You don't have to be awake," Daley told him.

"I know, but I am used to it. I will help you stay awake."

"Thanks," Daley said with genuine gratitude. Holding out the starlight scope, he said, "Here, can you hold this for me?"

"Certainly." After that they fell into an easy silence, watching and listening for anything out of the ordinary. Daley leaned against a tree trunk, while Ky squatted down, cradling the scope in his lap. Occasionally they heard a cough or rattle from one of the other men standing guard elsewhere in the grove, but otherwise there was only the soft sigh of a breeze brushing against the leaves and grass.

Despite the danger, and the fear that still gently squeezed his insides, Daley wasn't sure he could stay awake for three hours. Right after Sergeant Stagakis had briefed him on the radio, the starlight, and making sitreps, he had stretched out on his poncho and fallen into an uneasy sleep. A short time later there had been a rain storm move through the area, and the water dripping from the leaves overhead had soaked him before he finally woke up long enough to pull the poncho over his torso and wrap himself up like a burrito. His legs, however, had remained uncovered, and now the damp cuffs of his fatigues chilled his calves.

Uncomfortable, tense, tired, and a little bored, Daley pondered his situation and realized just how bizarre his life had become. Growing up in a middle-class suburban family, attending a small college in Missouri, he had led a bland, white-bread existence where the most excitement was found at the drive-in movies and the most danger was from reckless driving with his friends. Now, with little preparation or expectation, he was hiding in the jungle halfway around the world, in a land where small men with big guns were trying to kill him. It was kind of like in the movies, but not really. Here the peril was real, and far less glamorous. Nonetheless, he had to admit, it was still exciting and adventurous, although not enough to compensate for the danger and discomfort.

His thoughts were interrupted by a tug on his pants leg. Ky hissed at him very quietly and stood up so he could move closer. "Viet Cong," Ky whispered in his ear, and pointed toward the east.

Daley brought his rifle into a ready position as he looked out through the leaves, searching for any sign of movement in the tall weeds outside the jungle enclave. He couldn't see anything, but then he heard the distant sound of voices. That must have been what alerted Ky, as the sounds had the particular tone and speech patterns of Vietnamese. Daley fumbled around and took the starlight scope from Ky, then leaned in to whisper to him: "Wake up the sergeant." Ky hesitated, and Daley realized that Ky might not know who he meant. "The older man with the radio," he added. Ky bobbed his head rapidly and scurried away. Daley tucked his rifle under his arm so he could use both hands, switched on the scope, and raised it to his eye. Immediately he realized his mistake, and used one hand to remove his glasses and stick them in his pants pocket. The starlight scope's eyepiece had a spring-loaded aperture that remained closed until you pressed it against your eyelids, so the bright image remained invisible to anyone else.

Trying again, he pushed the scope against his eye and was dazzled by the bright green image that now appeared. It was grainy and monotone black and green, and it took a couple seconds for Daley to get oriented to what was the sky and what was the ground. Once he found the distant clump of trees he remembered seeing when it was still light out, he was able to swing the scope from side to side while he searched for any anomalies in the terrain. He almost swept past it, but quickly brought the scope back to a shape that didn't belong. As his eye adjusted to the contrast of the scene, he made out the shape of a human head moving slowly above the tall grass, and then another behind it.

"What is it?" Stagakis had come up behind him and was speaking softly directly into his ear.

"Looks like VC," Daley responded, still watching the figures approaching in the distance. More heads had appeared, and it looked like they were traveling along the same trail that the CRIP platoon had been following. As they got closer, the vagaries of the terrain allowed Daley to see the men more clearly, at least from the waist up.

"How many?" Stagakis asked.

"Can't see all of them yet," Daley replied. "At least ten so far."

"Keep watching," the sergeant told him, and then moved away. Behind him Daley could sense that Stagakis was waking the others.

Daley realized that Ky was again by his side, and the young man breathed a few words into his hear. "He sent two men to warn the others." Daley was glad to hear that. He had wondered how they could alert the rest of the platoon, with the four groups scattered so far apart. He hoped the foliage of the grove would sufficiently muffle the sounds the Americans were making. The VC were still talking and laughing, so he doubted they would notice.

"Need a spot report." Stagakis was now on the other side of Daley, the radio on his back and the handset pressed to his ear. Because he was in Army Intelligence, Daley at least had some clue as to what Stagakis was talking about. He tried to remember all the elements of a spot report, and began quietly calling out what he was seeing.

"I count twenty men in black pajamas. I see five weapons— three AKs, two carbines of some sort. The rest of the men are carrying bags and boxes. They're heading east to west along the trail we came in on, at about two meter intervals."

Beside him, Stagakis rephrased his report into the handset mouthpiece, relaying the information to both Lieutenant Jones and Battalion. After a pause while he listened to the responses, Stagakis turned and spoke quietly to Cassidy and Jimmerson, who had just returned from alerting the other men. "Go back and tell 'em to keep down and don't shoot unless they have to." The two soldiers again scampered off into the trees.

"What are they doing now?" Stagakis asked Daley.

Daley stepped forward to get a better angle around the edge of the grove. "Still moving down the trail. Still talking."

"Watch for anyone following them," the sergeant told him. "I can see these guys now."

Daley swept the scope back along the trail as ordered, and saw nothing. The voices of the VC column kept moving to his left, crossing past the north edge of the grove.

"Anything?" Stagakis asked.

"Negative," Daley responded, a little surprised at his own use of proper military terminology.

"Stay here," Stagakis said, letting the radio backpack slip off his shoulders and drop to the ground. "I'm going up to the LT. Call if you see anything else."

"Roger," Daley answered, still sweeping the scope slowly from side to side. He heard rustling on either side of him, presumably Jimmerson and Cassidy returning and taking up defensive positions.

"I got the radio," Jimmerson said on his right. Daley was glad to hear that. Between his rifle and the starlight, he had his hands full, and operating the radio too would have presented problems.

Daley felt Ky step away from him and heard two voices murmuring in Vietnamese. He guessed that Dodie had shown up, and Ky was filling him in on the situation. A moment later Ky was again beside him. "Duong," Ky muttered with a tone of distaste.

"Gooks are moving away," Jimmerson reported after a couple minutes.

Although still hyper alert, Daley began to relax a little. The enemy had walked right by them. The danger had passed, at least for now.

Daley awoke with a start when someone kicked the sole of his boot. Cocooned in his poncho and poncho liner, he was at first disoriented, and then simply uncomfortable. Untangling himself from the wrappings, he sat up and rubbed his eyes. What he could see of the sky through the leaves had turned from black to a deep indigo, hinting at the approach of dawn.

"Gear up," Staff Sergeant Stagakis said gruffly. He was apparently the one who had awakened him, and was himself pulling the radio onto his back. At the edge of the grove Daley could just make out the silhouette of Cassidy standing guard, and he also already had his pack on his back. Daley hastily rolled up his poncho and liner and stuffed them into his pack, buckled on his pistol belt, tied on his bandoliers of magazines, shrugged his arms into the straps of his pack, placed his helmet on his head, and picked up his rifle from where it leaned against a tree. By the time he did all that, everyone else was ready to go, including Ky. Daley was a little embarrassed that he was holding everyone up; he felt like an amateur amongst professionals.

He was still adjusting his load as he followed the others toward the middle of the grove to meet up with the rest of the platoon. It was just beginning to be light enough that he could make out faces under the helmets, joining the group of men standing around stretching and whispering lame jokes and insults to each other. Daley shivered involuntarily. His clothes were still damp, and it was relatively cool this morning—probably around seventy Daley guessed.

"Get a head count, Rosie," Stagakis told Gardner. The young sergeant went from person to person so he could get a good look at their faces, muttering to himself as he counted them off on his fingers.

Ky nudged Daley in the back and said, "Duong." Daley was about to ask what he meant when Gardner spoke out suddenly.

"Where's Dodie?"

"Not my day to watch him," Al Most joked.

"Dodie!" Gardner hissed in a suppressed shout. "Dodie!"

"Looks like Dodie didi-ed," Tanner remarked snidely.

"Son of a bitch!" Stagakis cursed. "Where'd the little fucker go?"

"Maybe it's his day off," Kessler suggested facetiously.

"When was the last time anyone saw him?" Lieutenant Jones said, cutting off any other discussion.

"He came over to us when we saw the VC patrol last night," Daley offered. "What was that, around one or two?"

"He was hangin' around us just after that," Tanner said.

"He was gone when I went on guard last night," Gonzalez said. "I figured he'd gone somewhere else to sleep, didn't think nothin' of it."

"Number ten," Ky growled behind Daley, using one of the few English phrases he knew. It was the phrase shared by GIs and Vietnamese for the worst possible anything.

"Sergeant Gardner," Jones said, "You and Gonzalez make a quick sweep of the area and see if you can find anything. Carl, would you please get the map out of my pack." While Gardner and Gonzalez walked away in different directions, Jones turned his back to Tanner so the RTO could rummage around in the pack. After a couple minutes of searching the various packets and spaces, Tanner stepped away shaking his head.

"Can't find it, LT," Tanner said. "You sure you put it in there?"

"Positive," Jones said. He swung the pack off his shoulders and set it on the ground, kneeling down beside it so he could search it himself. He also patted all the pockets on his uniform.

Benkowski, who had stepped away when Tanner had first failed to find the map, returned shaking his head. "I searched the area where we were sleeping. Nothin'."

While the lieutenant pulled everything out of his pack and set it on the ground beside it, Sergeant Stagakis removed one of the straps for his radio from his arm and let the other strap slide down until the pack frame hit the ground. He, too, began rummaging through his pack with increasing frustration. "Mine's gone, too," he said angrily. "That little fucker must'a tooken 'em."

"Dodie?" Jones said, still kneeling by his now-empty pack. "Why would he do that?"

"Give 'em to the VC, probably," Tanner said.

"Get us lost," Cassidy suggested.

"Never trusted that little bastard," Romano remarked casually.

Jones hurriedly repacked his ruck and stood up to put it on. "Carl, get the BC on the horn," he told Tanner. Tanner pressed the handset to his ear and began calling. Gardner and Gonzalez returned, shaking their heads.

"Spread out," Stagakis told the men, "he might be bringing gooks here. Keep an eye out." Daley started to take his place on the perimeter, but Jones stopped him. Before the lieutenant could say anything, however, Tanner handed him the radio handset."

"It's him," Tanner warned, "and he sounds pissed."

"Rifle Six, this is Dagger Six," Jones said into the mouthpiece. After a brief pause, he explained their situation, with pauses during which Daley could hear the angry tones of the battalion commander leaking past Jones' ear.

"I understand, sir, but our scout has disappeared with both our maps. . . .No, sir, just those two. . . We're not sure how he did it. . .Yes, we looked all over. . . Wait one." Jones let his hand with microphone drop to his chest and turned to Daley.

"Can Ky still find the fort?" he asked.

Daley relayed the question to Ky, who assured him he knew the area well.

"He believes he can, sir," Jones said into the radio. "Roger that, sir. . . Yes, sir, but what about fire support?. . . That's true, but now we can't even guess where we are. . .Roger. Out."

"He wants us to keep goin'?" Stagakis asked with disbelief.

Jones handed the mike back to Tanner. His expression was dark and full of doubt. "Yes. But if we don't find the fort by noon, we're to turn around and head back."

"What good will that do?" Stagakis complained. "Even if we find it, we won't know where it is."

"I don't know either, Sergeant," Jones told him. "I just do what I'm told."

"Fuck me!" Stagakis muttered under his breath. Daley felt a tinge of fear. If these experienced infantrymen were dubious about their chances, what did that mean for him?

"Daley, tell Ky what we're doing," Jones ordered. "Sergeant Stagakis, get everyone else into column. Let's move out."

SEVEN

The disappearance of Dodie with the maps had put everyone on edge. The men were maintaining a five-meter interval, rarely speaking, and constantly looking in all directions for anything suspicious. Daley could feel the tension, and even Ky had lost his smile. Benkowski had volunteered to take point again, and was so far in front that Daley only caught occasional glimpses of him. The terrain was still high grass and reeds interspersed with small clumps of trees, any of which, Daley knew, could be hiding enemy soldiers. On everyone's mind was the question of why Dodie had taken the maps and vanished, and in which direction had he gone. If he was running on ahead of them to warn the enemy, the Americans could be walking into an ambush. When the platoon had moved out onto the trail this morning, Benkowski, Ky, and others had searched for footprints, knowing Dodie's little combat boots would leave a distinctive pattern, but had found nothing.

Mid-morning the trail had crossed a small creek, and the muddy approaches to the ford had revealed hundreds of footprints, but all appeared to be from tire-tread sandals and tennis shoes. The absence of boot prints, however, did little to ease the concern of the Americans. Dodie could have changed shoes, or avoided the crossing, or who knows what. The only bright spot, Daley realized, was that the constant worrying about their situation had taken his mind off his aches and pains. His ankles felt like they were swelling, his thighs burned with muscle fatigue, and his back and shoulders ached. His hands were covered with tiny cuts made by the sharp blades of grass they were passing through, and his neck throbbed from the unaccustomed weight of his helmet. But all those complaints were pushed to the back of his mind by the external dangers that faced him. What was a little discomfort compared to the possibility of a bullet striking home?

Not long after crossing the creek the trail cut through the middle of one those small clumps of trees, and Jones took that opportunity to call for a rest break. At Sergeant Stagakis' direction, the men set up a hasty perimeter defense, then sat down to have a drink of water. Daley saw Tanner reach into his shirt pocket for his pack of cigarettes, but, without being told, thought better of it and put it back. Jones and Stagakis moved to the center of the stand and huddled together in worried conversation. Daley sat down and leaned back against a tree trunk, with Ky squatting beside him. Ortiz, the medic, came over and sat down next to Daley.

"How're you doing?" Ortiz asked solicitously.

"I'm making it," Daley told him, "but just barely. You guys do this all the time?"

"Not really. Mostly we just go out for the day with minimal equipment, guns and canteens. Long patrols like this are usually done by the LRRPs."

"Lurps?" Daley asked. He had heard the term in passing, but wasn't familiar with it.

"Long Range Reconnaissance Patrols. They'll go out for a week or so at a time. Got special freeze-dried rations, travel light."

"So how come we're doing this instead of them?"

"Fuck if I know," Ortiz said with a shrug. "We get all the shit jobs. I don't think the BC likes Lieutenant Jones."

"Why not?"

"Don't know. Maybe 'cause he's black. Maybe 'cause he's from California. The colonel don't always confide in me."

Daley took another sip of water from his canteen as he thought about that. Despite the Army's best efforts, there was still a lot of racial prejudice, with this being the first war when the troops were fully integrated. Daley had no problem with serving under a black officer, but others, like Tanner, clearly chafed at the idea.

Ortiz interrupted Daley's thoughts. "How much water you got left?"

Daley shook his canteen to gauge the amount of slosh. "About a quarter left in this one. The other one's still full."

"Good. Glad to see you're rationing it. We probably shoulda set up ponchos to catch the rain last night. Maybe do that tonight. I've got water purification tablets, too."

"Yeah," Daley groused, "it's a bitch being thirsty all the time. I could sure do with a cold Coke."

"Ain't many Coke kids in this area," Ortiz commented. "Guess we'll just have to suffer."

Daley turned his head and asked Ky how he was doing on water. Ky told him he was fine. Daley wondered if Ky could drink the creek water and not get sick, since he was born here.

"What's Ky think about Dodie going AWOL?" Ortiz asked.

"Haven't really had time to ask him," Daley responded. He turned to Ky again and began speaking in Vietnamese.

"Where do you think Duong went?" Daley asked. Ky gave a half smile, apparently pleased at being included in any conversation.

"He wants to rejoin the People's Army," Ky said, using the official name of the NVA. Unlike the Viet Cong, the NVA was an organized army with uniforms and a typical military command structure. "He will give them the maps to prove he is loyal to them."

"So he is probably ahead of us on this trail?"

"Maybe. Or maybe not. I do not think he knows this area. He might have gone back across the river. There he could disguise himself as a peasant and travel to a People's Army base he knows about."

Daley translated this for Ortiz, but the medic was clearly hoping for something more definite. "That little motherfucker!" Ortiz grumbled.

"How far are we from the French fort?" Daley asked Ky.

"Not far. Maybe an hour or two."

Daley turned to Ortiz. "He says the fort is an hour or two away. What are we going to do when we get there, anyway?"

"Nothin', I hope," Ortiz answered. "You don't want to go pokin' a wasp's nest with a stick."

"Then why are we out here?"

"Everybody's got to be somewhere," Ortiz told him philosophically. Just then the shade of the grove deepened as clouds moved in to block the sun. "Shit. Looks like we're gonna get wet again."

Daley looked up through the leaves and saw how dark the clouds were, pregnant with rain. In Basic Training a black drill sergeant had told him, "It don't rain in the Army, it rain ON the Army." Daley now understood that somewhat cryptic remark.

"We're moving out," Sergeant Stagakis announced in a voice just loud enough to carry throughout the grove. Like the others, Daley struggled to his feet and found his place in the column. Benkowski took off down the trail, alert and cautious, and a minute later Jones led the rest of the column out of the grove.

Within a few minutes the storm broke, engulfing the patrol in rain. The water came down in sheets, turning the trail into mud and reducing their vision to about fifty meters. Daley tried turning his face up to the shower to catch as much water as possible in his gaping mouth, but despite the apparent strength of the downpour, only a few drops wet his tongue. Every little bit helps, he thought. He considered taking off his helmet to catch more of the water, but decided that was too dangerous under the circumstances. His helmet wasn't all that clean, anyway. At least the plastic C-ration spoon sticking out of his shirt pocket would get washed.

Not long after the storm had broken, they crossed what appeared to be an old road. It was overgrown with weeds, and was little more than two parallel tracks of dirt that were now turned to mud. The road ran roughly north to south, but the heavy rain kept them from seeing where it led in either direction. Since it didn't appear to have been used in years, Lieutenant Jones didn't seem overly concerned about it. Daley wondered why it was there, and who had created it. Maybe it was something left over from the French colonial days, he thought.

The heavy rain slowed them down, but they kept pushing forward. Daley kept checking his watch, secretly hoping that noon would arrive before they found the fort, so they could turn around and head back to safety. By eleven the rain had eased to a steady drizzle, but the air was so saturated with moisture that Daley could still see only about a hundred meters, and his breathing was labored. The mud stuck to his boots, making each step more difficult, his feet feeling like they were encased in lead. Wallowing in his misery, Daley just kept slogging ahead, until he saw Benkowski.

His heart pounded, because Benkowski was running toward them in a low crouch, patting the air with his free hand as a signal to get down. Daley threw himself into the high grass next to the trail and brought his M-16 into a ready position. Looking through the dripping stalks, he saw Benkowski huddle with Jones, both kneeling just off the trail. This didn't look good at all. The lieutenant grabbed the radio handset from Tanner, who had moved up to a position just behind him, and spoke into it briefly. Daley heard him tell Sergeant Stagakis to come forward before he handed the mike back to Tanner. Jones then looked straight at Daley and motioned for him and Ky to join him.

Daley got up onto his feet, but kept his knees bent and his back hunched over to lower his profile. He crooked his finger at Ky to follow him, and scuttled over to where Jones knelt. Meanwhile Benkowski had scurried away, headed back up the trail. Kneeling next to Jones, Daley asked in a hoarse whisper, "What is it, sir?"

Jones gave his head a quick shake and pointedly looked back down the trail, indicating he was waiting for the arrival of Stagakis. Daley noticed that Ky was looking around himself and nodding with a half-smile, water dripping from the rim of his cowboy hat. Drops were also falling from Daley's helmet, and he was soaked to the skin, but his body still felt warm, for some reason. He watched the trail and saw the platoon sergeant, keeping his stocky body low, approach them in a hurry. He, too, knelt as he joined the small group, looking at Jones expectantly.

"The fort's just ahead," Jones told them quietly. "Three or four hundred meters, Benkowski says. It's hidden in a patch of jungle, surrounded by old rice paddies." Jones nodded at Daley. "Can Ky give me the layout of the fort, and what's around it?"

Daley remembered from his initial interrogation of Ky how the young man had described it, but he asked Ky to go over it again. Having drawn the fort during the first conversation with Ky, he knew its general layout already, but went over it again. Daley cleared a bare patch of earth in the middle of the trail and began drawing in the mud with the end of his finger as Ky told him the shape and size of the small fort.

"It's basically a square, about forty meters on a side," Daley told Jones and Stagakis, who were squatting down and staring intently at the jagged lines in the soggy ground. "There's two buildings, at opposite corners of the square. This big one is two-story, and the other one is single story. The bigger one has 'a big metal can' on top—I'm guessing it's an old steel pill box. The wall around the compound is about chest high, but it's collapsed in a couple areas. There was a gate directly across from the big building, but it's gone now."

"How many men?" Jones asked.

Daley repeated the question to Ky, who told him: "Maybe fifty, maybe only a handful. The fort is mainly a way station for soldiers going into Viet Nam from Cambodia, I think. When I was there, there were about a fifty People's Army soldiers, but most of them were traveling on the next night."

Daley was annoyed at Ky for not telling him this sooner, and at himself for not asking the right questions. He passed on the information to Jones, whose face clouded at this news.

"So these 'advisers,'" he said grimly, "might not still be there."

"That's possible," Daley admitted.

There was a long pause as Jones considered the options. Finally he asked, "What do you think, Sarge?"

Stagakis looked at the crude drawing in the dirt and rubbed his jaw. "Guess we'll have to check it out, sir."

"Yeah," Jones agreed with a resigned sigh. "We'll need to do a recon all the way around the fort, to determine the best approaches."

"I'll go," Stagakis volunteered without enthusiasm.

"Who do you want to take with you?" Jones asked. Before Stagakis could answer, Daley found himself interrupting.

"I'll do it," Daley said, regretting it the minute the words popped out of his mouth. "Me and Ky."

Jones and Stagakis both gave him looks of astonishment mixed with appraisal. "Makes sense," Jones remarked. "Ky knows the area."

Stagakis didn't look totally convinced, and Daley could tell the sergeant's main doubts centered around Daley, not Ky. Daley was a remf, not an infantryman, of unknown capabilities. But he was the only one who could interpret for Ky. The older man stared at Daley for a minute before finally nodding his head. "Okay," he said, "let's get ready." He stood up and turned in a full circle, observing the surrounding terrain, and then pointed to a small clump of trees to their north.

"LT, why don't you take the rest of the men over to that bunch of trees and set up a perimeter. I'll send Benkowski back to you when we pass him." He slid the radio off his back and began detaching his rucksack. "We're just taking weapons and ammo and the radio," Stagakis told Daley. "Ortiz, you take our gear."

Daley gratefully took off his pack and pistol belt and handed them to Ortiz. He explained what was happening to Ky, who handed his bags to Ortiz as well. "Helmets?" Daley asked the burly sergeant. Stagakis thought about it for a moment, but then shook his head.

"Naw, leave it here. We need to travel light and quiet. You got a boonie hat on you?"

"In my pocket," Daley told him, patting the cargo pocket on his right thigh. He took off the helmet and replaced it with the crushed hat. Stagakis went into his pack and pulled out one of the stateside issue olive drab baseball caps, well-worn and dirty, with the bill rolled almost into a cylinder.

"Okay, here's how we'll do this," he told Daley. "We'll circle around the fort clockwise, staying about 300 meters away, and see what we can see." Daley quickly relayed this information to Ky.

"Sergeant, you might need these," Jones said, and handed Stagakis a pair of binoculars.

"Thanks," Stagakis told him, taking them and trying to figure out how to carry them. Seeing Ky with nothing in his hands, he gave the binoculars to the young man, who beamed with pride at being asked to help. Ky turned the binoculars over and over in his hands, marveling at the seemingly magical device. "Tell him to be careful with those," Stagakis told Daley.

"That is very easy to break," Daley told Ky. "Do not drop it or get it dirty, or the sergeant will beat you."

Ky clutched the binoculars to his chest and nodded rapidly, putting an earnest look on his face. "I will protect them," Ky promised. "I do not think the old sergeant will beat me, though." Ky had recognized Daley's threat for what it was—empty and unnecessary.

Handing his rifle to Daley to hold for a minute, Stagakis pulled the radio back on, now missing the ruck, and straightened his cap. Taking back the rifle, he said, "Let's move out," and started up the trail. Daley and Ky fell in behind him, with Daley wondering just what he had now gotten himself into.

EIGHT

Feeling incredibly lighter and slightly cooler without all that extra equipment, Daley followed the burly sergeant up the narrow path away from the rest of the platoon and the relative security their numbers provided. Behind him Ky tread lightly in his sandals, his cowboy hat jauntily tilted back and his happy countenance full of excitement. Daley marveled at the young Vietnamese man's apparent lack of fear and trepidation, and hoped it would wear off on him. Daley's stomach was in knots, and he held his M-16 in a death grip while his eyes darted from side to side, seeking any hint of danger. He wasn't scared, he told himself, he was just very alert and cautious—and maybe juiced on adrenaline.

The grass and reeds here were almost shoulder high, and scattered bushes and small clumps of trees limited their view of the surrounding countryside to narrow slices that opened and closed as they moved down the trail. They had gone only a couple hundred yards when they heard a brief sharp whistle from their left. Hidden in a thicket of tall bushes Daley could just make out Benkowski waving to them. Leaving the well-worn path, they pushed through the tall grass to join him.

"Over here," Benkowski told them quietly, leading them through the thicket to a position that gave them a view out the other side. Crowding close to Stagakis to get a better look, all Daley saw at first was more grass and a larger cluster of trees and bushes less than a quarter of a mile away. As he stared at it, however, rectangular shapes began to resolve through the dense foliage, and there was a brief glint of a momentary reflection.

"Yes, that is it!" Ky said joyfully, pointing over Daley's shoulder.

"You seen any movement?" Stagakis asked Benkowski.

"I saw one gook come out into the weeds to take a dump a few minutes ago, but that's all."

Stagakis took off his ball cap and rubbed this thinning red hair. "You head on back to the rest of the platoon," he told Benkowski. "They're in a patch of jungle just north of the trail where we stopped. Me and these two are going to circle around the fort to get a better look-see."

"Roger," Benkowski said, relief just barely apparent in his expression. Daley suspected Benkowski had expected he would be the one sent forward on the recon. With no further discussion, the young soldier pushed his way out of the thicket and headed back the way they had come.

Stagakis replaced his cap and moved closer to the edge of the thicket to get a better view. "Looks like old paddies close to the fort," he remarked. Daley stretched his neck to get a better look, and after a few moments thought he detected rectangular patterns in the grass and reeds that would have escaped him if they hadn't been pointed out by the sergeant. His estimation of Stagakis's abilities, already high, went up another notch.

Stagakis bobbed his head toward the southwest and said, "We'll head over to that patch of trees." He shouldered his way through the bushes and ducked down as he emerged into the high grass. Daley and Ky followed, emulating his crouched posture. Threading their way through the curtains of stalks with their sharp leaves, the three men moved silently, ignoring the buzzing insects and humid heat. The skies had remained cloudy most of the day, but that had done nothing to lower the temperature. In a few minutes they had reached the small stand of trees, and when they shoved their way through the foliage into the center of the grove, Daley was very relieved to once again be able to stand up straight. All three then moved over to the west side of the stand and pushed some branches aside to see out. They now had a better view of the southeast corner of the fort, but it was still obscured by the heavy vegetation around it.

"Glasses," Stagakis demanded curtly, his open hand held behind him. Daley took the binoculars from Ky and placed them in Stagakis' hand. While the sergeant studied the fort through the binoculars, Daley took a minute to scope out his immediate surroundings. It was a small clump of jungle like so many others in this area, with five or six trees surrounded by bushes, and only low grass and vines in between the trees. And a large rock. Daley shook his head quickly in consternation. There just weren't any large rocks in this area of Viet Nam. He stepped over and knelt down to touch the mostly buried stone, brushing away the leaves and dirt that partially obscured it. It was only then that he grasped how rectangular the stone was. And as he ran his hand over it, pieces of it broke away—it was old concrete, not stone. It appeared to be the base of an old concrete post, about a foot square at its base. Daley wondered what it was doing here, why it had ever been set up in this remote location, but his ponderings were interrupted by Stagakis.

"Daley," he said gruffly, "come take a look."

Daley stood up and rejoined Stagakis at the edge of the grove, taking the binoculars and holding them up to his glasses with a clink as the plastic eyepieces hit his lenses. "Shit" he mumbled and placed the binoculars under his left arm while he removed his glasses, folded them, and stuck one of the stems into the pencil pocket of his shirt. He placed the butt of his rifle on the ground between his legs and clamped the barrel between his knees so he had both hands free to hold the binoculars. Holding them up to his face, he pointed them toward the fort, twirling the dial and adjusting them until it was relatively in focus. The clouds actually helped, as they reduced the contrast between light and shadow, allowing him to gradually make out the hidden shapes. He could see the two-story building, which was closest to them, and make out thin vertical slits in the upper portion. On top of the building was a rusty cylinder about six feet in diameter and four feet tall. It could have been a water tank, but from the rivets Daley could just discern around the top, he surmised it was more likely an old pill box designed for a machine gun. Back before World War Two the French had been greatly enamored of such fortifications, the ultimate expression of which was the Maginot Line.

A low concrete wall extended north from the eastern edge of the building, and a similar wall stretched west from the southern side. Daley could just barely make out that the eastern wall turned a corner and led to an open gateway, while the southern wall turned north before disappearing behind the big building. The second building Ky had described was apparently somewhere behind the larger building, invisible from this angle. A couple large trees grew in the courtyard, their tops just visible over the roof of the main blockhouse. The tops of the trees, both those in the courtyard and those around the fort, didn't look right, and Daley studied them trying to figure out what the problem was. Then it came to him.

"Camouflage netting!" he breathed.

"Good eye," Stagakis said approvingly. "That's how come we didn't know that fort was there."

Daley flushed with pride at the simple compliment. Next to him Ky was shuffling around, almost dancing, and Daley lowered the binoculars to see what the problem was. Ky had a pleading look on his face, and motioned toward the binoculars.

"May I look?" he asked excitedly.

Daley handed the instrument over, and Ky immediately lifted it to his face. Daley started to explain how to focus them, but Ky was already doing so. Because Ky had been carrying the binoculars since they had left the platoon, Daley guessed the young man had been experimenting with them along the way.

"Did you see any gooks?" Stagakis asked Daley while they waited for Ky to have his chance.

"Nope. You?"

"Nah. They're either in the parade ground or in the buildings, if there's any there."

There was a noise from overhead, and Daley and Stagakis both looked up, bringing their rifles up into a ready position. After a moment Daley realized what it was—raindrops. The big drops, scattered at first, were splattering on the leaves of the trees. The noise got grew gradually as the tempo of the rain increased.

Stagakis reached over and roughly took the binoculars from Ky so he could raise them to his own eyes. Ky pouted but looked contrite.

"Motherfuck! There's one," Stagakis said. "He was sleeping up on top, but the rain woke his ass up." He handed the binoculars to Daley, who trained them on the pillbox and immediately saw the North Vietnamese soldier, in his green uniform and pith helmet, standing up and looking miserable as the rain drenched him. His AK-47 hung barrel-down at his side. He made a slow scan of the countryside, his gaze slipping past the grove where the three Americans stood without pausing, and then strolled over to the north edge of the roof, where Daley now noticed two pieces of bamboo sticking up. It was a ladder, and the NVA soldier tentatively grasped the poles and climbed down out of sight.

"He got down and went inside," Daley told Stagakis, while handing the binoculars to Ky. The rain was now coming down pretty hard, and the water was dripping down past the leaves and onto Daley's head and shoulders.

"Doesn't like getting wet, I guess," Stagakis remarked. "Just as well. With the rain and him off the roof, we can move a little quicker. Let's go."

Stagakis slipped through the foliage to their left, heading toward another clump of trees to the west, one that was only a couple hundred yards south-southeast of the fort. Keeping low, the three men edged through the tall reeds quickly, depending on the now-heavy rain to mask both the noise and the sight of their transit.

This new clump was only two trees and a few bushes, and it was much closer to the fort than the last one had been. They paused there only long enough to take a brief look at the fort from this new angle. They could now see the second building, cater-corner across the parade ground from the bigger building. It was only a single story, more rectangular than square, with a couple windows and a door in the longer side. With fewer trees on this side of the compound, Daley was able to see the south wall more clearly, and noted that it was crumbling, with several significant jagged gaps. Neither he nor Stagakis saw any figures or movement; apparently everyone was inside, sheltering from the downpour.

"Probably not worried about getting attacked out here," Stagakis commented. "Still, it's pretty piss-poor security."

Taking advantage of the cover the sheets of rain were providing, Stagakis led them straight west, bypassing a small thicket just to the south of the fort. Daley stumbled when they crossed the first of several rice paddy dikes, which were hidden in the tall grass. Treading more carefully, he now noticed the subtle alterations in the color and height of the grasses that signaled a dike ahead, and avoided any further missteps. He estimated they had traipsed through at least ten paddies before they reached their next waystation, a small grove of trees west-southwest of the fort. He was now thoroughly soaked to the skin, but took pride in the fact that he was more hard core than the NVA soldier on the roof of the fort, the one who had sought shelter and left his post when the rain started. Being wet—and tired—was certainly uncomfortable, but Daley's self-confidence and self-image were improving as he demonstrated to himself that he was just as manly as anyone else. In high school and college he had always been the geek, the nerd with good grades and bad luck with girls, the skinny guy who didn't play sports. Now he was beginning to feel like the "lean, mean, fighting machine" his drill sergeants had demanded he become.

In the grove they paused to rest a moment and observe the west side of the fort. The foliage on that side was thicker than the others, but they were still able to see some details. The west wall of the smaller building had three of the vertical slit windows, and Daley had decided those were designed to be gun ports that allowed the defenders to fire out but prevent attackers from coming in. The camouflage netting over the courtyard was sagging under the weight of all the water, and Daley was pretty sure it was American-made. Stolen, he presumed, or bought from corrupt South Vietnamese soldiers. Taking turns with the binoculars, the three of them watched the compound for ten minutes without seeing any movement.

"Let's keep moving," Stagakis said, handing the binoculars back to Ky, and slipped through the bushes on the north side of the grove. Daley and Ky followed, heading across the open fields of grass toward yet another stand of jungle. This one was larger than the others, and almost directly northwest of the fort. As they ducked inside the cover of the trees, Daley saw that the grove was split by the main trail that led by the fort. It looked like two-thirds of the trees were on the north side of the trail, and Stagakis led them to the center of that larger section. He found a small clearing surrounded by thick bushes that mostly shielded them from the view of anyone traveling along the trail, as well as from anyone at the fort.

"Wait here," Stagakis told them, slipping the radio off his back and propping it against a tree. He stealthily crept away toward the trail, leaving Daley and Ky to wonder what he was doing.

"Where is he going?" Ky asked in a whisper.

"To scout the trail," Daley guessed with more confidence than he felt.

In less than five minutes the sergeant was back, saying nothing until he had repositioned the radio on his back. "Where does that trail go?" he asked Ky, and waited while Daley translated, even though he already knew the answer.

"It goes to a hospital camp in Cambodia," Daley told him, after confirming that with Ky.

"Probably hooks up with the Ho Chi Minh trail, too," Stagakis suggested. "Looks pretty well traveled."

Daley nodded in agreement.

Looks like there's a creek farther up the trail," Stagakis said. "Is that right?"

Daley translated the question for Ky, who confirmed that a small stream fed a little pond that the VC had used for bathing. Stagakis nodded, adding that detail to his mental map.

Noticing a change in the ambient noise, Daley tilted his head back and looked around. "Rain's letting up," he remarked.

"Afraid so," Stagakis replied. "Better keep moving." Leading them to the northeastern edge of the grove, the sergeant paused to assess the route they would next need to take. To their right Daley could see more overgrown rice paddies that paralleled the trail that ran in front of the fort. Stagakis pointed to a small clump of bushes to their northeast, just beyond the paddies. "That's our next stop," he said. "Keep really low, 'cause they might see us from the fort."

Stagakis stepped out into the high grass in a crouch, frequently looking to his right to ensure there was no sightline to the fort. Daley and Ky followed, staying as low as they could and still walk. At one point they had to get down on their hands and knees to remain out of sight, and in another area they had to duck-walk. Even when they reached the bushes, they couldn't stand up all the way without their heads sticking up above the leaves. On the other hand, they now had a much better view of the fort. They were almost directly north of the entrance, and there were fewer trees on this side. A short path branched south from the main trail to the gate of the fort, which now consisted solely of two rectangular gate posts with nothing in between. Looking through the opening, they could see the front of the larger building, with its door and a couple windows on the lower story.

Taking the binoculars from Ky, Stagakis studied the fort for a couple minutes, and then handed the glasses to Daley. In preparation, Daley had already pocketed his own glasses, which were of limited use anyway, due to the drops of water all over them. As quickly as it had begun, the rain suddenly stopped, leaving only the sound of water dripping from the leaves of the bushes around them. Daley raised the binoculars to his eyes and focused them on the fort's entrance. With the image closer and sharper now, he could see the rusting hinges left hanging on the gate posts, and the jagged gaps in the outer wall where the cement had crumbled. The smaller building to his right had only a couple of the slit windows facing the trail, and he could see something on its flat roof, what appeared to be a jumble of wood and maybe sandbags. Perhaps there had been a machine gun nest up there at one time, he surmised.

The larger building's doorway was dark and empty; it appeared there was no actual door, and the two windows beside it were unglazed. The enemy might be using the fort, but they had apparently invested no effort in restoring it. A wide bamboo ladder leaned against the left side of the building, and it looked fairly new. He focused on the metal cylinder on the roof, and could now see two elongated oval slits in the side: gun ports, confirming his previous guess about its purpose.

Ky nudged him and said, "Soldier!"

Daley shifted his gaze to the courtyard and then saw the man coming out of the door of the big building, hefting his AK with one hand while put on his pith helmet with the other. He stopped in the middle of the open area, then wandered over to the ladder and began climbing. Grasping his rifle in one hand made the ascent difficult, but he managed it in short order. Walking around the perimeter of the roof, he made a minimal effort to survey the area around the fort, then stopped on the eastern edge and stood facing the approach of the trail. At first Daley was concerned that the soldier had seen something, that perhaps Benkowski had come back and been inadvertently noticed. But then the man tucked his rifle under his arm, fiddled with his pants, and began pissing off the roof. Slowly exhaling with relief, Daley handed the binoculars back to Stagakis and took his own glasses out of his pocket. While the sergeant once again scanned the fort, Daley did his best to clean and dry his glasses with the tail of his shirt.

"The guy on the roof just sat down on the other side of the pillbox," Stagakis noted. "Another gook came out of the small building and went into the big one." With his glasses now relatively clean, Daley peered through the leaves, observing the activity in the fort as best he could. As he watched, two soldiers came out of the big building, each carrying an AK, but neither one wearing a helmet. One wandered over to the gate and leaned against a gate post, facing in toward the courtyard. The other strolled over to the back of the courtyard and took up a position next to a large tree growing there. He faced the one at the gate, and was similarly lacking in military bearing. The one at the gate shouted.

"Ready," Daley translated for Stagakis.

Two figures emerged from the dark doorway, the one in the lead taller than the one behind. The smaller figure behind had an AK pointed at the taller man's back. He poked the man with the barrel of his gun, causing the taller man to stumble and fall to his knees.

"That's the Chinese man," Ky whispered.

"Looks more like a prisoner than an adviser," Stagakis remarked.

Slowly the man rose to his feet and looked up at the camouflage netting overhead, as if hoping to see sunlight. With the cloud cover still hanging on, it was a vain hope. Stagakis passed the binoculars back to Daley, who quickly removed his glasses and focused on the man in the courtyard. His uniform was similar to Daley's, but with subtle differences. The shirt was tucked into his pants, and there was a colored patch on his left shoulder. The American Army had dispensed with colored patches several years earlier, as they made the soldiers easier targets in the jungle. While the man's facial features were obviously Oriental, they were clearly not Vietnamese.

"He's Korean," Daley announced suddenly.

"You sure?" Stagakis asked, obviously surprised.

"Pretty sure," Daley responded. "My roommate at Monterey was taking Korean, and I met all his teachers at a cookout. But what's a Korean doing here?"

"There's ROK soldiers in Viet Nam," Stagakis informed him.

"Rock?" Daley asked, not understanding.

"Republic of Korea," Stagakis explained. "I heard they're pretty tough soldiers."

Now Daley remembered reading somewhere that other countries had contributed troops and equipment to the war, although not in any great numbers. South Korea, in particular, had a vested interest in stopping communist expansion in Asia, so it was logical that they would send soldiers to aid the Americans.

"He's not Chinese," Daley told Ky in Vietnamese, "he's a Korean soldier, a prisoner."

"Ah," Ky said, as if that explained things that had bothered him.

"Guess they're giving him his daily exercise," Stagakis said. "Mighty nice of them."

"If the Chinese adviser is a Korean prisoner, I wonder what the Russian really is," Daley said, regretting his interpretation of Ky's description back in the base camp.

"No tellin'," Stagakis said. "Maybe gone, now."

They all watched for almost half an hour as the NVA soldiers forced the prisoner to walk around. Their taunts and angry gestures seemed half-hearted, as if they had been doing this for so long that it no longer gave them any pleasure. Finally they pushed the prisoner back inside the big building, and the two standing guards wandered over to the smaller building and went inside. Only the man on top of the big building remained outside, and only his legs were visible around the side of the pillbox. Asleep, Daley suspected.

"We need to get back to the others," Stagakis said. He called Jones on the radio and told him they were on the way, but nothing else. Dodging from thicket to clump, they hurried back east, finally rejoining the trail where they had left it.

NINE

"Korean?" Lieutenant Jones said in disbelief.

"That's what we think," Staff Sergeant Stagakis assured him. Daley nodded his head in agreement. Ky just kept smiling in non-comprehension. The four were gathered at the center of the small grove where the rest of the platoon had hidden while they did their recon around the fort. The men of the platoon were deployed around the edges of the grove, standing guard and eating C-rations. Daley suddenly realized just how hungry he was, and wished this discussion would end soon so he could get into his ruck.

"I guess I knew there were South Korean soldiers here in Nam, but never expected to ever run into any." Jones looked off into space for a moment. "What about the supposed Russian?"

"Didn't see anyone that looked like that," Daley said, taking off his boonie hat to wipe his forehead with his sleeve. "Might have left with the rest of them."

"Yeah, we only saw four gooks at the fort," Stagakis told him. "Might be more inside, but not many."

"Well, shit," Jones cursed. "What are we supposed to do now?" It was clearly a rhetorical question, so Daley didn't answer, but he believed the correct course of action was obvious. They should go in and get the Korean and then book back to the river. Jones looked over at Stagakis. "You didn't call this in to Battalion, did you?"

"No, sir, I thought you would want to do that." Daley realized that Jones had a radio, too, and should have known if Stagakis had called anyone. Of course, it was Tanner monitoring the radio, and

Jones might have reason to suspect that Tanner hadn't kept him fully informed.

"You're right," Jones told him. "I guess I better do that now." Daley clearly heard the reluctance in the lieutenant's tone of voice. Jones called for Tanner and walked away from them. Daley took that as a dismissal and went looking for his other equipment. As he had hoped, Ortiz had it, as well as Ky's two bags.

Daley and Ky got out some C-ration cans and had a quick late lunch. Daley had selected a can at random, and found it was pork slices, not one of his favorites. Regardless, he got his plastic spoon and shoveled the greasy meat into his mouth as fast as he could. He finished his meal with a John Wayne bar, the large coin-shaped slabs of hard chocolate that came in some of the cans of crackers. A brief swig of water from his canteen, and he was more refreshed than he would have expected. He put on his pistol belt and rucksack and traded his boonie hat for his helmet. Now he was ready to go again. Meanwhile, Ortiz had gathered their trash and was covering it with leaves.

"Specialist Daley," Lieutenant Jones called, "can you and Ky join us over here?" He and Sergeant Stagakis were kneeling in the center of the grove, looking over a bare patch of earth from which the leaves had just been swept. Daley motioned for Ky to follow, and the jogged over and knelt across from the officer. Using a small stick, Jones had drawn a line across the bare spot, and next to it had carved a square. Inside the square he had made two smaller squares, obviously intended to be the two building inside the fort. "Anything you can add to this?" Jones asked. Daley examined the crude drawing and compared it to the image in his head. Taking the stick from Jones, he drew in the path from the road to the fort, and added the gate. As he was doing that, Ky ran back to where he and Daley had just had their lunch. When he came back, he had two crumpled C-ration boxes and one empty can. He straightened one of the boxes and placed it on the drawing where the larger building was indicated, and then placed the empty can on top. The other box was carefully ripped in half and the one portion was placed where the smaller building was drawn. Then Ky searched the ground around them and found sticks that he laid down to indicate the walls of the fort. When he was done, he squatted down beside Daley and beamed with pride at his creation.

"Yeah, that's about it," Stagakis said approvingly, and reached over to pat Ky on the back. Ky's smile got even wider. Jones stared at the rudimentary diorama, working his mouth and wrinkling his forehead.

"So how we gonna do this?" Stagakis asked.

"Do what?" Daley interjected.

"We're going to rescue the prisoner," Jones informed him, clearly struggling with that decision. Because the lieutenant had been on the radio with Battalion, Daley figured that they had ordered Jones to carry out the rescue, despite any misgivings that Jones had. Daley had initially favored that course of action as well, but looking at the model of the fort now, he began to sees the problems and difficulties involved. They weren't sure how many enemy soldiers were in the fort, nor where exactly the prisoner was being held inside the larger building. Nor did they know if other troops might be returning to the fort soon, and since they didn't know exactly where they were, they couldn't call for support. At that point Daley noticed the patter of raindrops on the leaves above them; the rain had returned. And that rain meant they would have no air support.

Daley turned to Ky and asked him in Vietnamese, "You were in the fort before. Where do you think they are keeping the prisoner?"

Ky shrugged. "We didn't actually go in the fort. We camped outside it. But we just saw them take him inside the big building."

"I know, but where in the big building?"

Ky shrugged again. "But I could find out."

"How?" Daley asked, surprised by this offer. Jones and Stagakis watched the incomprehensible conversation without saying anything.

"I could go to the fort and tell them I am still Viet Cong, and ask questions." Ky said this seriously, with a grim smile of confidence.

Daley quickly considered the possibilities, and reached a conclusion. Turning to Jones, he announced, "Ky says he will go to the fort and find out more information. He'll pretend to be VC."

"What?" Stagakis said with astonishment.

"I don't know," Jones said doubtfully. "Can we really trust him?"

"I think you can trust him more than Dodie," Daley suggested mildly, hoping Jones wouldn't take the rebuke personally. He knew that Jones would ultimately be held responsible for the disappearance of Dodie with the maps. In the Army, shit always rolled downhill.

"He's done okay so far," Stagakis chimed in. "What have we got to lose? If he goes there and tells them where we are, there aren't enough of them there to do anything about it. The worst that could happen is we lose our Chieu Hoi."

Jones stared at Ky for a minute, as if assessing his suitability for the role. "He'll have to lose the hat," he remarked. Daley grinned at the implied acceptance of the plan.

Fifteen minutes later Ky was disappearing into the high grass to the west, leaving his cowboy hat behind with Daley. The plan they had devised had him retrace the steps Stagakis, Daley, and he had taken when reconning the fort. Circling back around the south side of the compound, Ky would find the trail on the far side and follow it back east to the fort entrance, as if coming from Cambodia. He would tell the NVA soldiers that he had just been released from the hospital camp after a prolonged illness, and was now returning to his unit in Viet Nam. He would claim weakness and request food, water, and a short rest. This would give him the opportunity to scope out the inside of the fort and ask apparently innocent questions. After a suitable time he would resume his journey east and rejoin the CRIP platoon. It was a simple plan, but still fraught with dangers. Daley was worried for Ky, afraid his naiveté and friendliness might give him away, but the die was cast. All they could do now was wait.

Daley went over and sat down next to Ortiz, the only member of the platoon with whom he had developed any sort of relationship. Most of the platoon was deployed around the perimeter of the grove standing guard, but as the medic, Ortiz was considered part of the command group and allowed to remain in the center of things, where he could respond to wherever was required. Ortiz had dropped his ruck and was sitting on his upturned helmet to keep his butt dry. Next to him were Daley's ruck and pistol belt, and Ky's canteen and food bag. Daley tossed Ky's hat on top of the young man's bags, before taking off his own helmet and upending it to sit on.

"Think this will work?" Ortiz asked him.

"Shit, I don't know," Daley answered despairingly. "He's a nice guy, but kind of goofy. I just hope they believe him."

"I can't believe the LT wants to rescue that Korean," Ortiz said, shaking his head.

"Probably just following orders," Daley surmised. SP4 Cassidy had walked up behind them and tilted his helmet in greeting. Cassidy looked Irish, with auburn hair and a pug nose.

"Nope," Cassidy said with certainty. "I heard him on the radio. I was monitoring Sarge's radio while he went to take a shit. The BC wanted us to pull back to the river and send in a whole company later, in a day or two. Jones was afraid they might move the prisoner, or reinforce the fort, before the other guys could get here. The LT is pretty much ignoring a direct order."

"No shit? Why would he do that?"

Cassidy looked around to be sure no one else was listening, then squatted down and lowered his voice. "The BC and the LT don't get along. Not sure why. I think the LT wants to prove himself, and prove the BC wrong at the same time."

"Okay for him, but what about us?" Daley had just realized that the lieutenant's willfulness was putting the rest of the platoon in danger.

"We do what we're told," Ortiz said. "And I think the lieutenant's right. We've got a chance to rescue a prisoner of war, and to not take it would be wrong."

Daley thought about that, and concluded Ortiz was probably right. They were here, they had the numbers and the intel, so there was no reason not to strike while the iron was hot. Besides, they didn't know exactly where they were anyway, so another, larger unit would have difficulty even finding the fort, and it would be almost impossible for them to approach it without alerting the enemy. A quick, surgical attack by CRIP right now would have a greater chance of success than a major assault by a full company later, he decided.

"I don't know," Cassidy said doubtfully. "It's pretty risky."

"Hey," Ortiz said theatrically, "You wanna live forever?" The old movie line didn't impress Cassidy.

"Fuck you," Cassidy said casually.

"And why aren't you on guard?" Ortiz added, ignoring the insult.

"I'm on airwatch," Cassidy said with false seriousness. Since the enemy didn't have any aircraft, there was no need to watch for approaching aircraft, even if they could see the sky through the trees and the low clouds. "I'm takin' a break, okay?" Cassidy grumbled. "Rosie said I could."

"Yeah, sure," Ortiz sneered. "Since when is Rosie in charge of anything?"

"He's a sergeant," Cassidy countered. "Besides, Sarge put him in charge while he talks to the LT."

Ortiz slowly shook his head in disbelief. "Sure, and I've got a bridge in Brooklyn you might wanta buy."

"Hey, that's my story, and I'm stickin' to it," Cassidy responded with a grin. "Lucky for you, I'm done with my break." He stood up and strolled away.

Daley's stomach rumbled, and he realized he was still hungry. Rooting around in his rucksack, he found a can of crackers and a small flat can of pineapple marmalade. After opening the cans and smearing some of the yellow jam on one of the crackers, he wondered who had invented pineapple marmalade, and why, and who had thought that was a good thing to put into C-rations. As far as he was concerned, neither one was a good idea, but he ate it anyway. It would probably be at least half an hour before Ky returned, and maybe an hour, so there was nothing else to do now but wait.

As he forced down the snack, Daley wondered where Ky was right at that moment. Had he made it to the far side of the fort, where the trail approached from the west? Would he be able to carry off his deception and return to the platoon? Daley was a little surprised that he was so worried about the young Vietnamese's fate. He had known the young man for only a few days, but he had to admit that he had already developed some sort of affection for him. He felt protective of Ky, like an older brother, and he wanted Ky to succeed and gain the respect of the other men in the patrol. Daley also knew that his own status in the platoon depended in part on how Ky performed, since he was Ky's escort and translator. He suspected the infantrymen around him considered them a package deal, a pair of outsiders, since neither of them were grunts who wore the Combat Infantryman's Badge. And as rough and tumble as those guys were, Daley desperately wanted their respect, for himself and for Ky.

The rain, off and on all day, let up to only a slight drizzle that made its way through the canopy overhead in the form of occasional large droplets. Daley decided this was as good a time as any to dry and lubricate his M-16. He pulled out an old green T-shirt from his rucksack that had remained relatively dry and, after removing the magazine, wiped down the outside of the rifle, then broke it open and pulled out the bolt to wipe it down as well. From the compartment in the butt he withdrew his cleaning kit and assembled the cleaning rod. Ortiz, beside him, was now doing the same, inspired, Daley hoped, by the interrogator's own actions. Daley pushed a couple dry patches through the barrel, then borrowed Ortiz's bottle of LSA lubricant and swabbed the inside of the barrel with that. He then applied LSA to the bolt and breech, reassembled the rifle, put away the cleaning kit, and worked the mechanism a couple times to ensure it was all working properly. After wiping down the magazine, he reinserted it into the well and tapped it home.

"Ready for Freddie," Ortiz said as he finished up his own weapon.

"Yep," Daley agreed. "But I hope we don't have to use these."

"Don't see how we'll avoid it," Ortiz said. "It's not going to be like in the movies, with us sneaking up on them and cutting their throats with bayonets. Hell, we don't even have bayonets."

"Well, maybe they'll surrender without a fight." Daley knew he sounded naïve and instantly regretted his remark.

"Yeah, it could happen," Ortiz said sarcastically. "You got a pencil and paper so I can figure the odds?"

"So how do you think we'll do it?" Daley asked sincerely, seeking enlightenment.

"Fuck if I know. That's for the Sarge and LT to figure out."

"Have they done something like this before?"

Ortiz rubbed the side of his nose. "Not since I been here. But Sarge is on his third tour, so he might have."

"Yeah, Sarge seems pretty knowledgeable."

"He knows his shit," Ortiz affirmed. "At least, when he's sober. But like I said, he usually is when we're in the field."

"I would hope so."

"Here he comes!" It was a loud whisper from someone off to his left. Daley jumped up and hurried over to the western edge of the grove, only to see Ky's head bobbing above the tall grass to the south, headed their way. Ky had continued on the trail past their location and then cut back, either because he wanted to disguise their location from anyone who might have been watching, or because he simply forgot where they were. Either way, he now parted the weeds and stepped into the relative openness of the grove.

"Hello, Sergeant," he greeted Daley with a smile. "I am back, just as I said I would be."

"Yes, you are," Daley replied, grinning with relief.

"Bring him over here," Lieutenant Jones said, pointing to the make-shift model of the fort Ky had built. Daley and Ky joined Jones and Stagakis in a circle around the little diorama, Ky squatting and the other three kneeling. "So. What did he find out?" Jones looked expectantly at Daley.

Before Daley could ask, Ky began telling his story in an excited hushed voice, emphasizing things with hand gestures and adding descriptive noises. He paused every few sentences for Daley to translate.

"I went the way the old sergeant told me to go, and no one saw me. When I got to the trail, I waited to make sure no one was coming or going on the trail, and then I walked to the fort. I yelled 'hello' to the fort before I walked up to the gate. A soldier whose name was Tho met me at the gate and asked who I was and what I wanted. I told him my name was Thieu and asked for some food and water. I told him I had been at the hospital camp recovering from an illness, and was walking back to Tay Ninh to rejoin my unit. He believed me, and invited me into the fort."

Ky took a moment to allow Daley to translate, and then continued. "Inside the fort I met two other soldiers. There was another one on the roof of the big building, but I did not meet him. They said there was an officer inside the building, but he was sick. I do not think they like that officer. They gave me some rice and some soup, and asked me questions about the hospital and about the fighting near Tay Ninh. I made up stories for them. I asked them if anyone else was at the fort, and they said usually there are about forty soldiers, but the others had gone to Cambodia to get supplies. They said it was just the officer and the four men, and the two prisoners."

"Two prisoners?" Jones said with a surprised look.

Daley asked Ky for more information, and then quickly translated for Jones and Stagakis.

"Yes. They said they have a Korean soldier, just as we saw, and they have a white soldier who is wounded. The white soldier is not American. They said he is from Oster Leah." That description left Daley confused for a minute. All he could think of was a blender and a Roy Orbison song. He repeated the phrase to Jones and Stagakis, saying it several times with different pronunciations and emphasis until he realized Ky meant Australia.

"Australian," Jones repeated. "Not Russian."

"I think Australian rank insignia are like European," Daley said in defense of his earlier assumption. "They have pips on their shoulder boards."

"And there are Aussies fighting here in Nam," Stagakis added, "just like the ROKs."

"Ask him where the prisoners are held," Jones told Daley.

"They are in rooms on the second floor of the big building," Ky said after Daley translated the question. "I do not know where on the second floor."

"How wounded is the Australian?" Stagakis asked.

"He doesn't know," Daley told them after a brief exchange with Ky. "He didn't want to seem too curious."

"What weapons do they have?" Jones asked.

"They each have AK-47s," Ky told Daley. "There is also an armory in the small building, where they have a machine gun and ammunition. I think they have an RPG launcher, too, but I did not see it. I only know about the armory because they said the rest of the unit, the ones that went to Cambodia, will be bringing more ammunition."

"When are those men supposed to arrive?" Jones now sounded worried.

"Tomorrow or the next day," Daley translated. "The soldiers think someone is also coming to take the prisoners somewhere else."

"So we can't wait," Jones said. Daley thought Jones acted like he had been vindicated in his earlier decision to rescue the prisoners. And he had.

By midafternoon Jones and Stagakis had devised a plan. Daley noticed that neither of them had contacted Battalion on the radio with the information Ky had provided. He assumed they were avoiding such radio contact to keep from receiving new orders. They were truly on their own now. The rain had resumed and was now a steady heavy drizzle that left the trees dripping and the soldiers soaked. Jones called all the men in from the perimeter and explained his plan to the men gathered around him, pointing out their approaches on the model of the fort.

Benkowski and Griffin would take positions along the trail near their current location and act as a blocking force in case anyone approached from the east. Stagakis would lead Jimmerson, Cassidy, Most, and Gonzalez southwest along the route he and Daley had taken during their initial recon, and then deploy into jump-off positions in the patch of jungle just south of the big building. Jones would lead the rest of the group northwest to a clump of trees northeast of the fort and also prepare to attack from there. Splitting off from this group, Kessler and Romano would continue circling around to the northwest until they reached the far grove that straddled the main trail, where they would be both a blocking force for anyone approaching from the west, and also be prepared to kill or capture anyone escaping from the fort. When everyone was in place, Stagakis and his group would assault on line toward the south and west walls of the fort, firing one or two shots each for effect. Once the defenders' attention was concentrated on this attack, Jones' group would rush the entrance from the north, with Ky and Daley calling for them to surrender.

"What if they don't surrender, sir?" Al Most asked. Jones just gave him a hard stare, but Romano answered.

"Then shoot 'em, dumbass."

"But watch where you're shootin'," Stagakis warned. "We'll be coming at them from opposite directions, so be sure you don't shoot at our own guys. Keep your rifles on semi, verify your target, and don't shoot unless you have to. We don't want a lot of gunfire to draw anyone's attention."

"That's right," Jones affirmed. "The less shooting the better. We need to conserve ammo and not kill the prisoners by accident.

Hopefully they'll give up without a fight, once they see they're outnumbered."

"Yeah, that'll happen," someone in the back said sarcastically.

"Any other questions?" Jones asked. Some shook their heads, and no one spoke up.

After dropping off Benkowski and Griffin along the trail, the remaining groups split up and headed for their initial positions. The rain began to increase in tempo, which made them more uncomfortable, but masked their movement from the soldiers in the fort, who were probably sheltering inside anyway. Daley checked his watch, and it was after four when his group reached the large clump of jungle that was their jumping off point. Kessler and Romano continued on, circling wide to the north of the fort to avoid detection, and soon disappeared from sight. To give the other group and the western blocking force time to get into position, Jones had decided that the attack would begin at 4:30. They still had fifteen minutes, so Daley went over the plan again with Ky, ensuring the young man understood his part in the action.

"Remember, stay right with me, and don't begin calling to the fort until I tell you."

"Yes, Sergeant. What should I tell them?" As almost always, Ky was smiling, but it was a smile of determination and concentration.

"Tell them they are surrounded by the American Army, and if they do not surrender, they will all die. Tell them that if they do surrender, they will be treated fairly as prisoners of war."

"Is that true?" A cloud of doubt passed over Ky's face. Daley had his own doubts, but did not confide them to Ky. It would be hard enough getting the two prisoners back to American lines, so escorting the NVA as well would be tricky at best. Executing prisoners of war was against Army policy and the Geneva convention, but in this war, many rules had already been broken.

"Yes, they will be treated fairly," Daley assured Ky with as much sincerity as he could fake.

"What are you two talking about?" Jones asked conversationally, sidling over to Daley.

"What he'll yell to the soldiers in the fort," Daley answered. "He'll tell them they're surrounded, and if they surrender they will be treated fairly."

"Fairly," Jones repeated. He had a bemused look on his face, which caused a twinge in Daley's chest. "Yes, that's sounds good." Jones checked his watch. "About time."

To the entire group he announced, "Spread out. As soon as we hear the shots from Sergeant Stagakis' group, we'll move out on line. Don't run, but don't dilly-dally."

Ortiz and Gardner shuffled off to the right, and Daley and Ky deployed to the left, leaving Jones and Tanner in the center. All of them moved forward to the verge of the grove, ready to move out across the tall grass and overgrown rice paddies. Daley felt a real tightness in his chest. He had never been in a real battle before, and he was very worried about how he would react. He smiled ruefully to himself as he thought: at least if he pissed his pants, no one would notice, since he was already soaked by the rain. With a start he remembered he didn't have a round in the chamber, and quickly pulled the charging handle to the rear and let it fly forward. Then he turned the rifle to one side so he could see the safety lever and moved it to SEMI with his thumb. He cursed his own stupidity, thinking what a fool he would have looked like if he had tried to fire with nothing in the breech.

The rain was coming down steadily now, obscuring his view of the fort like a glass-bead curtain. The drops of water on his glasses didn't help, either. What Daley could see, however, was a large stand of trees that shielded the geometric forms of the fort. Made of concrete, the walls had eroded and broken down in places, and all of it had moss or something growing on it, turning the old gray cement dark and splotchy. He could just barely make out the trail passing in front of the fort, and the worn path that led from the trail to the fort's entrance. There were trees and bushes around the front of the fort, both between the trail and the walls, and on the nearer side of the trail, limiting what he could actually see inside.

The camouflage netting spread between the trees over the fort was sagging with the weight of the rain, keeping the interior dark and foreboding. It looked deserted, like an ancient Inca ruin, and he could detect no movement, no sign of life. Maybe they've all left already, he thought hopefully.

A crackle of gunshots broke out on the far side of the fort, muffled by the rain, but easily distinguishable.

"That's it," Lieutenant Jones said urgently. "Let's go."

In a ragged line the six men strode out into the wet high grass, parting the dripping stalks with their knees and holding their rifles at shoulder level, ready to fire. Daley kept glancing to his right to ensure he stayed on line with the others, who were advancing with long strides, but not running. Ky was between him and Tanner, and the slender young man with the cowboy hat was slipping through the high weeds far more gracefully than the Americans, like a leopard stalking its prey.

After the initial burst of gunfire from Sergeant Stagakis' men, only the drumming of the rain was heard. Daley could still see no movement, and there was no return fire from the men within the fort. Maybe they had left?

"Ky!" Jones commanded, and the young man responded. Without slowing his pace, he called out as loudly as he could to the men inside the fort, ordering them to surrender. Daley used his own Vietnamese language skills to say the same thing, emphasizing that the fort was surrounded. There was still no response from inside the fort. When they reached the outer line of trees, the other Americans paused and took cover behind the trunks and higher bushes, so Daley and Ky did the same. Both continued to yell their warnings. Dodging from tree to bush to tree, the men moved closer to the fort, crossing the trail and spreading out in the trees to other side of the entrance path. Daley found himself at the northeast corner of the fort, looking down the east wall to where it connected to the two-story building. Between the corner and the structure the wall had collapsed, leaving a ragged gap. With Ky right behind him, Daley crept along the wall and peeked around the jagged edge of the hole.

His heart skipped a beat as he saw an NVA soldier a few feet away, standing at the base of the bamboo ladder, his AK-47 held by the forestock in his left hand. The man saw Daley at the same time, and immediately dropped the assault rifle and raised his hands. "I surrender," he yelped, his face full of fear. Daley trained his rifle on the man and carefully edged forward and over the rubble at the middle of the opening. As he rounded the edge of the wall, he saw three other enemy soldiers scattered around the courtyard, all holding up their hands. Jones and Gardner had just entered through the gate and covered the soldiers with their rifles. Tanner and Ortiz came in behind them and spread out, their M-16s at the ready, and a moment later Stagakis and his men, who had climbed over the back wall, took up positions behind the men with their arms raised. Daley heaved a great sigh of relief. The fort had been taken without anyone being killed or wounded, and all was now right with the world. Or so he thought.

"Sergeant," Ky barked in warning, looking at the doorway to the large building. Daley heard a wet cough from inside, and then another soldier staggered forward, a pistol in his hand. Bracing himself with one hand on the doorframe, the man raised his pistol and aimed at the group of American's at the fort's entrance.

Without any thinking or planning, as if on auto-pilot, Daley raised his rifle to his shoulder and fired off three quick shots. At such close range, only about twenty feet, it was almost impossible to miss, and Daley was sure he hadn't. Yet the man kept standing for a moment, his head turning toward Daley and his gun hand swaying. The look in the man's eyes was a combination of confusion and hatred. Daley began squeezing the trigger again, but before he could fire the man collapsed in a heap, like a marionette whose strings had just been cut. Daley kept his rifle aimed at the fallen man, in case he wasn't yet dead. Ky suddenly darted forward and picked up the pistol the man had dropped.

"Hold your fire!" Jones screamed. Daley wasn't sure if the lieutenant was yelling at him, or at the other soldiers in the platoon. He wasn't taking any chances and continued to watch the crumpled shape of the man he had just shot. Out of the corner of his eye he could see the soldier by the ladder, his hands even higher in the air and his eyes wide with terror. Ky jumped back, holding the pistol by its barrel, and then dropped it at Daley's feet. Only then did Daley wonder if Jones' order had been directed at someone who had been ready to shoot Ky.

"Tell that guy to come over here with the others," Jones told Daley. Without taking his eyes off the guy lying in the doorway, Daley told the man by the ladder, "Go over there with the others." Nervously the man stepped sideways, keeping his gaze directed at the end of Daley's rifle, and skipping when he passed between Daley and the doorway. Once he was clear of Daley's line of fire, he scuttled over to join the other three, who were now clustered in the middle of the courtyard, surrounded by the American soldiers.

"Jimmerson, Gonzalez," Stagakis ordered, "check out that building." He nodded toward the smaller structure, and Jimmerson and Gonzalez approached the doorway cautiously. Meanwhile, Doc Ortiz hustled over and stood against the wall of the big building just to the right of the doorway. He and Daley exchanged glances, and Daley understood that Ortiz wanted him to watch for anyone who might be inside. Then the medic knelt down, keeping his shoulder to the wall, and reached out to grasp the foot of the fallen man. He was wearing the black tennis shoes typical of NVA soldiers, but his were unlaced, as if he had dressed in a hurry. Ortiz wrapped his fingers around the man's ankle and pulled it toward him. There was no resistance.

"He's dead," Ortiz pronounced, releasing the ankle and standing up, but remaining against the wall. Daley lowered his rifle and relaxed his grip. His rational mind told him he had just killed a man, but as yet he felt no emotion. It would come later, Daley realized.

"Watch the windows," Jones admonished him, approaching with Tanner and Gardner. Up until that point Daley had not considered the two windows, one on either side of the doorway, to be a threat, even though it should have been obvious. The glass was long gone from the weathered wooden frames, and burlap curtains covered the openings from inside. One of the curtains had a shield with stars and stripes printed on it, now faded to near invisibility. Shaking his head sharply to clear out the cobwebs, Daley jumped forward to put his back against the wall on the opposite side of the doorway from Ortiz, out of any line of fire coming from either the doorway or the window to his right. Ky scurried after him, crowding close by his right side. Jones and Tanner ran up and crouched by the right corner of the building, avoiding the window between them and Ortiz, and Gardner jogged over to take a similar position at the left corner, stooping to scoop up the dead man's pistol as he went.

Daley could see that Stagakis, Cassidy, and Most had lined up the four prisoners facing the big building, and stood behind them, using them as a human shield in case someone inside the building opened fire. Jimmerson and Gonzalez had ducked into the smaller building and were now out of sight.

"Sergeant Gardner," Lieutenant Jones said, "You and me will go in first. Drop your pack and get out your flashlight." Daley heard Gardner's pack hit the ground the swish of material as he opened a flap. Jones was doing the same thing. "Doc, you and Daley stay out here. You, too, Tanner." Daley was glad he wasn't one of the people going in, and felt guilty as a result. Jones held his Army-issue flashlight in his left hand and switched it on to make sure it worked. It was the typical green plastic tube with the head pointed at a right angle from the long battery compartment. After verifying that a beam of yellow light glowed from the lens, Jones switched it back off and clipped it to his pistol belt.

Gardner ducked below the window and stopped in a crouch right in front of Daley. Gardner had a civilian-style flashlight, with the lens at the end of the tube, and he held it next to the handguards along the barrel of his rifle, the weak beam of light ready to illuminate whatever his rifle pointed at. Jones duckwalked over in front of Ortiz, and nodded to Gardner. Daley heard the slender young black man take a deep breath, and then he jumped across the dead body and ducked inside, sweeping his flashlight beam from side to side. "Nothin' here," he called out, so Jones stepped carefully over the body and went inside.

Daley, his back still against the outer wall of the building, slowly became aware that he was trembling, and try as he might, he could not control it. Mentally he was alert and relatively calm, but his body seemed to have a mind of its own. He told himself it was just the aftermath of an adrenaline rush, but it still worried him. He couldn't let the others think he was afraid, that he had been terrified by the brief burst of combat. He took a deep breath, and then another, and his shaking began to subside, albeit not totally and not quickly. He glanced over at Ortiz, who gave him a knowing but sympathetic look. Daley was extremely grateful for the silent support.

Over in the center of the courtyard Stagakis now had the NVA soldiers on their knees with their hands behind their heads, and Al Most had dropped his pack to rummage around in it, quickly coming up with a roll of green duct tape. Most and Cassidy then began binding the wrists of the prisoners behind their backs, while Stagakis stood guard over them. Meanwhile, inside the big building, Daley could hear Jones and Gardner shuffling around, murmuring to each other, and then cautiously ascending a flight of wooden steps. There were slow muffled footsteps from the upper floor and then Daley heard Gardner call out, "In here!" Rapid footsteps followed and then Jones said something Daley couldn't make out. A third voice Daley didn't recognize exclaimed something and sobbed. Daley and Ortiz gave each other puzzled, questioning looks, and then both stepped away from the building and faced the doorway, bringing their rifles up to their shoulders.

More footsteps upstairs, and then Lieutenant Jones called down the stairwell: "Daley, Ortiz, come up here, quick."

"Wait here," Daley told Ky, before following Ortiz. Both had to stretch to step over the body still sprawled in the doorway, and then paused to let their eyes adjust to the relative darkness of the interior. To their left was an old wooden desk with a couple of wire in-baskets and papers and pencils scattered on top. Behind the desk were wall-mounted shelves, most empty, but some with old ledgers and binders, and one held two large military radios of foreign manufacture. This was apparently the orderly room, Daley decided. A door in the wall to the right of the desk led to a back room of some sort. A second door, further to the right, led to another dark room at the back of the building. Just to his right Daley saw a long, low table with a variety of old chairs around it and some empty beer bottles in the center. Beyond the table was a wooden staircase leading from the front corner of the room up to the second floor. Ortiz dodged around the table and chairs and climbed the stairs; Daley followed, hoping the steps weren't as rickety as they looked.

The steps creaked and swayed from the heavy combat boots, but held. At the top of the steps there was a wide landing, and it took Daley a moment to orient himself. They were now at the back right corner of the building, and two thin vertical windows allowed just enough of the cloudy daylight in to illuminate the landing, which led to a narrow hallway that ran from back to front in the center of the second floor. Peering through the window slit, Daley could see only the leaves of nearby trees and the rain that continued to fall from the sky. For the first time in a long while, however, that rain wasn't falling on Daley, and he was amazed at how luxurious the dry dirty landing felt to him.

Ortiz was ahead of him, rounding the wall of the landing and hurrying down the hall where Lieutenant Jones and Sergeant Gardner were waiting for them. "In there," Jones told them, motioning toward an open door to their left. Ortiz looked in, and Daley stretched to peer over his shoulder. The small room was sparsely furnished, with only an old metal bedstead with no springs, a rumpled pile of blankets on the floor, and an overturned metal bucket. Sitting on the bucket was the man Daley had identified as a Korean soldier, his elbows on his knees and his head in his hands. His body was bouncing up and down in a staccato tempo, and he snuffled and moaned. His uniform was dirty and torn, his hair was a spiky mess, and his boots had no laces.

"Can you talk to him?" Jones asked Daley.

While on casual duty at DLI in Monterey, his roommate, a Korean student, had frequently asked Daley to help him study for tests. As a consequence, Daley had picked up a few words of the language. "I'll try," he said.

"Ortiz, the next room." Jones led the medic away from the Korean, and Daley stepped into the room and knelt down in front of the emotional man. He wasn't sure why the man was crying, but hoped it was simply relief at finally being rescued.

Hoping his pronunciation was somewhere near correct, he said in Korean, "Hello. How are you? What is your name?" That was about all the Korean language he knew, other than some curse words and the word for beer, but apparently that was enough. The man jerked his head up and looked at Daley for the first time, his eyes wide with astonishment. He replied in rapid-fire Korean that left Daley far behind, gesticulating excitedly with his hands and apparently telling the story of his capture and imprisonment.

Daley shook his head and held his free hand out palm up, saying, in English, "That's all the Korean I know." Then he remembered one more Korean phrase from his roommate: "Do you speak English?"

A look of extreme disappointment clouded the man's face. He shook his head and said in heavily accented English, "I know little." Daley wasn't sure if he meant he knew a little English, or he knew very little English.

"What is your name?" Daley repeated in Korean.

"Sung," the man said, pointing to the name tape on his uniform shirt. The tape had Korean symbols, but also the word SUNG spelled out in the Roman alphabet.

Daley pointed to his own name tape and pronounced it for Sung. The man repeated it, almost correctly, and held out his hand for Daley to shake. "Tank you," he said in his heavily accented English. Shakily he stood up, one hand on the wall for support. Daley stood as well.

"How are you?" Daley asked again in Korean. "Okay?" He was pretty sure the American word was generally recognized throughout the world, and especially in a country like Korea, which had had American troops stationed there for nearly twenty years.

"Okay," Sung said without real conviction. He said something Daley didn't understand, and then made spooning motions toward his mouth. Daley laid his rifle on the bed frame and shrugged out of his backpack. Setting it on the floor, he knelt down and reached inside, feeling around for one of the cans of C-rations. He found one and pulled it out, peering at the black printing on the dark green can. He couldn't read it in the dim light of Sung's prison cell, but guessed it didn't really matter. Standing up with the can in his left hand, Daley stuck his right hand inside the neck of his shirt to retrieve the P-38 can opener hanging on the chain of his dog tags. As he pulled it out and fumbled to unfold it, Sung reached out for the can, smiling and showing his own P-38 on a string around his neck. Daley smiled back and handed him the can, watching as Sung expertly operated the opener to cut through the lid and pull it back. It looked like it contained some kind of fruit, and Sung simply lifted the can to his mouth and poured the contents in, finishing it in three swallows. He wiped the juice from his chin with his sleeve and said, with more enthusiasm this time, "Okay."

Daley pulled on his rucksack again and picked up his rifle. With a gesture like a movie usher, he waved toward the door and said, "Let's go," in English. Sung nodded and preceded him into the hallway. Sung turned right and started for the stairs, but Daley looked to his left and saw Gardner standing in the next doorway down.

Gardner, his dark face totally in shadow, looked over at Daley and said, "The Australian," tilting his head toward the interior of the room.

"How is he?" Daley asked.

Gardner shook his head. "Not good. His leg's infected. Doc's workin' on it, but I don't know how much he can really do."

Gardner stepped back to let Lieutenant Jones step out of the room. "How's the Korean?" he asked Daley. Daley glanced behind him to see Sung waiting at the end of the hall. "He seems to be okay. He was hungry, so I gave him some C's."

"So you can talk to him?"

"Not really," Daley admitted. "I know about ten words in Korean, and he maybe knows that many in English. We mostly communicated with hand gestures."

"Close enough for Army work," Jones commented with a smile. He was in a good mood, it appeared. Daley suspected the lieutenant was glad his risky moves had paid off. Rescuing two prisoners of war would save him from the wrath of the battalion commander for ignoring his orders. "I need to talk to Captain Taylor, as soon as Doc Ortiz is done with him. Why don't you take what's-his-name out and tell Sergeant Stagakis what's going on. Tell him to wait for me before we call Battalion."

"Sung, sir," Daley told him. "And the Australian's a captain?"

"Yes." Jones looked passed Daley. "Sung's waiting for you." Daley realized he was being dismissed, so he nodded and went back down the hall to the landing.

TEN

At the bottom of the stairs Daley met Tanner, who had his M-16 hanging from his left hand by the carrying handle and the radio handset in his right, close to his ear. "Where's the LT?" Tanner demanded.

"Upstairs," Daley told him with an upward jerk of his head. Tanner pushed by him and Sung to ascend the wooden steps. The doorway had been cleared of the dead officer, leaving smeared blood on the floor along with muddy footprints. A pool of rainwater just outside the door sill was tinted pink. Daley had dried off just enough during his short stay indoors to hesitate before stepping back out into the rain. Steeling himself, he stepped wide to avoid the blood and emerged into the courtyard. To his right Ky was draping an old blanket over the inert form of the man Daley had killed, Apparently Ky had dragged the body out of the doorway and laid it out under the window, and had then gone inside to find the blanket, which was already getting soaked. When Ky looked up at him, Daley nodded his head in appreciation.

Turning to his left, Daley trotted over to Sergeant Stagakis, who stood with a group of soldiers a short distance away from the captured NVA soldiers. The prisoners were sitting on the ground with their hands bound behind their backs and their ankles wrapped together with the duct tape. Gathered around Stagakis were Most, Cassidy, Jimmerson, and Gonzalez; the latter two had been searching the smaller building, and were now reporting their findings just as Daley and Sung came up, with Ky following close behind. Stagakis and the other four all stopped talking and turned to stare at Sung with open curiosity.

"So this is the Korean, huh?" Stagakis said, more as a statement than a question.

"Yep," Daley answered. "His name's Sung."

"Does he speak English?"

"Not really," Daley told him. "Maybe just a few words."

"Too bad. What's the LT doing?"

"The Australian is wounded pretty bad in the leg. Doc Ortiz is fixing him up and the LT's talking to him. LT says to not call this in yet."

"Why not?" Cassidy asked.

"Don't know," Daley said with a shrug.

"Doesn't want Battalion fucking with us yet," Jimmerson suggested. A couple of the others nodded wisely.

"The colonel could fuck up a wet dream," Al Most observed.

"That's enough," Stagakis reprimanded them mildly. "So, tell me again what you found in there." The latter was directed at Jimmerson, who took up his story from the beginning.

"There's two small rooms on the left when you go in. The rest is a big open bay, with a pile of old bunkbeds at the end. There are some cots along the back wall, and odds and ends on the floor. Looks like it's being used as a barracks for the guys here in the fort. The small room by the door must be a sergeant's room or something—one cot, a little desk, and some personal items. The other room is the arms room. There's an RPD with a couple drums, a couple RPG-2 launchers, a small mortar, some bangalore torpedoes, crates of ammo, a couple broken AKs, and some tools."

"What kind of ammo?" Stagakis asked.

"I didn't take inventory," Jimmerson said, "but I saw some RPG rounds, some 7.62, some belted ammo for the RPD, a crate of mortar rounds, and what looked like a box of American grenades. There's enough there for at least a company-sized unit."

Stagakis stared at the four prisoners for a minute, mulling over what Jimmerson had told him. "More than those four dildoes needed," he estimated. "Wonder when the rest of 'em are coming back?"

"Well, let's don't be here to find out, Sarge," Most said. "Let's get the fuck outa Dodge."

A couple others grunted in agreement.

Stagakis ignored the comment. "Cassidy," he said, "you go get Kessler and Romano and bring 'em in. Most, you go get Benkowski and Griffin. All of you be ready to move out."

Cassidy and Most trotted away, out through the main gate.

"Daley, take your two friends here and search the other building, see if there's anything useful there. I want to look around." Motioning to Jimmerson and Gonzalez to watch the four prisoners, Stagakis started a slow tour around the inside perimeter. Daley waved at Ky and Sung and led them back to the main building. The two men followed him like puppies, and Daley realized he now had two new best friends, whether he wanted them or not.

As they approached and entered the building, Daley explained to Ky what they were doing, and hoped Sung would figure it out by watching the other two. Daley and Ky went over to the small desk and started searching through the drawers and the shelves on the wall. Sung watched them for a minute, then wandered away into the back room at the right.

"Unit roster," Ky said, holding up a single sheet of paper he had found on top of the desk.

"Save that," Daley told him. That would be valuable intelligence to someone. Daley looked through the ledgers and binders on the shelves, but all seemed to be very old. Some were even in French. One of the radios was on, with the volume turned down; Daley switched it off. The other radio was off, and didn't react when Daley tried to turn it on. The only other things on the shelves were a couple spare radio batteries, some cups and bowls, and a few candles with a Zippo lighter next to them. Ky handed him some more papers he had found in the middle drawer, and Daley studied them in the waning light coming in through the open door. They appeared to be supply requisitions, as best as he could tell. He added them to the unit roster. Nothing else of interest was found in the area of the desk.

Next Daley turned to the room behind the desk, its doorway dark and uninviting. There were no windows in the room, apparently, and little light from the building entrance made it all the way back here. Behind him Ky grabbed a candle and lit it with the Zippo. Once it was burning steadily, Ky handed the candle to Daley while slipping the cigarette lighter into his food bag. Holding the candle far in front of himself, Daley eased into the room; even with the candle, he had to let his eyes adjust to the darkness that was only partially pierced by the flickering flame. He set his rifle down, leaning it up against the doorjamb, to free one of his hands.

The room contained only a cot and a small field desk with a bamboo stool. A single blanket on the cot was draped over the end, with most of it crumpled on the floor. A uniform hung from a nail on the left wall, and next to it was an empty pistol belt and holster. This must have been the officer's quarters, Daley realized. The room stank of urine, feces, and vomit, and Daley guessed the foul odor was coming from the plastic bucket under the cot. Ky had said the officer was sick, and it looked like he had been suffering in here for a while. Above the cot on the back wall of the room there was a tall, narrow niche lined with wood. It puzzled Daley for a minute, until he realized it was one of the vertical slits that served as gun ports for the building, one that had been sealed to block the rain. He moved closer to it, being careful to avoid upsetting the bucket of foulness, and saw a latch at the bottom. He reached across the cot and pulled on the latch, and the wooden panel came away and fell to the floor, barely missing Daley as he jumped out of the way. The room was suddenly brighter, the weak daylight outside providing far more illumination than the single candle had. Daley blew out the candle and handed it to Ky.

The added light revealed the room to be even more squalid than before, and did nothing to alleviate the horrible stench. But Daley's eyes were immediately drawn to the wall beside the door: tacked to it was a map. Rushing over to it, he put his face close to read the faint markings, moving his head from left to right to avoid casting shadows on it. It was a Vietnamese map, with different ways of indicating terrain features than an American military map, but he had been shown one once in his intelligence training, so he was able to interpret it after only a few moments. There, near top center, was a populated area labeled as Tay Ninh, so Daley could now orient himself, and began searching for other recognizable features. There was Nui Ba Den mountain, and here was the Vam Co Dong River. Daley was elated—now they could figure out where they were, and call in support from Battalion.

After carefully pulling out the tacks that secured it to the wall, Daley rolled the map up and handed it to Ky, telling him to keep it safe and not let it get damaged. A quick search found nothing else of interest in the room, and with relief Daley and Ky exited, leaving the stench behind. He had intended to immediately take the map up to Lieutenant Jones, but a clatter from the other back room made him stop and look in. This room had two of the slit windows, and the burlap curtains had been pulled down roughly to brighten up the cluttered space. It was the unit's mess kitchen, with shelves, a work table, and a small wood stove. Standing by the stove, waiting for a pot of water to boil, was Sung, a large metal cup of rice in his hand. Sung looked up at Daley with a smile, and made spooning motions toward his mouth. On the table was what appeared to be a cut-up chicken, a salt shaker, and some large cans. Sung was making himself dinner, and Daley had no problem with that. He smiled and nodded his encouragement, then pointed at the ceiling to indicate he was going upstairs.

When he turned to go, he nearly bumped into Ky, who was watching Sung with great interest. Daley chuckled and held out his hand for the map and other papers. "Why don't you help him?" Daley suggested to Ky, and Ky bobbed his head in joyful acceptance. Leaving those two to their KP, Daley headed up the stairs. He got only a few steps before he met Jones coming down, with Tanner right behind him.

"I found a map," Daley blurted out happily, holding the rolled up paper in front of him. He turned around and stepped back down into the main room.

"Great!" Jones said. "Let's take a look."

Daley unrolled the map onto the big table at the base of the stairs, pushing a chair out of his way with his hip. Laying his rifle along one edge as a paperweight, he spread and smoothed the map out with his hands while Jones and Tanner drew close on either side of him.

"It's a Vietnamese map," Jones noted with disappointment.

"Yes," Daley said, "but at least we can figure out where we are approximately. And I think I can use the legend to figure out our coordinates with longitude and latitude."

Jones looked doubtful. He was used to using the military map grid coordinates, which used a different numbering system. "But how accurate would those be?" he asked.

"Close enough for Army work," Daley answered, repeating what Jones had said earlier.

"I don't know," Jones muttered, shaking his head slowly. "Anyway, where are we now?"

"I haven't figured that out yet," Daley admitted, leaning over to peer closely at the tiny lettering in the pale light coming through the front door. He pointed out obvious terrain features. "Here's Tay Ninh, here's the river, and here's Go Dau Ha. So we should be somewhere over here." The map had numerous pencil markings on it, and the handwriting was hard to decipher. Daley noticed one area was slightly darker than the others, smudged as if it had frequently been touched by dirty fingertips. Taking off his glasses, he bent down and analyzed the various faded colors and lines, noting a faint dotted line that apparently represented a trail, and numerous darker green splotches he supposed indicated clumps of trees. And then, there, in the middle of one of those splotches, he saw the black square that indicated a structure. Just to the west was the squiggly blue line of a small stream that widened to an oval pond.

"This is the fort!" Daley said excitedly, pointing to it with his index finger. "See, here's the trail, and over here's the creek and pond."

Lieutenant Jones leaned over to take a closer look, and then nodded his head. "But what's this?" he asked, pointing to a wide red line that ran fairly straight from north to south just east of the fort.

"Probably an old road," Daley surmised while he searched the legend. What he found there caused him to say, "Uh-oh!"

"What?"

"That's the Cambodian border," Daley groaned. He straightened up and grimaced. Jones kept looking at the map, biting his lower lip. Daley remembered the old road they had crossed that morning; it probably was an old border patrol road.

"So we're in fucking Cambodia?" Tanner griped. Daley just nodded disconsolately.

"That's a problem," Jones commented dryly.

"No shit, sir," Tanner said. "We ain't supposed to be here."

"I know, Carl," Jones told him. "At ease."

"Want me to tell Battalion?" Tanner unclipped the handset from his pack strap in preparation for making the call.

"Not yet," Jones told him. "I need to talk to Sergeant Stagakis first."

"I'll get him," Daley offered, feeling somehow guilty for their predicament. He grabbed his rifle and stepped out the door. Out in the courtyard he saw Stagakis addressing the rest of the platoon, including the men who had been out as blocking forces. The four bound prisoners still sat on the ground beneath the tree. "Sarge!" Daley called out. "LT needs to see you." Stagakis nodded and finished up what he was telling the others before strolling calmly over to where Daley waited.

"In here," Daley said unnecessarily, leading the stocky NCO inside to the table.

"What's the situation out there?" the lieutenant asked as a greeting. Stagakis took off his helmet and dropped it on the table with a thud, then ran his hand through his thinning hair.

"Brought in the guys from the trail," Stagakis reported. "The gooks are tied up in the yard. I posted sentries on all four walls. There's a bunch of munitions in the other building. We probably ought to blow them up when we leave." The sergeant made a show of looking at his watch. "We ought to move out pretty soon, before it gets dark." He scowled when they all heard laughter coming from the back room.

"That's Sung and Ky," Daley hastily explained. "They're fixing food back there in the kitchen. Sung's starving." Stagakis rolled his eyes. Jones just looked serious.

"Daley found a map," Jones told Stagakis, gesturing toward the table. "Looks like we are well inside Cambodia."

"Oh, fuck!" Stagakis complained with a wince.

"Yeah. So even if we could pinpoint our location, we can't call for any support. I'm trying to figure out what to tell Battalion."

"I've had my radio off to save the battery," Stagakis told him. "What do they know already?"

Tanner jumped into the conversation. "I been just giving them bullshit sitreps. Bravo Company made contact today, so the colonel has been busy with them and not payin' much attention to us. But Bravo just made it back to their hardspot, so he's gonna be wanting to know what's up with us pretty soon."

"I'm going to have to tell him we're in Cambodia," Jones said with resignation.

"He'll be pissed," Stagakis noted.

"I'm not too happy about it, either," Jones remarked.

"So we better move out, try and get back over the border," Stagakis said, picking up his helmet.

"There's another problem," Jones told him. "The Australian captain upstairs is in pretty bad shape. Doc Ortiz is working on him, but I don't think he can travel."

"Maybe we could make a stretcher," Daley suggested. "Sung and I could carry him."

"That'd work," Tanner commented approvingly. He clearly was anxious to get away from the fort.

"I don't know," Jones said. "We'll have to see what Doc says. And it's getting close to sundown. Do we really want to be walking the trail at night?" Daley understood what he meant: the gooks controlled the terrain in the dark, and they were far from any

American support. If they ran into an enemy patrol at night, it could be disastrous. In addition, it would be easy to get lost at night.

"But if we stay here tonight," Stagakis pointed out, "the rest of this garrison might come back. Didn't Ky say they were due to return soon?"

"In a day or two," Daley admitted. "Kind of vague, but . . ."

"We'd have a better chance here than out in the open," Jones said.

They all turned at the sound of clunking footsteps on the stairs. First feet, then legs, and finally Ortiz's face became visible as he wearily staggered down the stairs, wiping his bloody hands on a rag he had found. When he reached the ground floor, he sat down heavily on the second step, leaned his rifle against the staircase, and placed his helmet on the step beside him.

"How is he?" Jones asked, referring to the Australian.

"He'll make it, I think. He's out now. I gave him a bunch of morphine 'cause I had to do a lot of cutting and stitching. Rosie's watchin' over him." Daley had forgotten about Sergeant Gardner.

"Can he walk?" Stagakis asked.

Ortiz shook his head. "Not right now. That leg's gonna be really weak for a while. He needs to see a real doctor. Plus, he's malnourished. They ain't been feedin' him shit here."

"Sung and Ky are making dinner," Daley said. "They can feed him."

"Not right now," Ortiz told them, "he's out like a light. Should wake up in an hour or so, though, and food would really help."

"If we had a stretcher for him," Jones asked, "could we move him that way?"

"Could," Ortiz answered dubiously, "but I wouldn't recommend it. He needs to rest some more, get his strength back. Do we have a stretcher?"

"No," Daley said, "but we were thinking maybe we could make one."

Ortiz looked at Lieutenant Jones. "So, are we leaving tonight?"

"I haven't decided. I still need to talk to Battalion."

"If we wait until morning," Ortiz said, "he might be able to walk with a crutch. Maybe."

Jones pondered what he had been told, then leaned over to study the map again. Stagakis moved up next to the table across from Jones and looked at the map as well. "We're here," Jones told him, pointing out the fort's location, "and this is the border." Stagakis measured the distance from the fort to the border with his thumb and forefinger, and then, holding them apart the same distance, moved his hand down to the legend of the map and compared it to the distance scale.

"At least five clicks," Stagakis said, straightening up.

"Yeah, that was my estimate, too." Jones looked over at Stagakis questioningly, but didn't say anything. Stagakis worked his mouth as if doing mental calculations. Finally he reached a conclusion.

"Better stay here tonight," Sergeant Stagakis said.

Jones nodded. "I'll tell Battalion. Tanner, tell them I need to talk to the colonel." Tanner began speaking into the handset as there was another burst of noise from the kitchen, a crash followed by giddy laughter. "Daley, tell those two to keep it down."

ELEVEN

The kitchen smelled wonderful. Daley found Ky and Sung busy with pots and pans, a blazing wood stove, and a bloody chicken carcass on the table amongst the scattered cans and bags.

"Ky, you two need to keep the noise down in here, please," Daley told him. "The lieutenant is making plans and talking on the radio."

"Yes, Sergeant," Ky said happily, stirring a pot of boiling water with unidentifiable things floating in it.

"Can you make enough food to feed the Australian man upstairs?"

"Oh, yes," Ky answered, bobbing his cowboy hat vigorously. "We will make enough for everyone. There is plenty of food here."

"Good. Thank you." Daley watched the two men dodging each other as they moved back and forth from the table to stove with cans and jars in their hands. He wondered if maybe Sung had been a cook in the Korean Army, and decided to find out.

"Sung," Daley said to get his attention. With the Korean watching him, Daley pointed to his chest, and then to his rifle and made walking gestures with two fingers of his left hand. He wasn't really an infantryman, but there was no way to describe his job as an interrogator with simple hand motions. Then he pointed at Sung's chest and waved at the stove and cooking utensils with a questioning look on his face. Sung's face was blank. Daley repeated the performance, and finally Sung's expression changed to one of understanding. He shook his head violently, and then pointed to himself before making a downward motion with his hand cupped. He made a "poompf" sound and drew a high arc in the air, then opened his hand quickly with a percussive breath to imitate an explosion.

"A mortar," Daley said, and Sung nodded. So Sung was a mortarman. Who just happened to also be a cook. Interesting. Daley smiled and reached out to shake his hand. Both smiled goofily at each other as they shook.

"He shoots mortars," Ky said in Vietnamese, to prove he understood the mute conversation as well. He also shook Sung's hand.

"Back to work," Daley told Ky with a half-smile, and then went back out into the front room. Lieutenant Jones and Tanner were over by the desk, with Jones listening intently to the radio handset with a pained expression on his face. Every couple minutes he would simply say, "Roger, over," and listen some more. Daley wandered over to the long table, where Sergeant Stagakis had paper and a pencil he had found on the desk and was drawing a crude map of the fort and the surrounding area. Ortiz was no longer on the steps, presumably having gone back upstairs to check on the Australian, and Sergeant Gardner came down the steps just as Daley reached the table.

"Ortiz says we're staying here tonight," Gardner said as he reached the main floor.

"Yep," Stagakis said, not looking up from his drawing efforts.

"That's fucked up," Gardner commented mildly.

"Hmm," Stagakis grunting, neither agreeing or disagreeing.

There was movement at the door, and Benkowski leaned in. Daley could See Jimmerson and a couple others milling around outside. The rain appeared to have stopped, but the light was fading as sundown approached.

"Anything we should be doing out here, Sarge?" Benkowski asked.

"Yeah," Stagakis said, straightening up. "How many grenades we got?"

"I got one," Benkowski replied, then turned to query the other guys behind him. "Jimmerson's got two, and Gonzalez's got two."

"Okay. Go over to the other building and look around for some string or wire, as thin as possible. Daley, you check this building. We need to make some booby traps."

"Roger," Benkowski said and ducked back outside, motioning for the other men in the courtyard to follow him.

Daley didn't remember seeing anything like that during his initial search, but he could have missed it, and Ky had done some of the searching. Jones had handed the radio mike back to Tanner and walked over to peer down at Stagakis's drawing. Daley took that opportunity to go over to the desk. Laying his rifle on top, he began going through the wooden drawers, most of which were difficult to open due to swelling and warping. In the bottom of one of the pedestal drawers he found a small ball of twine, but it was only a couple feet long, and broke in half when he stretched it out. He stuck his head in the kitchen and told Ky to look around there. Steeling himself against the smell, he went into the other back room and searched it again, finding nothing useful. He had held his breath as much as possible inside the room, so when he stepped back out he had to take a couple deep breaths. Ky came to the other door and shook his head at Daley.

"Nothin', Sarge," Daley dolefully reported to Stagakis, after respectfully waiting for Jones to finish relaying what the colonel had said. Daley had only caught fragments of the report while he had been searching, but the tone of Jones' voice made it clear his conversation with the colonel hadn't been pleasant.

Benkowski came running in from the courtyard holding a spool out in front of him. "Fishing line!" he announced proudly. "Found it in the sergeant's room."

"All right!" Stagakis enthused, taking the spool from Benkowski to examine it. He pulled a foot or so of the line from the spool and tested its tensile strength. Nodding with approval, he said, "This'll work." He looked toward the doorway, where three other guys crowded together to look in. "Come on in, guys, let me show you what you got to do." Jimmerson, Griffin, and Gonzalez all came in and formed a half circle around Stagakis with Benkowski.

"Benkowski and Griffin," the Sergeant began, "you two go back to where you were on the trail; Jimmerson and Gonzalez, you provide security for 'em. Use the green tape to tape a grenade to a tree trunk facing the trail, about knee high, leaving the spoon free. Run some of this line across the trail, from the grenade's pin to another tree, as tight as you can. Be sure to remove the safety bail on the grenade, then squeeze the ends of the pin together so the pin will pull out easy. That way, anybody hits that line, it'll pull the pin. The grenade won't go off for a few seconds, so they'll have time to take cover, but it will alert us to anyone bein' there. Once you got that one set up, go to where Kessler and Romano were earlier and do one there, too. Got it?"

"No sweat, Sarge," Benkowski assured him, and the others nodded. The four men crowded out through the door, discussing whose grenades were going to be used.

"Think we should post LPs?" Jones asked Stagakis. Listening Posts were two or three men hiding a couple hundred yards out to warn of an enemy approaching. Stagakis shook his head.

"Gooks can come from too many different directions," the sergeant explained. "Most likely they'll come down the trail, though, and the grenades will give us warning. If they do come, we'll need everyone here in the fort."

"I agree," Jones said. "Think they got off a message on those radios?" He nodded toward the two sets on the shelves behind the desk.

"One of 'em doesn't work," Daley interjected. "I turned off the other one."

"The officer might have," Stagakis mused, "but I don't know if he had time. If he was sick in bed when we attacked, he'd of had to get up, get his pistol, stagger into this room, make radio contact, and then come to the door so Daley could shoot him. I don't think he had that much time."

"Well, let's hope so," Jones said. "Oh, by the way, the colonel suggested we send out an AP tonight."

"Are you shittin' me? What's he been smoking?" Stagakis waggled his head bag and forth in disgust at the idea of sending out an ambush patrol. "Sitting back there in his cozy-ass bunker," he grumbled. Putting his helmet back on and picking up his rifle, Stagakis said with a more positive tone, "I'm going back to that arms room, see what we can use tonight." With that he went out. Not knowing what else to do, Daley followed him.

Daley was able to catch up when Stagakis stopped in the middle of the courtyard, under the bigger of the two trees that grew there, and gazed at the four NVA prisoners. Huddled miserably together under the other tree, sitting in the mud, they looked utterly defeated. Daley swept his gaze around the inside of the fort to determine where the rest of the platoon was. Over by the gate Romano slouched against one of the gateposts, alternately looking out through the gate and gazing inside at the prisoners. Al Most sat on the crumbled blocks in the middle of the east wall, not far from where it connected with the big building, staring off through the trees. At the opposite corner of that building, along the south wall, Cassidy half-leaned his pack against the side of the building so he could simultaneously watch the prisoners and observe the area outside the wall. Daley heard hawking and spitting from around the south side of the small building, and knew that Kessler must be there guarding the west wall.

Stagakis turned to Daley. "Where they were keeping the Korean," he asked, "is that secure enough to hold these guys?"

"Should be," Daley answered. "It's got a pretty stout door with an outside bar. There's one of those slit windows, but they're too narrow to crawl through."

"Romeo, Hopalong," he called out to Romano and Cassidy, "take these gooks upstairs and put them in the Korean's cell. Lock 'em up tight. Rosie can show you where."

"Sure thing, Sarge," Romano replied. He and Cassidy trotted over, pulling out pocket knives to slice the duct tape on the prisoners' legs.

"Come on," Stagakis said to Daley, resuming his walk to the arms room in the small building.

The interior of the building was pretty much as had been described. It took Daley's eyes a few seconds to adjust to the gloom, relieved only by the fading light coming in through the doorway and slit windows. To his right the building was totally open, and at the far end was a jumble of broken wooden frameworks that had once been bunkbeds. The rest of the room was cluttered with makeshift sleeping areas—piles of straw with blankets on top, a long wooden bench, and a couple US Army folding cots with the end cross-braces missing. Might be able to make a stretcher out of one of those, Daley thought. To his left were two small rooms. The one closest to the outer door had no window, but a large hole had been chipped through the back wall, providing enough light to see that the room was almost bare except for a wooden bed frame with rope strung between the sides to form springs, and a small folding wooden desk. The second room had a riveted steel door that stood open, but little light made its way inside.

Stagakis stopped at the arms room door and unclipped a flashlight from his pistol belt. Sweeping the yellow beam around the room slowly, he said, "Fuck me!" almost under his breath. He stepped all the way into the small room, and Daley crowded in behind him. Three walls were lined with rusty metal shelves, and the fourth one, just inside the door on the right, had gun racks, one on top of the other, made to hold long rifles standing upright. The gun racks were empty except for a couple AK-47s that were missing parts and a light machine gun laid crossway on the upper rack. In a corner, propped on its bipod support, was a small mortar.

"Sixty mike-mike," Stagakis said, holding the beam of the flashlight on the mortar for a moment. It took Daley a second to translate that to 60 millimeter. Behind it, leaning against the wall, were a number of metal tubes that looked like plumbing supplies. "Bangalore torpedoes," Stagakis explained without being asked. Daley had read about them in books about D-Day in WWII, but had never seen them before. From what he had read, the pipes were filled with explosive and could be connected end to end and pushed under a barbed-wire entanglement, then detonated to blow a hole in the wire.

On one of the shelves lay two RPG launchers, basically just narrow tubes with two handles and a rudimentary sight. "RPG-2," Daley said, hoping he was right. Stagakis grunted his concurrence. Below them was a crate with what appeared to be Russian lettering. The larger writing looked like a letter 'P', a 'pi' symbol, and an upside-down 'L', followed by a dash and the number '7'. Daley guessed that meant RPG-7, and said so. Stagakis unlatched the top of the wooden crate and looked inside. The rounds had been packed horizontally, and the top one had been unwrapped. It consisted of a narrow tube with folding fins at one end and a bulbous warhead at the other.

"Will an RPG-7 round work in an RPG-2 launcher?" Daley asked curiously.

"Beats me," Stagakis replied. "Don't intend to find out, either." He examined other wooden crates and metal ammo cans, having Daley translate when the markings were in Vietnamese, although most were in Russian or Chinese. Fortunately, the Russian and Chinese markings often had Vietnamese scrawled above them in pencil. There was one crate of 60mm mortar rounds, eleven boxes of belted ammo for the machine gun, which Stagakis had identified as an RPD, twenty-three cans of AK-47 ammo, a box of Chicom "potato-masher" hand grenades, and a box of American hand grenades. Stagakis took one of the GI grenades out of the box and examined it. It was round, rather than egg-shaped like the ones Daley was familiar with.

"Concussion grenades," Stagakis said. "No shrapnel. Just make a big noise. Useless." He put it back in the box. "Could have used them for the booby traps, though, I guess."

There wasn't much else in the room, just anonymous parts and pieces. Stagakis handed Daley the flashlight and set his rifle down on a crate. "Gimme some light here," he instructed Daley as he picked up the RPD. It looked kind of like an overgrown AK-47, with a large wooden stock, wooden pistol grip, and wooden handgrips at the base of the barrel. A folding bipod was attached to the end of the barrel. Stagakis opened the top of the feed mechanism and closed it again, pulled on a lever, and then reached over to pull one of the two black metal drums that were slotted into the gun rack. Daley hadn't noticed the drums before, which looked like the ones used on Tommy guns in the old 1930's gangster movies. Stagakis tried to attach the drum, but couldn't find the right combination of moves. He set the drum and gun back on the rack.

"Griffin's a gun nut," he said. "He probably knows how to work this damn thing, or can figure it out pretty quick." He picked up his rifle and took the flashlight back from Daley. "Let's get out of here."

Trailing behind Sergeant Stagakis as they crossed the empty courtyard, Daley noticed how much darker it had become just since they had gone into the arms room. The trees, both those inside the fort and those around it, brought deep gloom to the immediate area, but between their trunks Daley could see the outer fields of grass still somewhat illuminated, glowing in shades of emerald and amber. Nighttime was only minutes away, and despite the concrete walls around him, Daley began to feel a twinge of impending danger.

"Sung is a mortarman," Daley said impulsively.

"Motorman?" Stagakis asked, coming to a halt just outside the door to the big building.

"Mortarman," Daley repeated, with emphasis on the first syllable. "Mortars. You know."

"How do you know? I thought he didn't speak much English."

"Pantomime," Daley explained, making the same gestures Sung had used.

"Hmm. Good to know." Stagakis turned and entered the building, and Daley followed him.

Inside the main room the dimness was now partially alleviated by a couple candles flickering on the big table. The two enemy radios lay smashed on the floor below the shelves. Tanner, Romano, and Cassidy were all sitting at the table eating from wooden bowls, their rucksacks and helmets on the floor beside them, their rifles leaning up against the edge of the table. Tanner had placed his radio on an empty chair and clipped the handset to his collar, the coiled cord stretching over to the radio. Sergeant Gardner was sitting on the bottom step eating as well. Lieutenant Jones continued to study the map in the candlelight, a bowl of food sitting untouched next to him.

"Dinnertime, boys?" Stagakis said with a hint of sarcasm. The men who were eating looked up guiltily, but kept spooning the food into their mouths.

"Going back out as soon as we're done," Romano promised between swallows. "That Korean's a pretty good cook."

Stagakis sighed. "Eat up and get out," he said, echoing the words they had all heard in Army mess halls during Basic Training. "Send the other guys in to get something to eat when you relieve them. Rosie, you're sergeant of the guard." Gardner nodded his head and tried to wolf down the food. From what Daley could see, it was a stew of rice and other things.

Ky came out of the kitchen carrying another bowl, smiling when he saw Daley. "Food for the captain," he said in Vietnamese as he stepped around Gardner and started up the stairs.

"So the Aussie's awake?" Stagakis asked the room.

"Could be," Gardner answered. "Doc went up to check on him a few minutes ago."

Sung stuck his head around the edge of the door to the kitchen and gave Daley a questioning look. He pointed at him and Stagakis and made spooning motions. Stagakis had seen it, too.

"Might as well eat while we can," Stagakis said, nodding emphatically at Sung, who immediately ducked back in the kitchen and began rattling pots and pans. A moment later he came out with two unmatched pottery bowls and handed them to Stagakis and Daley. The bowl was hot, and Daley quickly set it down on the table. Stagakis didn't seem to notice the heat, and just leaned over to sniff the contents. "Smells pretty good," he commented. He went over to the vacant desk, placed the bowl on it, and shrugged out of his radio and pack, leaning his M-16 against the desk. Daley was pulling his plastic C-ration spoon out of his pocket when the four men who had left to set the booby-traps pushed in through the door.

"Table for four?" Daley addressed them with a smile.

"What the fuck?" Griffin said, taking in the relaxed atmosphere and people dining.

"Take a break in place," Stagakis told them, sitting down at the desk to begin eating. "Get some chow. It's going to be long night."

Sung stuck his head out again, and Daley held up four fingers to him. Sung nodded and ducked back in to rattle the dishes. Romano, Cassidy, and Gardner wolfed down the rest of their meals and stood up, reaching for their equipment.

"You can leave your rucks here," Stagakis told them. "Put 'em over there in the corner." He used his spoon to indicate the northeast corner of the room. The four new arrivals hurriedly dropped their rucks in the corner as well, and Daley set his bowl down on the corner of the desk so he could do likewise. He felt so much lighter, and cooler, without that weight on his back. He picked his bowl back up and began eating. It tasted wonderful, but he knew enough to not even wonder what those various green, yellow, and brown chunks floating amongst the rice were. If he knew, he probably wouldn't eat them.

Sung brought out two bowls and handed them to Jimmerson and Gonzalez. On his way back to the kitchen he policed up the empty bowls that Gardner, Romano, and Cassidy had left behind.

"Griffin," Stagakis said between spoonfuls of the stew, "what do you know about the RPD?"

"Gas-operated, shoulder-fired, belt-fed, 7.62 light machine gun. Developed by the Russians, copied by the Chinese communists. Counterpart to our M-60." Daley was amazed by this rapid-fire response, similar to how he had heard weapons described by bored drill sergeants in Basic. Stagakis, however, showed no surprise at the specialist's knowledge. He had said Griffin was a gun nut, after all.

"Ever fired one?"

Griffin took the bowl that Sung offered him and shook his head. "Nope, but I played with one once. Pretty simple, just like an AK. They made it so even dumb Russian peasants could operate it. Why?"

"They got one over in the other building. After you eat, go over and check it out, see if it works."

"Roger that, Sarge," Griffin said enthusiastically. "If it works, can I use it?"

"Only if we have to," Stagakis told him.

"They won't let you take it home with you, Griff," Benkowski reminded him like a parent talking to a kid who had found a puppy.

"Maybe I'll think of something," Griffin said with vague confidence.

"Don't even," Romano warned laconically.

TWELVE

The room had become fairly quiet. Daley had convinced Lieutenant Jones to eat his stew, and Sergeant Stagakis, still sitting at the desk, was now studying the crude map he had drawn earlier. Kessler and Most had come in to ground their packs and have their dinner, while everyone else had gone back outside to stand guard. Daley had held his nose to retrieve a couple more candles from the officer's quarters and place them strategically around the room to provide more light. Not sure what else he should be doing, Daley then helped Sung gather up the used bowls and pile them in the tin sink in the kitchen.

There were halting footsteps and scuffling from the top of the stairs, and then Ortiz appeared, coming down the steps backwards. Hopping down the stairs on one leg, both hands gripping Ortiz's shoulders, was the Australian captain, stabilized from behind by Ky. Laboriously the three men maneuvered down to the ground floor until Captain Taylor was able to collapse into a chair next to Lieutenant Jones.

"Evening, gentlemen," Taylor gasped with exhaustion.

"Shouldn't he be in bed?" Jones asked Ortiz. Ortiz spread his hands and tilted his head toward Taylor to indicate Taylor had insisted.

"I had to get out of that damn cell," Taylor said, still catching his breath. He glanced over at Jones. "Didn't we meet earlier, lieutenant?" he asked, pronouncing it 'leftenant'. "I may have been a little delirious."

"Yes, sir," Jones replied respectfully. "First Lieutenant Jones."

Sergeant Stagakis rose from the desk and walked around the table to offer his hand to Taylor. "Staff Sergeant Stagakis, sir. Glad to see you up and around." They shook hands.

"I may be up, Sergeant," Taylor said, "but I'm not really around yet, I don't think. Your medic here had done wonders, but I'm still pretty bad off." Taylor looked around at the other men in the room.

"That's PFC Kessler and PFC Most," Jones told him, motioning toward the two soldiers sitting at the end of the table. "That's Specialist Daley, our translator, and Specialist Tanner, my RTO. You've already met Doc Ortiz and Mr. Ky, and I guess you know Sung back in the kitchen."

"The rest of the platoon is outside," Stagakis said, and then looked over at Kessler and Most with a stern expression. "Where you two should be by now." The two men hurriedly finished their stew, handed their bowls to Daley, and headed out the door with the rifles and helmets.

"Where's the rest of your unit?" Taylor asked.

"This is it," Jones answered regretfully. "We're an independent recon platoon. Didn't really expect to end up in this situation."

"So, about forty men?" Taylor asked hopefully.

"I wish. I've got a dozen men, plus Daley, Ky, and now Sung."

"You do know the regular garrison here is about forty or fifty, right?" Taylor's expression now reflected his concern. Daley handed the empty bowls to Sung, who had come out of the kitchen, and sat down across from the Australian. Tanner swung the chair Most had been in around backwards and straddled it, to leave room for the radio on his back.

"Yes, Ky told us."

At the mention of his name, Ky stepped forward and almost came to attention at the head of the table, trying to suppress his perpetual smile. Taylor looked at Ky and raised one eyebrow.

"Ky's a Chieu Hoi," Daley explained. "Former VC. He's the one that told us about this fort and about you and Sung."

"He's been very helpful," Stagakis added warmly.

Taylor nodded and said, "I guess I owe him." He didn't sound convinced, however, and Daley wondered if Taylor equated Ky with the men who had been holding him prisoner.

"So how did you get captured, sir?" Jones interjected.

Taylor blew out a breath. "I was on my way to Long Binh and my jeep hit a mine. Killed my driver, but just blew me into the weeds. Three gooks captured me and frog-marched me here."

"You came all this way on that bad leg?" Jones asked, his eyes wide with wonder.

"Nah, nah. I was fine. This happened a few days ago. They took me and Sung down to the pond to wash up, and I tried to escape. Little fuckers shot me in the leg."

"He was lucky," Ortiz said. "Didn't hit the bone or any major arteries."

"Yeah, mate, if you call getting shot 'lucky'."

"How long you been here?" Stagakis asked. To Daley, it seemed like the sergeant's interest was more than casual.

"About three months, I think. They brought Sung in about a week after me."

"So you know the gooks' routine, then?"

"Such as it is, I guess," Taylor replied. "They've got groups coming through here hauling supplies, and sometimes these guys go out on patrol for two or three days at a time. I heard them leave yesterday morning."

"Do you know where they were going?" Jones asked.

Taylor shook his head. "I was in my cell with this fuckin' leg, mate. Got no idea."

"The guys they left here told Ky the others went west to get supplies," Daley told him.

"Could be," Taylor said. "Wherever, we don't want to be here when they get back."

"We're leaving first thing in the morning," Jones assured him.

"Can't you get some helicopters in here to take us out now?" Taylor asked, with worry creeping into his voice.

"We're in Cambodia," Jones explained. "They won't violate Cambodian neutrality."

"Fuck that!" Taylor exploded. "The gooks are violating it. I want to get the hell out of here."

"Not my decision," Jones told him. "My Higher says we have to walk back into Vietnamese territory before they can come get us. Besides, the weather has been bad, and now it's getting dark."

"Shit on a stick! You better hope those little fuckers don't come back tonight, then, or we're fucked royally."

"We're preparing for that right now," Stagakis said with what sounded like confidence. "We'll move out at first light. The question is, can you make it?"

"I'll need a crutch or something, but sure, I can make it. Anything to get away from here."

Tanner spoke up for the first time since Taylor had come downstairs. "Gonzalez found a branch when they were out setting the booby-traps. He was gonna see if he could whittle it down into a field-expedient crutch."

"Doc," Stagakis turned his head to Ortiz. "Would you go check on that, see if it will work?" Ortiz grabbed his rifle and went out. Stagakis then looked at Daley and said, "Daley, take Sung over to the arms room and see if he can work that mortar. Better take Ky with you." He unclipped his flashlight and tossed it to Daley.

Daley told Ky to get Sung while he collected his helmet and rifle. Like a mother duck and her ducklings, the three filed out the door into the gathering gloom. As they left Daley heard Stagakis say something to Jones about plans for the night.

Outside there was still enough light to make out their surroundings. Daley could see the soldiers of the CRIP platoon manning the wall on all sides, their rifles pointing outward, and in the middle of the courtyard, leaning against the tree trunk, was Sergeant Gardner. "Going to the arms room," Daley told Gardner as they passed by him. Gardner didn't respond. Daley didn't know if the black sergeant just wasn't interested, or was so hyper alert he couldn't be distracted. Outside the door of the small building they found Griffin sitting with his back to the wall, the RPD machine gun lying in his lap. Griffin's M-16 and shotgun leaned against the wall next to him, and two ammo drums sat on the ground on the other side. Griffin worked the bolt mechanism back and forth and mumbled "That'll work" to himself. Like Gardner, he ignored Daley and the other two.

Daley led the other two into the arms room, clicking on the flashlight to sweep the room and then settle on the mortar in the corner. "Can you operate it?" Daley asked in English. He leaned his rifle on the doorjamb and laid the flashlight on the gun rack so its beam bounced off the ceiling and dimly lit up the room. He repeated the question, using his now-free hands to add suitable gestures, pointing to the mortar and the crate of mortar rounds, and then at Sung. After a moment Sung seemed to understand, and pointed at himself and the mortar while speaking Korean with emphatic positivity. He then pointed to his eyes and pantomimed picking up the mortar and taking it outside. Daley nodded and picked up the flashlight to aim it at the mortar. Sung gathered it up, folding the bipod with one hand and cradling the baseplate in the other, then scooted past Ky and Daley through the door and out of the building. Daley picked up his rifle and followed, with Ky close behind.

In the courtyard Sung dropped to his knees, plopped the weapon onto the muddy earth, and extended the bipods. He fiddled with the adjustment knobs and felt around inside the tube. With one last push to make sure it was firmly planted, he stood up and nodded to Daley. He said something in Korean, and then added "Okay" in English. Daley belatedly noticed that Griffin was no longer by the door. He finally spotted the gun enthusiast over at the front wall, trying to find the ideal position to place the now-loaded machine gun.

"He is going to shoot the mortar?" Ky asked in Vietnamese, pointing at Sung.

"Maybe," Daley replied. "If we get attacked."

"Will I get a gun, too?" Ky sounded both envious and nervous at the prospect. Daley knew that Ky's technical status as a POW ruled out arming him, but he had shown his true loyalty so far.

"That's up to the lieutenant," Daley temporized, passing the buck. "Do you want one?"

Ky was silent for almost a minute. "I don't think so," he finally admitted. Daley was relieved. He liked Ky, but was afraid of what might happen if he had a gun. Not only would the NVA soldiers be anxious to shoot a traitor, the American soldiers might mistake him for the enemy and try to kill him. It was just better to avoid all the possible complications.

At the main building yellow candlelight filled the open doorway, and Daley briefly wondered about light discipline. Thinking about it, however, he realized that any enemy coming here would expect to see light and activity, while a dark and silent fort would be an anomaly. Then the doorway darkened and flickered as Lieutenant Jones led Sergeant Stagakis and Tanner out to the center of the yard.

"Platoon meeting," Stagakis called out just loud enough for everyone in the fort to hear. "Over here." The men at the wall drifted over, as did Daley, Sung, and Ky. Everyone gathered in a rough circle around Jones and Stagakis, their faces barely visible under the shadows of their helmets. "Daley," Stagakis barked, "can Sung work the mortar?"

"He says he can," Daley answered promptly.

"Griff, I see you've got the RPD. Will it work?"

"Smoother than shit," Griffin assured him with a grin. He patted the gun lovingly. His shotgun was strapped diagonally across his back.

"Where's your assigned weapon?" Stagakis asked reprovingly.

"I got it," Romano said, holding up two M-16s. "Call me two-gun Romano." Several guys laughed.

"All right," Stagakis said, "listen up. The lieutenant's going to explain the defensive plan. Sir."

Jones took one step forward and paused to gather his thoughts. "Men," he began, "as you may have heard, we are in Cambodia. Due to the loss of our maps, we cannot pinpoint exactly where we are, but the Vietnamese map we found indicates we are about five clicks west of the border. Because of our location, not to mention the overcast, we cannot get any fire support or an eagle flight."

"Candy-ass motherfuckers," Most groused. "Who'd fuckin' know?" Jones ignored the comment, as did everyone else. They all knew from bitter experience that in the Army, challenging authority was pointless, at best.

"It's possible that an NVA unit of up to company strength will be coming to this fort tonight or tomorrow, but we can't be sure of what direction they will be coming from. Captain Taylor, the Australian officer who was being held prisoner here, is wounded in the leg and can barely walk. Under the circumstances, it is too dangerous for us to travel at night, so we will be staying here until morning. We'll roll out of here at first light and move as quickly as possible back to the river."

Daley appreciated the succinct way Jones had summed up their situation without making it sound like a death trap. No one said anything, letting the difficulties sink in.

"We're all tired," Jones continued, "but we have to stay alert. We'll have at least three men on each wall—one awake and two asleep. The gooks have at least provided us with some additional firepower. As you can see, Specialist Griffin has their RPD and assures us it will work just fine. In addition, Mr. Sung, the Korean soldier who fixed dinner, is an accomplished mortar operator, and he will man the sixty millimeter mortar we found in the arms room. Captain Taylor will be given one of the AKs we captured."

"Sir," Sergeant Gardner said, stepping forward. He pulled the pistol out of his belt that had been brandished by the officer Daley had shot and handed it to Jones. "He could use this easier than an AK, if he's on crutches."

"Thank you, sergeant. Anyone have any questions?"

"What kind of mortar rounds we got?" Kessler asked. "Any illume?"

Stagakis answered. "Nope, just HE, and only twelve of those. But at least we got something."

"We gonna have anybody on the roofs?" Gonzalez asked.

"We thought about it," Stagakis said, "but decided against it. Too hard to see through the trees, and takes too long to get down if we have to book on short notice."

"I got the starlight," Cassidy said. "Where do you want me?"

"Sergeant Stagakis will make the assignments," Jones said. "I'll be in the main building with the radio and Captain Taylor." With that he turned and walked away. Stagakis stepped forward and began calling out names.

"Cassidy, Kessler, and Jimmerson, west wall. Rosie, Doc, and Al, south wall. Tanner, Benkowski, Gonzalez, east wall. Griff, Romeo, and Daley, by the gate. I'll be in the center, under the tree, with Sung and Ky. Daley, have Sung set up the mortar wherever he thinks best. Ky can be his loader. Everyone get your packs and keep them close. If it starts raining again, sleep under your poncho. Don't be goin' in the buildings to sleep dry—you can't hear the gooks comin' in there, and you'll just get fleas anyway. We got those booby-trap grenades set up on the trail, but the gooks might come another way, or see the traps and go around, so we got to keep our ears open. Got it?"

There were nods and grunts of acknowledgement.

"How's the battery on the starlight?" Stagakis asked Cassidy.

"Pretty good, and I've got a spare."

"Use it as much as you can," Stagakis told him. "The gooks will most likely come from the west, if they're comin'."

"Roger."

"Griff, you got enough ammo for that RPD?"

"Two drums," Griffin answered, "plus a couple cans of belted I can use if someone helps me feed it in."

"I can do that," Romano offered.

"Any of it tracer?" Stagakis asked.

"One in six," Griffin said, meaning every sixth round was a tracer round.

"Good news bad news," Stagakis said. "They'll be confused by the green tracers comin' at 'em, but it will give away your position." American tracer rounds left a red streak behind them.

"I'll keep my head down," Griffin assured him.

Stagakis tilted his head back and looked up at the sky. Daley did the same, and through the camouflage net he saw only thick clouds barely visible as the sun set somewhere to the west. It would soon be totally dark. But it turned out Stagakis wasn't just looking at the sky: he was focusing on the camouflage netting still strung between the building, the trees, and the gate posts. "Tanner," the sergeant called, "you got your knife handy?"

"Sure, Sarge."

"Then cut down that damn netting. Jimmerson, give him a hand."

"Everybody else," Stagakis said. "go to your posts." The group broke up as guys went inside the building to get their packs and then scatter to the four walls. Tanner and Jimmerson, with the help of the bamboo ladder, cut down the old netting and balled it up, then tossed it under the tree near the south wall. Daley took Ky and Sung aside, explaining to Ky the basic plan and his role as loader for Sung. With extensive gestures and English spoken slowly, he finally conveyed to Sung what was expected of him. Daley wasn't sure if the Korean fully understood the situation, but he did walk around with his head up, apparently assessing lines of fire. Finally satisfied, he went and gathered up the mortar and placed it a few yards in front of the doorway to the main building. Meanwhile Ky had gone into the small building and came out with the crate of mortar rounds, struggling with the weight of the wooden box. Sung hurried over and took it from him, and Ky followed Sung over to the mortar. Sung demonstrated how to unpack the individual rounds from the cardboard canisters they were packed in. Daley left them to go in and get his own pack, then joined Griffin and Romano at the wall just to the west of the gate.

"When's my watch?" Daley asked as he dropped his pack against the wall next to the other two.

"I'm on now," Griffin told him. "You're second watch, from eleven to two. Romeo's got third watch."

"Okay," Daley said.

"Think the Korean can really shoot that thing?" Griffin asked.

"Seems to know what he's doing," Daley told him. "Don't know how much good it'll do if he can't see the gooks, though."

"Good point," Griffin remarked. "Still, random mortar rounds dropping on them will give them something to think about."

"Let's hope it doesn't come to that," Daley wished.

"Bet that," Romano agreed.

THIRTEEN

"Daley." A hand roughly shook his shoulder. Daley came instantly awake and tense, listening for anything unusual or threatening. "It's your watch," Griffin said. Daley's tension ebbed as he realized where he was and what was happening. Groggily he unwrapped himself from his poncho, his uniform still damp from the rain that had soaked him not long after he had tried to go to sleep, what must have been two hours earlier. Now it was 2300 hours, eleven p.m. civilian time, and it was his turn to stand watch. He staggered to his feet, picked up his rifle and helmet, and went to stand beside Griffin who had returned to his post at the front wall of the fort, the RPD machine gun nested in a shallow V where a part of the wall had crumbled.

"Okay, I got it," Daley told him. "Anything happening?"

"Pretty quiet," Griffin told him. "Oh, Sarge came by a few minutes ago, checking all the guards, and said your two little buddies were doing all right. Said to tell you they were taking turns standing guard, too."

"No shit? Cool." Daley turned to look back at the center of the courtyard, and only then realized he could actually make out the tree and the figures below it. Looking up, he saw that the clouds had cleared and there was a bright three-quarter moon casting a ghostly blue glow over the area.

"Don't forget to wake Romeo at two," Griffin said, picking up the RPD. "I'll be right over here if anything happens." He moved over closer to the gate, wrapped the machine gun in his poncho along with his shotgun, and lay down alongside with his helmet for a pillow and his poncho liner as a blanket. Daley noticed that Griffin took better care of his weapons than he did himself.

Daley laid his rifle on top of the wall, which was chest high there, and scanned the area in front of him. To his right was the path from the entrance of the fort out to the main trail, speckled with the shadows of the leaves on the trees to either side. In front were more trees and a couple low bushes, but Daley could just make out the main trail crossing from right to left, and more trees and bushes just beyond it. To his left there was less foliage, and between the tree trunks he could see the wide wales of grass that surrounded the small clump of jungle encompassing the old French fort. The moonlight was a godsend. It was a generally accepted notion among the American troops that the Vietnamese must have better night vision, as they seemed to be able to move and shoot in darkness that totally blinded the GI's. The Army's tactical doctrine in Viet Nam usually called for troops to huddle in defensive positions at night, with the limited exception of ambush patrols that were rarely successful.

After studying the shadows outside the wall for a few minutes and detecting no unusual shapes or movement, and hearing no unnatural sounds, Daley turned to look at the center of the courtyard. Sergeant Stagakis was sitting on the ground under the tree, his knees drawn up, his arms crossed on top of his knees, and his head lying on his arms. Daley could hear a faint gentle snore. A couple feet away Sung was stretched out on the ground, on his back with his hands behind his head. Daley couldn't tell if he was asleep or not. Over in the middle of the courtyard was a pyramidal shape that Daley knew was the mortar, covered by something.

There was movement near the tree trunk, and Ky stepped away from the tree that he had been standing behind. Daley gave him a friendly wave, and even in the faint moonlight he could see Ky's bright smile split his face. Ky trotted over to him.

"Hello, Sergeant," Ky whispered. "How are you?"

"Tired," Daley answered truthfully. "How about you?"

"Oh, I am very fine. I am standing guard, too."

"I heard. Thank you." Daley waved his hand toward the mortar. "What did you cover the mortar with?"

"It is my poncho that you gave me," Ky answered proudly. "We did not want the mortar to get wet."

Griffin stirred and angrily whispered, "Knock it off!"

Daley felt a pang of guilt, and saw from Ky's chagrinned expression that he had understood Griffin's meaning, if not the actual words. Ky gave Daley a small wave and trotted back over to the tree. Daley resumed his scanning of the area outside the fort, listening intently for any man-made sounds among the murmur of insects and rustle of leaves in the breeze. It was still peacefully quiet. Too quiet, Daley thought to himself in what he imagined was the voice of John Wayne, and chuckled.

Leaning his elbows on the top of the wall, he kept his M-16 pointed outward as his head slowly swiveled from side to side, his eyes watching for any disturbance in the shadows and his ears attuned to every click, rustle, and thump in the night. Behind him, inside the walls, he occasionally heard snoring, the swishing of a poncho being repositioned, or the soft clack of an M-16 tapping against concrete. The overall silence was eerily comforting, perhaps because no noise meant no activity, and no activity meant no imminent danger. For all intents and purposes, Daley was alone in the dark, enveloped by the moonlit night and the humid atmosphere, free to think about whatever came to mind.

And what came to mind was his killing of the NVA officer a few hours before. The images of the incident played over and over again in his mind—the sudden appearance of the man in the doorway, brandishing his pistol, and Daley's almost instinctive reaction, bringing up his rifle and firing off three quick rounds. The man's eyes found Daley's, and they were filled with both hatred and pleading for the brief moment before they went totally blank and the man crumpled to the ground. It was an instant in time, one fraught with significance and sudden transformation. Immediately following the shooting there had been so much going on that Daley had been unable—and unwilling—to contemplate the emotional impact. Now he had the time, and he didn't really like it.

He had killed a man. That was the long and short of it. Sure, it was war, and the man was threatening them with a gun, so technically it wasn't murder, but however you framed it, he had ended the man's life. As an ordinary American, raised in a Christian middle-class suburban home by good parents, Daley should be overcome with anguish at this heinous act. But he wasn't. He was sorry for the man, but no more so than he would be for a murder victim he heard about on the news. He regretted the necessity that led to the killing, and felt some remorse for his part in it, but he did not feel any existential guilt. And that bothered him. He had always considered himself a very empathic person, one who understood and shared the feelings of others, but apparently he had deluded himself. He tried to work up a sympathy for the man's family, assuming he had one, but it didn't come. So what did that say about Daley? Was he a sociopath who couldn't really empathize? Somehow he didn't think so. He could empathize, he told himself, with people who were suffering. He understood how Ky felt, and how he must be torn by his fractured loyalties. He appreciated how Lieutenant Jones must feel about being a black man in a white society, and how he must struggle against racism every day. So it wasn't a lack of empathy on his part, Daley decided, but simply the circumstances that dictated his indifference. It was the morality of war, an oxymoron if ever there was one. War required a suspension of morality, an elimination of common decency, a subversion of ethics. Daley knew he was rationalizing, but decided it was the only rational approach to take.

Forcing his mind away from such deep and painful thoughts, Daley reviewed his experiences as a pseudo-infantryman the last couple days. He had surprised himself by how well he had adapted to the totally different lifestyle. He had kept up physically, he had held up his end in brief combat situations, and he had been somewhat accepted by the other men. Being a grunt was generally acknowledged as the worst job in the Army, combining a mean and dirty daily existence with the constant threat of death or maiming. What other soldiers had to hump the boonies, sleep in the mud, eat bad food, and risk death at every turn? Daley had heard of infantrymen who volunteered to be helicopter door-gunners, an even more dangerous job, just because they would get to sleep on a cot in the base camp at night, providing they survived. And only infantrymen dreamed of the million-dollar wound, the injury that wasn't life-threatening but was severe enough to send them back to the States to recover.

Yet infantrymen took pride in their being the lowest men on the totem pole. To be an infantryman meant they couldn't do anything worse to you, that you were surviving the toughest challenge there was. Any change to your existence, whether it be a transfer to another duty station, a discharge, or even a short stay in a hospital, was something to look forward to, because it had to be better than the current situation. There was a reason the Combat Infantryman's Badge was one of the most coveted awards in the Army: it proved you had taken the worst the Army could throw at you and came out on top. Or at least survived. So far.

A week earlier Daley had been like most soldiers, looking down on the infantry as the poor suckers who hadn't managed to get a better job, either because they were too dumb, or too unlucky. They were the brutes, the peasants, the lowest class of the Army, and were to be pitied, but not envied. Now, however, having spent just a couple days with them, Daley knew the truth. He had felt the pride of these men, the satisfaction they got from doing the things no one else was willing or able to do. And, Daley suddenly realized, he wanted to share that pride. He wanted to be part of this down-trodden brotherhood, because doing so would give him a pride and self-confidence he had always lacked. Here, acting like an infantryman, he felt like a man, not just a boy who had graduated from college. And the risk was its own reward: the adrenaline that flowed when they made contact gave him a high that no drug could possibly equal. It was a difficult thing to admit, but he actually enjoyed the danger.

Daley checked his watch. He had to hold it at several different angles, trying to see the barely glowing hands or get enough moonlight to see where they were on the face, and finally decided it was just after midnight. Two more hours to go. Then he could go back to sleep, a luxury that he had only recently learned to appreciate. He thought about a soft mattress with clean sheets, and a plump pillow, imagining how wonderful that would feel, especially after taking a hot shower. You just don't realize how magnificent the simplest comforts of life can be until you don't have them. He heard something behind him, and turned to see someone hunched over the mortar after having removed the poncho that covered it. Daley felt a twinge of alarm in his chest before he realized it was

Sung. The Korean was just checking to make sure it was ready, he assumed. It looked like Ky was asleep over next to Sergeant Stagakis. The faint yellow flicker of light in the doorway of the main building told him at least one candle was still burning in there. Otherwise the fort was dark and silent. He hoped it would stay that way. It was odd, he knew, but although he almost enjoyed the action of contact, he desperately hoped they wouldn't make any. It wasn't the danger he wanted to avoid, it was the interruption of his daily routine and his sleep.

An hour and a half later, nearing the end of his guard shift, Daley was fighting to stay awake. Nothing had happened, and he had run out of things to think about. He kept checking his watch, willing the hands to move faster. He had convinced himself that if the gooks were coming, they would have been there by now, so standing guard was an exercise in futility, albeit a necessary one.

"Psst." Daley turned at the hiss and saw a short stocky figure approaching from the area near the small building. It was Sergeant Stagakis, he quickly realized, checking on the guards. Stagakis came up and stood beside him, looking out through the trees. "Heard anything?" the sergeant asked in a whisper.

"Nothing," Daley answered quietly.

"Good. Maybe we've lucked out." Stagakis held a black tubular object up. "You want to use the starlight for a while?"

"Might as well. I'm bored."

"Cassidy just put new batteries in it, so it should be good for the rest of the night, if you don't leave it on all the time."

"Thanks." Daley took the scope, and Stagakis walked away toward whoever was standing guard on the east wall. Daley was really glad he had not fallen asleep; he would hate to have had to explain that to Stagakis. Laying his rifle down on top of the wall, he fumbled around on the starlight scope until he found the switch to turn it on, and listened to the ascending whine as it warmed up. Removing his glasses, he pressed the eyepiece against his cheek and eyebrow to open the aperture and winced at the bright green image that appeared. It took a minute to get his bearings, but soon he was sweeping the scope slowly from left to right, pausing every couple degrees to focus on any suspicious clump of bushes or shadowy tree trunk. Five minutes later he took the scope from his eye, switched it off, and put it down next to his rifle while he closed his right eye to let the night vision return. He put his glasses back on, blinking to resolve the difference between his left and right eyes' vision.

He remembered from training that the small starlight scope he had now was made to mount on a rifle or light machine gun, although he had not seen anyone actually do that. Curious, he picked up the scope and felt the various protrusions with his fingers. There did seem to be some sort of clamps on one side, and as he explored them with his fingertips, he tried to visualize how they would work. Holding them up to the moonlight, he studied what he could see in the dim light, the black clamps barely visible against the black tube of the scope. He picked up his M-16 and held it in one hand while he tried to position the scope on the carrying handle. His first few tries were unsuccessful, but finally he found the right combination of angles. With a few twists the scope was now firmly mounted on the rifle, making the rifle almost unwieldy with the additional weight. Daley removed his glasses again and switched on the scope, bringing the rifle up into a normal firing position. The scope was much higher than the peep sight on the carrying handle, so he had to stretch his neck to line his eye up with the scope. He pressed his eye to the scope and pretended to fire his rifle. He pointed it at a small bush in the distance, and lightly touched the trigger as he focused the scope on it. "Pow," he whispered to himself, imagining how he would bring down the target with a single shot.

He swung the rifle slowly side to side, watching the countryside slide across the scope's image in a blur. When he stopped, the image became clearer, or at least as clear as the grainy black and green image ever got. Despite his pretending to be a sniper, Daley knew that using this starlight scope to mark a target was a waste of time. The scope would have to be zeroed with the rifle to ensure that the bullets fired would intersect the crosshairs of the scope at a given distance. Daley knew his rifle wasn't even zeroed for the iron sights, much less for the starlight, which stood several inches higher. Still, having the scope mounted on his rifle was kind of cool, and if he did see something in the scope, he could immediately fire in the general direction, which was as likely to be accurate as using the iron sights in the dark.

He switched off the scope and checked his watch again, intending to dismount the scope before waking up Romano. Again, it took several tries before he was sure of the time, and saw he still had five more minutes of duty. He was just reaching for the starlight scope's clamps when he heard a voice in the distance to his left, and realized that it was a man shouting "Watch out!" in Vietnamese. He heard other panicked voices, and then an explosion rocked the night. Daley saw the flash a split-second before he felt and heard the blast. It was way off to his far left, and he knew instantly that it was the grenade booby-trap that had been set on the main trail to the west. Daley started to shout a warning, but realized quickly it wasn't necessary. Every man in the fort was now awake and scrambling into their positions on the wall.

FOURTEEN

Sergeant Stagakis called out "Hold your fire!" in a hoarse whisper to Daley, causing him to turn his head to see what was going on behind him. Even without his glasses on, he could make out the blurry shapes in the dim moonlight. He saw Stagakis sprinting with surprising agility toward the back corner of the fort to give them the same instructions. As the sergeant came around the corner of the main building he saw Sung and Ky already preparing the mortar, and he slowed down just enough to hold his hand out, palm facing them, to tell them to wait. Sung nodded his understanding and paused in his manipulations, while Stagakis continued over to the east wall to direct the men there. When he turned to return to the center of the fort, he met Lieutenant Jones coming out of the building, positioning his helmet on his head. They stopped to confer in low whispers, and Daley swung back to face the outside of the fort. On his right Griffin had set the RPD's barrel bipod in the breach of the wall and was ready to fire; on his left Romano was crouching with his rifle pointing through another semi-circular hole where part of the wall had crumbled.

In the distance Daley could hear anxious voices yelling in Vietnamese. Behind him Jones and Stagakis came up, dragging Ky by one arm. "What are they saying?" Jones demanded. They were speaking too quickly and excitedly for Daley to really understand; he was getting only every third word or so. He turned to Ky.

"Can you understand them?" he asked.

Ky cocked one ear and listened for a moment. "They are confused," he said judiciously. "One man is telling the others to be quiet." Daley relayed this to Jones and Stagakis, just as the chattering subsided and stopped.

"What'll they do now?" Jones asked, addressing no one in particular.

"They still don't know we're here," Stagakis pointed out. "My guess is they'll send someone to recon the fort."

"What about the rest of them?"

"If it was me," Stagakis surmised, "I'd have them spread out and take cover."

"Can you see anything with the starlight?" Jones asked Daley. Remembering that he had it mounted to his rifle, Daley clicked it on and pointed his rifle to the west, estimating where the trail led.

"Nothing yet," Daley told them, his eye pressed to the scope, the bright lime green image swimming in and out of focus. "Wait! I think I see something." He had caught a flicker of movement through the trees, something round bobbing just above the waves of grass. He steadied his hands and watched the area until he saw it again. Now there were two, the distinctive pith helmets of NVA soldiers, moving cautiously toward the fort on either side of the trail. When they reached the edge of the woods that surrounded the fort they halted and took cover. "Two of 'em," Daley whispered. "Checkin' us out."

"Hello!" one of them suddenly called out in Vietnamese.

"Tell Ky to answer them," Jones breathed. "Pretend he is one of the fort's garrison."

"Ky," Daley whispered, "greet them like you were greeted the first time you came to the fort."

"Welcome, comrades," Ky yelled in Vietnamese, trying to sound jovial. "You are late."

"Why was there a booby-trap on the trail?" one of the NVA soldiers demanded, still keeping his head down.

"We were attacked by Americans in the afternoon. They must have left it. At first we thought you were them, returning." Ky was making it up as he went along, but it sounded authentic.

"Good," Daley told him. In English he told Jones and Stagakis what Ky was saying, without taking his eye from the scope.

"We are glad you are here," Ky called out. "We were worried."

"Where is Lieutenant Cao?" the soldier asked, standing up but keeping his AK-47 at port arms.

"He is very sick," Ky told him. "He is in bed."

The soldier turned to consult with his partner, who had remained in hiding. Turning back to the fort, he called out, "What is your name? I do not recognize your voice."

"I am Tran," Ky said, pulling a name out of his ass.

"We have no Tran," the soldier said accusingly. "Where is Sergeant Minh?"

"Uh, he was killed by the Americans," Ky said nervously. "Why don't you come in, and we will feed you." This sounded strange even to Daley, and the enemy soldier's posture noticeably changed.

"I think they're on to us," Daley whispered in English. "Looks like they're getting ready to book."

"Griff, you got 'em?" Stagakis said.

"Yep," Griffin answered.

Daley saw the hand gesture from the man who was standing, and then the other man rose into view and they began backing away. "They're takin' off," Daley warned.

There was a quick whispered exchange between Jones and Stagakis, and then Stagakis said, "Get 'em, Griff." Immediately the machine gun erupted beside his head, making Daley wince at the blast of noise so close beside him. In the scope he could see the bright sparks of the tracer rounds flying toward the two NVA soldiers, who both dropped to the ground out of sight. After three bursts, the machine gun went silent

"Did I get 'em?" Griff asked.

"Can't tell," Daley answered. "You were in the right area, though." He kept watching through the scope, the image one of sharp contrasts and deep shadows. A man's head, without a helmet, popped up and moved jerkily away from them. "There he goes!" Daley said unnecessarily loud, and Griffin opened up with the machine gun again. Daley watched as a tracer flashed past the man on the left, and another on the right, and the man's AK went flying as his body crashed into the tall grass. "Got him," Daley announced with satisfaction.

"What about the other one?" Jones asked.

"Don't see him," Daley reported, sweeping the starlight over the area where the soldier had last been seen. "Must be down."

"Or he's low-crawling back to the others," Stagakis said pessimistically. "With those green tracers, they'll be wondering just what the hell is going on up here."

On a hunch, or just a gut feeling, Daley used the scope to search closer to the fort, looking at the bushes and areas between the tree trunks. It occurred to him that his M-16 was still on SAFE, so he blindly thumbed it to SEMI as he continued to scan the ground just outside the walls. There was a mechanical click, and then he saw it. "There he is!" he shouted. The soldier had stepped from behind a tree and raised his arm, a Chicom potato-masher hand grenade held like an Olympic torch over his head. Daley jerked the trigger and fired five rapid shots. To his left he heard Romano doing the same. The man's body jerked and shuddered, and the grenade fell from his hand behind him. Then the soldier fell backwards, only to be blasted upright again as the grenade detonated behind him. This time he fell forward, his body contorted in ways the human body was never meant to achieve, and crumpled on the ground.

"I got him!" Romano exclaimed proudly. Daley believed it was his own bullets that had brought the man down, but this was no time to argue the point.

"Definitely down now," Daley reported to the others.

"The cat's out of the bag, though," Stagakis said. "They heard those M-16s, so they'll know who's here."

"What do you think they'll do, Sarge?" Jones asked in a worried tone.

Stagakis paused a moment. "It was me," he finally said, "I'd split the troops into two groups and do a pincer movement. Have one group attack from the southwest, the other from the northwest. Right now, whatever they intend to do, they're bunching up to make plans." He tapped Daley on the shoulder. "Daley, tell Ky to have Sung start lobbing rounds down toward where that booby trap was."

Daley told Ky what was wanted, and the young man ran over to join Sung at the mortar. Daley watched as Stagakis pointed to Sung and waved his hand in a big overhead arc toward the west. Sung nodded and repositioned the mortar, adjusting the elevation with a twist of the knob. Ky handed a mortar round to Sung, and then put his hands over his ears. Sung dropped the round down the tube and turned away from it, but didn't cover his own ears. With a loud poompf the round launched upward, and everyone gazed to the west and waited. After what seemed like a minute, but was surely only a few seconds, there was a flash and boom somewhere beyond the fields of grass. As they blast's echoes quickly faded, Daley heard a cry of anguish. Someone had been wounded.

Sung made some adjustments to the mortar tube, then took another round from Ky. Daley resumed scanning the area outside the fort with the starlight as another round was launched into the sky. That round exploded just before Sung launched another. Surely, Daley thought, the enemy was now in disarray.

"Daley," Stagakis ordered, "take that scope over to the west wall, see if you can see anything there." As Daley grabbed his backpack with his free hand, Stagakis called over to the east wall. "Gonzalez. Move over to the corner so you can cover both directions, but watch the northeast in particular. Tanner, you and Benkowski let me know if you see anything coming from southeast."

As Daley hurried over to the west wall to join Cassidy and the others, he glimpsed the Australian captain standing in the door of the big building, the make-shift crutch under one arm and the pistol in his other hand. Made from a thick branch with a fork at one end, the crutch had burlap wrapped around the forked end for Taylor to tuck under his armpit. Daley dropped his pack along the south wall of the small building and found a place on the east wall, between Cassidy and Jimmerson. Kessler, to Cassidy's right between him and the building, saw Daley arrive and asked, "What the fuck's happening?"

Daley put his rifle across the top of the wall and peered through the scope. "We got two gooks over there. Sung's hitting the rest with the mortar."

"How many are there?" Cassidy asked calmly, as if it didn't really matter.

"Don't know," Daley said. "Sarge thinks they'll come at us in a pincer movement, some over here, and some over there." Daley observed the area to the west, orienting himself to the different terrain. The trees on this side of the fort were less dense than where he had been, and he could see further across the open fields and abandoned rice paddies. He was observing a large patch of woods to the west-northwest of the fort, which he was pretty sure was the one in which the booby-trap grenade had gone off, when a mortar round exploded inside the trees with a flash that nearly blinded Daley. Somehow Sung had gotten the range and direction just right. Daley hoped it was having the intended effect.

Daley heard Stagakis call out Sung's name, and the mortar fire stopped. Daley assumed the sergeant had halted the firing to conserve ammo. Meanwhile he kept scanning the area to his front, searching for any sign of the enemy.

""We got us a fucking blind spot," Kessler told the others. "This goddamn building blocks our line of fire." Taking up the entire northwest corner of the fort, and with only the slit windows on the north and west side, the building did limit their view in those directions. The narrow apertures of the slit windows limited the viewing angles from inside, and the bunks and other furniture would get in the way of anyone moving around there.

"What do you expect?" Cassidy said. "It was built by the French."

"I'm gonna get on the roof," Kessler announced. "Boost me up."

Daley leaned back from the scope and watched as Cassidy laid his rifle down on the wall next to Kessler's and cupped his hands together at knee level. Kessler placed one foot in Cassidy's hands and jumped up to grab the edge of the flat roof. Jimmerson came around Daley and grabbed Kessler's other foot, and with both pushing upwards, Kessler was able to scramble on top. Still on his stomach, he turned around and reached down to retrieve the rifle that Cassidy handed up to him.

"Keep your ass down," Cassidy warned him.

"No sweat," Kessler panted. "There's some old sandbags up here." He crawled away.

"Crazy fucker," Cassidy muttered affectionately as he, Daley, and Jimmerson resumed their watch along the wall.

Daley could hear no more voices from the far tree line, nor could he see any movement. The minutes dragged by.

"Maybe they turned around and went back the way they came," Daley suggested hopefully.

"Sure," Cassidy grumbled, "and maybe they'll make me a general tomorrow. It could happen."

"They're comin'," Jimmerson predicted calmly. "Sooner or later, they're comin'."

Daley regretted his naïve comment. He really wanted to fit in with these guys. Nothing further was said for a few minutes as all three watched and listened.

"Hey guys," Kessler called in a loud whisper from the roof above them. "I think I saw something."

"Where?" Cassidy snapped back. Daley, whose mind had been wandering, was instantly fully alert.

"If looking straight out is twelve o'clock, then it was around eleven. Looked like someone moving through the grass."

Daley lifted his rifle and aimed the scope in the approximate direction Kessler had indicated. At first he didn't see anything unusual, just the stalks of grass waving in the breeze. Then he realized there was no breeze.

"I see the grass moving!" he whispered excitedly.

After a moment Jimmerson said, "I see it, too."

Daley heard someone approach from behind, and then the hoarse whisper of Sergeant Stagakis. "How many?" he asked.

"Can't tell," Daley said, keeping his eye pressed to the scope. "Must be at least four or five, the way the grass is moving."

"Okay," Stagakis said judiciously, "maybe we need a recon by fire. About half a magazine. Aim low, guys."

Daley had kept the scope locked on the area where he had seen the movement, and now he lowered the aiming point what he hoped was about five feet at that distance. He was startled when Jimmerson opened fire first, his hot brass casings bouncing off Daley's helmet and shoulder. Then Cassidy began shooting as well, so Daley pulled the trigger and fired. Repeatedly he squeezed the trigger back and felt the recoil. The noise of the three rifles was deafening. The image in the scope shuddered and blurred as he adjusted his aim in small increments to the left and right with each shot. When he realized Jimmerson and Cassidy had stopped shooting, he did the same. He wasn't sure how many rounds he had fired, but hoped it was only ten or so.

"Anything?" Stagakis asked.

The bright green image in the scope seemed unchanged from before—fields of grass and distant trees. Daley started to tell Stagakis that when there was movement on the left side of the screen. He swung the rifle a little to the left to center the movement, which he now saw was a man standing up, only his shoulders and head visible above the stalks, aiming an AK-47 right at Daley.

"Gook in the open!" Cassidy yelped and fired his rifle. The man let loose a burst of automatic fire from his AK, and Daley heard them crack through the air over his head. He pulled the trigger on his own rifle, as did Jimmerson beside him. The enemy soldier dropped back out of sight.

"Got him!" Jimmerson gloated.

"Maybe," Cassidy said, being conservative.

"Just a probe," Stagakis said. There was an outbreak of firing from the north wall, a mix of M-16 and RPD machine gun along with a reply from an AK. Stagakis ran over that way, but the firing stopped as soon as he got there.

"Another probe?" Daley asked. He was still watching his front through the starlight scope.

"Probably," Cassidy said. Daley heard him release the magazine from his rifle and click another one into place. On his left Jimmerson did the same. Following their lead, Daley stepped back from the wall, caught the magazine in his left hand as he released it from the rifle, and set it on the wall. It felt very light, and Daley guessed it was nearly empty; he had fired more than half a magazine just now. Reaching down he freed a fresh magazine from one of his bandoliers and inserted it into the magazine well, tapping the bottom to make sure it was fully seated. He started to pull the charging handle back, but remembered he already had one in the chamber from the previous magazine. Imitating Jimmerson, Daley put the nearly empty magazine into one of the cargo pockets on his pants leg.

"They're counting our guns," Cassidy said, affecting a strange accent. "It's a line from a movie," he hastily explained, without really clearing things up. But Daley knew what he meant. The probes told the enemy commander how many men might be holding the fort, and what sort of armament they deployed. This would allow him to better plan his main attack. Or, Daley hoped, deter him from attacking at all.

Sergeant Stagakis came back and said, "Daley, we need the starlight." Daley turned his back to the wall and began detaching the scope from his rifle. Stagakis looked around and asked, "Where the hell's Kessler?"

"Up here, Sarge," Kessler called out.

"What the fuck you doin' up there?"

"I got up here to see better. I thought. . ."

Stagakis interrupted him gruffly. "You ain't paid to think, Kessler."

"Sorry. Want me to get down?"

"No," Stagakis grumbled. "As long as you're already up there, might as well stay for now. You got any cover?"

"Couple of old sandbags," Kessler told him, having now scooted over to the edge of the roof so he could look down as he talked to the sergeant.

"What'll you do if we have to leave in a hurry? Fly?"

"I can jump down, Sarge," Kessler assured him. "No sweat."

"Okay, but if you break your ankle, don't expect me to carry your sorry ass."

"Roger that. I'll make Cassidy do it."

"No fuckin' way," Cassidy said with mock seriousness. "You'll just have to die in place."

"Idiots," Stagakis laughed as he turned and walked away with the starlight. Daley wiped his glasses before he put them back on.

Two minutes later Stagakis was back. "Daley, come hold the flashlight for me," he said, leading him back into the small building. Leaning his rifle against the inside wall, Stagakis went into the arms room and handed his flashlight to Daley. "Keep it pointed at the bangalores," he instructed, kneeling down to examine the long black metal tubes. Stagakis rolled them back and forth and examined the ends closely. "Five sections," he mumbled more to himself than Daley, "and only one end cap. But that'll work." He attached an acorn-shaped end cap to one of the tubes, then bundled three of them in his arms and stumbled to his feet. "Get the other two," he told Daley, the walked sideways out the door, the five-foot-long pipe sections banging against the door frame as he exited.

Daley clipped the still-lit flashlight to his pistol belt and fumbled to gather up the two sections of pipe along with his rifle. Like Stagakis, he had to turn sideways to maneuver out the arms room door, then again to get outside the building. Only then did he realize the flashlight beam was still shining like a beacon from his waist. He lowered the bangalore sections to at least block some of the light, since his hands were too full to operate the switch. He followed Stagakis across the courtyard to the corner of the main building, and both laid their cargo down gently on the ground. Daley quickly switched off the flashlight and handed it back to Stagakis. "Wait here," Stagakis told him, and ran back to the small building. In moments he was back with his rifle.

"Gardner, Benkowski, bring me your Claymores." Stagakis knelt down and slid one of the pipe sections along the ground until it was clear of the stack, then reached over to pull one end of it to connect with another section. Daley knelt down to help him line the two sections up so they locked together. Gardner and Benkowski ran up and laid their Claymore bags on the ground beside Stagakis.

"What's up, Sarge," Benkowski asked. "Bangalores?"

"For outside this building," Stagakis answered, sliding the two combined sections backwards so he could attach the end cap. "One on the south side, one on the east. In case any gooks get up against the walls there, in the ballistic shadow." Even Daley now understood. The outside walls of the large building could not be observed from inside the fort's walls, and firing at anyone there would require leaning way over the walls, making yourself a prime target. Stagakis opened one of the Claymore bags and took out the firing device and coil of electrical wire with the blasting cap.

"Daley, run over and tell Cassidy and Romano to set up their Claymores just outside the wall, pointed along the sides of the small building. Understand?"

"Yeah, Sarge," Daley answered as he jumped to his feet and ran over to Romano, and then Cassidy, explaining what Sergeant Stagakis wanted. Both men laid down their rifles and began preparing their Claymores. Daley jogged back to where he had left Stagakis and the others, but they were already crowded in the corner between the building and the south wall, maneuvering the longer of the Bangalore torpedoes over the wall and pushing it along the outer side of the building. The electrical wire trailed from the near end, and Gardner had the opposite end of the wire tied around his wrist.

Once the pipe was in place, Gardner pulled out his firing device from his pocket and began attaching it to his end of the wire.

Daley joined Stagakis and Benkowski and helped them put the other, shorter torpedo in place along the outer east wall of the building. While Benkowski attached his firing device, a block of plastic with a spring-loaded lever on one side, Stagakis picked up his rifle and looked around the fort appraisingly. Lieutenant Jones walked over and joined them.

"Battalion says they can't help us," Jones said.

"Not surprised," Stagakis answered. "That gate worries me," he said tilting his head toward the wide opening between the tall gateposts. The wooden gate, if there had ever been one, was long gone. "Wish we had some concertina or something to block it."

"Hey, how about the ladder," Daley suggested as the thought occurred to him. The tall bamboo ladder had been returned to the side of the main building after being used to cut down the camouflage netting. The rungs were nearly three feet long, making it wide and stable. "We could stretch it across the opening. Maybe cover it with the camouflage net."

"How would you hold it in place?" Stagakis asked logically.

"There's bags of rice upstairs," Jones said. "We could pile them against the ends of the ladder."

Stagakis nodded. "Anything would help. Daley, get Ky and Sung to help you with the rice. The LT and I will get the ladder."

Daley got Ky's and Sung's attention and led them inside the building, brushing past Captain Taylor who quickly stepped out of their way. Daley set his rifle down near the base of the stairs and climbed the steps two at a time. Faint moonlight streaming in through a slit window at the far end of the hall gave him just enough light to see what he was doing. He found that the second room on the right was piled high with burlap bags of rice, and he grabbed up the nearest one and slung it on his shoulder. He told Ky what was needed, and Ky stepped past him and grabbed another bag, hoisting it up to his own shoulder. Sung clearly understood and went in the room to load up. Daley and Ky hurried back down, the heavy bags of rice making the stairs somewhat precarious.

Outside Daley saw that Jones and Stagakis had placed the ladder on edge across the gate opening, holding it in place against the gateposts with their knees. Daley rushed over and dropped his bag against the right end of the ladder as Jones moved out of his way. Ky did the same on the left side. Only then did Daley see Sung arrive, with two bags of rice, one on each shoulder. Marveling at the Korean's strength, Daley smiled at him and indicated where to place the bags. While Sung did that, Daley and Ky ran back upstairs to get more bags. After three exhausting trips, they had enough bags to firmly secure the ladder in place. Daley told Ky about the camouflage nets, and Ky motioned Sung to help him retrieve them while Daley went to get his rifle. Soon they had spread the netting over the ladder, giving at least the visual impression that the opening was now partially sealed.

"I figure they'll send a feint against the southwest corner," Jones said, thinking out loud. "Then attack the front here in force. At least, that's what I'd do."

"Makes sense to me, sir," Stagakis said. "I think we're as ready as we can be." He turned to Daley, who stood with Ky and Sung awaiting orders. "Think Sung can put mortar rounds close in, like right along the main trail out there?"

Daley shrugged. "He seems to know what he's doing." Daley turned to Sung and pantomimed firing the mortar nearly straight up, with the rounds coming down and exploding close in. Sung nodded his head vigorously and asserted something in Korean. Daley explained what he was asking Sung to Ky in Vietnamese.

"He is very good," Ky told Daley. "I will help him. When you tell me where you want the explosions, I will show Sung."

"Good. How many rounds do you have left?"

"Only five," Ky told him regretfully.

"They've only got five rounds left," Daley told Jones and Stagakis.

"Better than nothin', I guess," Stagakis said. "Wish I knew how many gooks there are out there."

"Can't be more than forty or so," Jones estimated, "according to Captain Taylor. The question is, when and where will they attack?"

"Soon," Stagakis said, "and anywhere they damn well please. Daley, you better stay here on the north side, over there by Gonzalez. Tell Ky that him and Sung should stay by the mortar."

"Roger that, Sarge." Daley told Ky and then ran to retrieve his backpack over by the west wall, before taking a position on the north wall, just to the right of the gate. He checked his watch. It was two-thirty, and quiet. But not for long, he guessed.

FIFTEEN

The moonlit stillness was abruptly fractured by gunfire from outside the far corner of the fort, to the southwest. Daley turned to look just as supersonic bullets cracked overhead, and saw the brief sparkle of muzzle blasts between the trees. "Fuck!" someone yelled, and then the men on that side of the fort began returning fire.

"Over there!" Ortiz yelled, firing steadily into the trees.

"I think I got him!" Most replied ecstatically.

"Watch your front!" Sergeant Stagakis bellowed. Guiltily Daley turned back to watch the northern approaches. He noted with some satisfaction that Gonzalez had to do the same. The volleys from behind him subsided to sporadic outbursts, signaling, perhaps, that it was indeed just a feint. This was confirmed only moments later.

"They're in the trees!" Griffin shouted and began firing the RPD. The chatter of the machine gun brought a response from the area of the main trail: AK-47s on full auto burst into life, spraying the front wall with bullets that thudded into the concrete and zipped overhead. Daley resisted the urge to go into a fetal position behind the wall and began firing his M-16 blindly. The roar of the gunfire was deafening. Lieutenant Jones, just to his left, was firing steadily but judiciously, squeezing off shots in a steady rhythm. His spent casing ejected over toward Daley, bouncing off his left leg, but Daley barely noticed.

Taking a cue from Jones, Daley forced himself to control his shooting, aiming first at any perceived movement or muzzle flash before pulling the trigger. Even with this measured shooting, Daley was surprised when the trigger froze as the bolt locked to the rear, indicating the magazine was empty. Shaking his head to clear it,

Daley dropped the empty magazine on the ground and fumbled to retrieve a fresh one from his bandolier, belatedly ducking his head down below the parapet while he did so. Rising to place his rifle across the wall again, Daley searched out new targets.

"I'm hit!" It sounded like Romano, over next to the small building. The staccato drilling of Griffin's RPD stopped. Daley guessed that Griffin was tending to Romano.

That was confirmed as Griffin yelled, "Medic!"

Daley glanced to his left and saw Ortiz running across the courtyard from the south wall to the north. At the same time he noticed that the gunfire at the opposite side of the fort had stopped. Then he jerked his head around as he detected movement out of the corner of his right eye and pulled off three quick rounds without really aiming. The movement, whatever it was, stopped, at least for the moment.

He was startled by a loud noise directly behind him, but quickly realized it was the mortar being fired. He kept shooting, until he was nearly blinded by the fiery blast of the mortar round impacting just beyond the main trail.

"Again!" Sergeant Stagakis yelled. "Fire for effect!" Daley hoped Sung understood the sergeant's intent, if not his words. Another mortar launch proved that he did. Daley kept firing at the sparkles of the enemy guns, and felt a surge of elation each time a mortar round exploded to his front, hopefully breaking up the enemy assault.

Then the mortar fire stopped. At first Daley feared that Sung or Ky had been hit, but then Ky ran up and crouched beside him at the base of the wall. He looked back to see Sung in a crouch hurrying over to where Ortiz was tending to Romano. Daley thought back to how many mortar rounds had just been fired, and realized they had exhausted their limited supply.

Outside the fort, the attackers had also noticed the absence of mortar fire, and Daley realized Griffin's RPD had not resumed its deadly fusillade. He took a step backward to look in that direction, and saw Griffin crouched down pounding on the side of the gun with the palm of his hand, apparently trying to free a jam. Out in the trees

Daley heard Vietnamese voices shouting. It took him a minute to absorb what they were saying and translate it in his head. Ky pulled at his pants leg and repeated the key phrase being used by the enemy: "RPG." Looking across the wall Daley saw a figure rise up from behind a bush, a weapon on his shoulder.

"RPG!" Daley shouted as warning, and ducked down next to Ky. On either side of him Jones and Gonzalez did likewise, just in time. With a brief introductory whoosh the rocket-propelled grenade slammed into the wall and exploded. A narrow jet of fire squirted out through a hole in the wall between Daley and Jones, and pieces of cement rained down on his helmet.

"Are you okay?" Lieutenant Jones asked. He had to yell over the ringing in their ears.

"Yeah," Daley reassured him. Everyone along the north wall was still crouched behind it, preparing to rise and resume defensive fire, when a maniacal scream was heard approaching the gate.

An NVA soldier, his AK-47 held in one hand, leaped over the net-covered ladder like it was a high hurdle and hit the ground inside the fort in a stumble. Quickly regaining his balance, he swung around to face the Americans along the inside of the wall. Tucking the stock of his AK under his right arm, he grabbed the forestock and prepared to fire from the hip. Daley, like the others, was stunned and slow to react, feeling like his M-16 was stuck in molasses as he tried to bring it to bear on the wild-eyed enemy.

Three quick shots rang out, with the distinctively short bark of a pistol, and the enemy soldier froze, his eyes going dull, dropping the AK-47 with a clatter before he sprawled forward on his face. In the doorway to the main building, Daley saw Captain Taylor, his wounded leg bent at the knee, his left hand holding onto the doorjamb for support, and a pistol pointing at the fallen man in his right hand. Daley couldn't see his face clearly due to the shadows, but Taylor's body language spoke volumes.

"Here they come!" Stagakis yelled, breaking the spell of astonishment that had overtaken the others. Daley sprang up and began firing over the wall, methodically spraying the gaps between the trees as dark figures rushed toward him. He saw one man pitch backward, and another dive to the ground. To his left Griffin had gotten the RPD working again, sending a stream of tracers across the front like water from a hose. It was a mass of confusion, the noise drowning out all rational thought, the darkness repeatedly split for a milli-second by the flash of guns, only to envelope the scene in blackness again. Daley kept firing, replacing magazine after magazine, in a daze of combat fury.

"Cease fire!" Lieutenant Jones hollered, and other men down the line echoed the command. Daley came out of his fog, but kept watch on the trees in front of him. Only then did he notice that the enemy had stopped shooting as well. His ears were numb and a constant piercing whine dominated his hearing. Ignoring this internal noise, Daley listened to hear anything that might be occurring outside the walls.

A painful groan emerged from the darkness. One of the attackers had been wounded and left behind, it seemed. His moans came in short bursts with each breath. "Unhhh, unhh, unhh," he grunted.

"Shut the fuck up!" Gonzalez yelled pointlessly at the man. And with a liquid gargle the man suddenly went quiet. "About damn time," Gonzalez remarked petulantly.

Daley's hearing gradually returned to normal, and still there were no more shots or voices from beyond the walls of the fort. The calm seemed to drag on, with everyone waiting for the other shoe to drop. After about ten minutes, Lieutenant Jones spoke to Sergeant Stagakis across the gateway opening.

"What's our status?" he asked.

"I'll check," Stagakis replied, and started walking around the fort in a roughly clockwise circle, quietly calling out to each man. "Daley, you hit?" he asked.

"Good to go, Sarge," Daley answered quickly. "Ky's okay, too."

"Gonzalez?"

"I'm okay."

"Tanner?"

"Hunky-dory," Tanner replied sarcastically. "I love this shit."

Stagakis ignored the comment and kept moving, checking each man in turn. When he got back around to Lieutenant Jones, he gave his brief report: "Romano's the only one wounded. His right arm, pretty bad. Ortiz has got it bandaged, but he won't be able to use it. Sung is using Romeo's M-16."

"Thank you, Sergeant." Joes looked back across the inner courtyard where the Australian was still standing in the doorway. He raised his voice enough to carry to the entire fort. "And thank you, Captain Taylor. You really saved our asses."

"Glad I could help," Taylor answered. "I believe that fucker was quite mad."

"Damn straight," Benkowski muttered in agreement.

While Stagakis was taking headcount, Ky had gone over and dragged the dead body over near the right front corner of the building, out of the way. Again, he carefully and respectfully folded the man's arms over his chest and straightened his legs.

"Daley," Stagakis said, "ask Ky to take that AK over to the arms room. And take the other ones we captured there, too."

"Right, Sarge," Daley answered, then translated the request for Ky. Ky didn't question why he was being asked to do it; he just picked up the weapon by its barrel and trotted across the courtyard to disappear in the small building. A moment later he reappeared and hurried back to duck inside the big building as Taylor stepped back out of his way. There was some scuffling and muttering inside before Ky came back out, the four AKs awkwardly cradled in his arms, and walked across the courtyard again, stepping more cautiously this time. After depositing the weapons in the building, he jogged back to Daley and stood looking expectantly at Stagakis. The sergeant ignored him.

Sergeant Stagakis instead had noticed that many of the other men, including Daley, had turned their attention inwards. "Eyes front!" he hollered with patient anger. "They'll be back." Daley grimaced and turned to gaze at the tree-shrouded area near the fort and the lighter fields of grass beyond. Ky came over and sat down with his back against the wall, between Daley and Gonzalez. Jones knelt down beside the gatepost, and beckoned Stagakis to join him. Although they spoke quietly, Daley was close enough to overhear.

"You really think they will?" Jones asked.

"Seems likely," Stagakis said. "We've got their fort, and they need it. They've lost at least five or six guys, but they probably had at least forty to begin with. The real question is when."

"Yes," Jones agreed. "When. The good news, if there is any, is that they don't seem to have any heavy weapons, other than an RPG."

"Yeah. Since they're probably the fort's garrison gone to get supplies, they wouldn't be carrying anything but small arms. If they only went to get food, then they might be running out of ammo, but if they got ammo, too, then we're fucked."

"No way to know," Jones mused out loud. "Think they requested reinforcements?"

"If they have a radio," Stagakis remarked, "then they might. We didn't find a pack radio here, just those bigger ones, so if they have one, they must have taken it with them when they left. Otherwise, they'd have to send a runner. What we don't know, is how far away any reinforcements are, and how many."

"Let's figure worst case scenario," Jones suggested. "They have a radio, and additional troops are close enough to respond. It took these guys half the night to get here from wherever they were before, but they weren't in a hurry. If they just now called, it would take maybe thirty minutes for the troops to gear up and organize, and at least an hour or two to get here."

"So, two to three hours from now we could have half the damn North Vietnamese Army down on our ass," Stagakis estimated pessimistically.

"Worst case, yeah." Jones paused to consider the possibilities. "If the guys who are here now knew reinforcements were coming, would they just sit and wait for them?"

"I would," Stagakis said, "but these guys are pretty pissed about us taking their fort and freeing their prisoners. Their commander might be taking it personal, or worried about his OER, and wants to try and take us out before the others arrive."

"It's still two or three hours until it gets light," Jones noted. "I'm wondering if we should try and sneak out now."

"I don't know," Stagakis said with true uncertainty. "If we left just as they were getting ready to attack again, we'd get caught out in the open. But if we wait, we might get surrounded by superior forces. I just don't know."

Daley, pretending not to hear this conversation, was disturbed by his leaders' indecision. He thought they would always know the right thing to do, and depended on them for his own safety. To know that they were unsure what to do next gave him plenty to worry about.

"How about this," Jones suggested. "If they don't attack again within the next hour, we can assume they're waiting on reinforcements, and we'll exit stage left."

"What if they do attack again?" Stagakis asked.

"We repel the attack, and when they fall back to regroup, like last time, we quietly go over the east wall and beat feet to the river."

"Might work. It'd still be dark when we left, and they might not notice we're gone until sunrise, by which time we should be back in Nam and can get air support."

"Okay," Jones said with finality. "That's the plan. Subject to change, of course. Let's start working out the march order."

"I'll take care of it, sir. Taylor's gonna be slow, and so is Romano. Maybe Sung can help Taylor. . ." Stagakis' voice dropped to a mumble as he rose and walked along the ladder blocking the gateway to take a position at the other gatepost.

"Tanner," Jones called to the RTO, who was only about fifteen feet away along the east wall. "When was the last sitrep?"

"About an hour ago," Tanner replied. "Before the attack. Didn't think it was worth the effort to tell 'em about it while it was happening."

"Understood. Call them now, brief them on the attack, and tell them we plan to exfiltrate just before dawn. Ask them if they can provide us support once we cross the border."

"Roger," Tanner answered, then muttered under his breath, just loud enough for Daley—and Jones—to hear, "Exfiltrate! What the fuck kind of word is that?" Nonetheless, he unclipped the handset from his collar and began calling Battalion.

Jones stood up and joined Daley on the wall, gazing out at the moonlight shadows. Nothing was said for several minutes. Then Tanner called out to Jones.

"They said they'll try," he reported, clearly not believing it.

"Thank you." Jones said, and continued staring out into the darkness. Daley checked his watch, and it was past three. Over to his right Gonzalez shifted his weight and stretched a little. Somewhere in the far corner someone coughed.

"So, Specialist Daley," Jones said abruptly, "where are you from?"

Daley was startled by the sudden question, and almost stuttered his answer. "Kansas City, sir. Missouri."

"And you went to college?"

"Yes, sir. Got a BS in Geology from Drury, in Springfield."

"Hmm." Daley suspected Jones had never heard of Drury, but that wasn't really surprising. It was a small school. "I'm from Oakland, California." Jones offered, apparently forgetting he had already told Daley that. "Went to San Diego State, got my degree in Education. ROTC scholarship. You didn't take ROTC?"

"Nah, I thought the war would be over by the time I graduated. Guess that's what I get for thinking."

"What about OCS?" Jones asked. "You obviously qualified."

"I don't know," Daley told him, "just didn't seem right for me. Language school in Monterey seemed like a better option at the time. And then I got sent to Texas instead."

"Still hoping the war would be over by the time you finished?" Jones asked with a chuckle.

"It occurred to me," Daley admitted.

"Maybe that's what I should have done," Jones mused. "This officer crap doesn't seem to be working out."

"Sir?" Daley was a little taken aback by this personal information.

"Never mind. One day at a time." Jones went silent, and Daley could tell the conversation was over. He had always thought officers had it made, and to hear one complain about his status was unnerving. Daley wondered if Jones was simply unhappy with the lot of all lieutenants, or if perhaps his skin color was the major factor. Daley acknowledged that racism still existed, despite the gains of the civil rights movement, but he always assumed that such prejudice remained primarily in the southern states among the less educated. He had had plenty of black NCOs in training, so he had accepted that the Army was unlike the nation as a whole, and had virtually eliminated such stereotypes. As one of his drill sergeants had told him, "In the Army there ain't no blacks or whites, no yellows or browns. Here we're all green." But Ortiz had hinted that Jones, as a black officer, was not welcomed by all the members of the officer corps. Daley wanted to reassure Jones that he, Daley, did not hold any prejudices, but knew he would just sound like a bleeding-heart liberal trying to suck up, so he kept quiet. He felt sorry for Jones, because he knew that being an infantry lieutenant in Viet Nam was hard enough for anyone, but might be doubly difficult for a black man.

"Daley," Stagakis called quietly from across the entrance. "Ask Ky if there's anything flammable in the kitchen."

It took Daley a moment to figure out how to ask that, since he didn't know the Vietnamese word for 'flammable'. Finally he said, "Ky, is there something in the kitchen that burns?"

"Burns?" Ky replied, his forehead scrunched in confusion.

"Yes, like gasoline, or oil."

"Oh, yes. There is cooking oil. It burns."

"Cooking oil," Daley told Stagakis.

"How much?" Stagakis asked.

Daley relayed the question. Ky told him there was a ten-liter can that was almost full. Daley did some calculations in his head, and hoped he remembered the conversions correctly. "About two and a half gallons," he told Stagakis.

"That ought to do it. Have him take the oil over to the arms room, and then gather up all the blankets, curtains, and empty rice bags he can find and take them over there, too."

"What for?" Daley couldn't help but ask.

"Just do it," Stagakis ordered him.

Daley repeated the instructions to Ky, who simply nodded and hurried off. Unlike Daley, he knew better than to question orders. Daley resumed his watch of the spooky area beyond the front of the fort, wondering what Stagakis was up to.

SIXTEEN

Daley heard Ky over to his left, saying he was finished in Vietnamese. Looking over, he saw Ky facing Stagakis at attention, his hand to the brim of his cowboy hat in an earnest but poorly executed salute.

"He says it's done," Daley translated for the sergeant. Stagakis gave Ky a dismissive wave and waggled his head in bemusement. Ky scurried over to once again sit next to Daley.

"Tell him thanks," Stagakis said. "Sir, I'll be back in a minute." With that he walked away, headed for the small building.

Jones jerked, as if he had suddenly been awakened. Daley couldn't blame him; he, too, had been fighting the urge to doze off. "What?" Jones asked, but Stagakis was already too far away.

"Something to do with the arms room," Daley told him.

"Oh." Jones rubbed his face with his left hand. "Long night," he commented.

"Sure is," Daley replied.

Five minutes later the platoon sergeant returned and took up his watch by the other gatepost without comment. Daley hoped that Jones would ask him what he had been doing, but the lieutenant just noted the return and resumed watching the woods outside.

A few minutes later Doc Ortiz came over, lugging one of the black plastic jerry cans the GIs used for water. Since the patrol hadn't brought one with them, Daley figured it was something the gooks had appropriated.

"LT," Ortiz said, "I found this in the kitchen. The water didn't smell bad, but I put some purification tablets in it anyway. We probably ought to have everyone fill their canteens."

"Good idea, Doc. Get me last." Jones gestured toward Daley and Ky. Daley unsnapped his canteen covers and pulled out his empty one first. Doc took the canteen and held it low so he could tip the jerry can over until water flowed out of the small spigot. Some splashed on the ground, but most went inside. Daley took the full canteen and handed Ortiz his other one, which was nearly half full. When that one was filled, Doc took Ky's canteen, and Daley replaced his canteens on his pistol belt and snapped the covers closed. Then, after thinking about it, and hearing the water splashing into Ky's canteen, he again unsnapped one of the covers and took out the canteen to get a drink. The water tasted bad, like a public swimming pool, but it felt good going down. While Ortiz moved on to Gonzalez, Daley returned his attention to the shadowy trees.

Sergeant Stagakis came across the entrance and held the starlight scope out to Daley. "You want to use this a while?" he asked. "Makes my eye hurt."

"Sure, Sarge." Daley took the scope and quickly attached it to his rifle.

"You know the scope's not zeroed for your rifle," Stagakis said.

"Yeah, but it will at least get me in the general direction. And keeps my rifle pointed where it needs to be."

"That's true," Stagakis agreed. He sighed and turned to look at the center of the courtyard. "Wish I could figure out a way to disable that mortar," he said thoughtfully. "Don't want the gooks using it after we leave."

Daley, his eye now pressed to the scope as he slowly scanned between the tree trunks, suggested, "Can't we just bend it or something?"

"Too strong," Stagakis said. "That tube's made to handle the propellant charge, so it'd take Superman to bend it with his bare hands."

"Sung probably knows what to do, if we knew how to ask him," Jones suggested.

"Sung!" Stagakis called softly, and the Korean trotted over, holding Romano's M-16 like he knew how to use it. Stagakis pointed at the mortar and made various hand gestures, like he was breaking a stick. Sung raised his eyebrows and shook his head. Stagakis repeated the gestures, and added stomping motions with his boot, all the while muttering in pidgin English, "Break mortar, no good, no fire."

Finally Sung's face cleared and he smiled. "Okay!" he said enthusiastically as he handed his rifle to Ky and walked over to the mortar. Expertly he disassembled the weapon, removing the bipod, the aiming mechanism, and the base plate. He picked up the tube, now bare of any attachments, and carried it inside the building. Daley heard metallic clangs and thunks that sounded like they were coming from the kitchen, and then Sung reappeared. He came over to Stagakis and proudly showed him his handiwork: the mortar tube had numerous dings and dents that were deep enough to have permanently distorted the inner diameter. Sung pantomimed hitting the tube with something—a meat cleaver?—and said, "No okay." Dropping the mortar tube to the ground, he then picked up the other pieces and threw them over the east wall.

Stagakis gave him a thumb's up gesture and smiled. Sung retrieved his rifle from Ky and returned to where Romano sat, over by the small building.

"That takes care of that," Jones remarked, obviously pleased. "What about the AKs?"

"Got that covered," Stagakis told him cryptically. He ambled back over to the other side of the gateway.

A few minutes later Ortiz returned, now filling Lieutenant Jones' canteens from a jerry can that was obviously much lighter than before. "That's everybody," Ortiz reported as he screwed the cap back on the water can.

"Good job, Doc," Jones praised him. Without responding, Ortiz turned and left, dropping the nearly empty can by the big tree as he returned to his place on the south wall.

There was a scuffling sound from the roof of the smaller building, and Kessler poked his head over the edge. In a hoarse whisper, he called out, "I think I see something!"

"What?" Stagakis asked with a touch of annoyance.

"Movement off to the southwest. Looks like they might be trying to circle around to the south."

"How many?" Jones asked.

"Can't tell. Maybe a squad."

"Cassidy, Jimmerson, you see anything?" Stagakis moved away from the wall toward the center of the compound.

"Not yet," Cassidy answered.

Now hyper alert, Daley peered through the scope at the expanse of grass beyond the trees, and saw the stalks move in a way that seemed unnatural.

"I got something," Daley yelped. "Straight north, about a hundred yards out. Moving east."

"Same same here," Gardner called out. "Off to the south, moving east."

"Surrounding us," Jones remarked.

"Remember the Alamo," Gonzalez mumbled.

"But those were Mexicans," Jones replied in a rare moment of humor. "Think these gooks are as good as those Mexicans were, Gonzalez?"

"No fuckin' way, senor," Gonzalez laughed with an exaggerated Spanish accent. "And we're sure as hell better than a bunch of damn Texans."

"The colonel's from Texas," Jones reprimanded him with mock severity.

"See what I mean," Gonzalez said. Everyone within hearing laughed. Daley felt his spirits lifted by the mood of defiance and bravery that seemed to exude from the men around him.

"You guys with the bangalores and Claymores be ready," Sergeant Stagakis called out. "And everybody, don't start shooting until you can actually see something to shoot at. Conserve your ammo."

"Shit!" Tanner cursed from the east wall. "There's somebody out there. Little fuckers are coming at us from the east, too."

"Fire as soon as you've got a clear target," Jones commanded loudly.

A green flare arced up from a grove to the northeast, nearly blinding Daley's right eye with the white flash in the scope's screen. Only a second later Kessler yelled from the roof: "Here they come!" He started firing, and others around the perimeter joined in.

Knowing it was a long shot, in more ways than one, Daley fired several rounds at the trees where he had seen the flare launch. Then, using the scope to pick out movement in the tall stalks of grass, he peppered the area, firing low to hopefully catch the men crawling or crouching out of sight. To his left Griffin had the RPD chattering away, and Daley could see the tracers in the scope, looking like super-fast fireflies flitting through the night. With all the gunfire from within the fort, it was hard to tell, but Daley didn't think he had seen or heard any return fire from the enemy. Just as he was about to remark on that to Lieutenant Jones, a large chip of concrete burst from the edge of the wall a foot to his right. Someone was indeed shooting at them, and one of them had Daley in his sights. Daley began firing wildly, swinging his gun around and shooting at shadows. The bolt locked to the rear, and Daley ducked down behind the wall to change magazines—and get out of the line of fire for at least a moment. Ky was huddled beside him, looking worried. Daley reloaded, and then took a minute to pat Ky on the shoulder reassuringly. Daley didn't know why he did that, since he himself was extremely worried, but was glad that Ky seemed to take some solace in the gesture. Sensing that it was no longer useful, Daley quickly detached the starlight scope from his rifle and handed it to Ky. "Keep it safe," he told Ky in Vietnamese as he put his glasses back on and popped back up to begin shooting again.

Without the scope, Daley hoped he made less of a target, and his peripheral vision was greatly improved. He saw Sergeant Stagakis drop back from the wall to the center of the courtyard, crouch down, and slam the end of an aluminum tube flare launcher against his knee. Like a roman candle the flare spat out of the tube and arced above the trees until the parachute popped open and the brightly burning flare began its lazy swaying descent over the open fields. Daley could now see enemy soldiers flitting between the trees, firing around the trunks, and in one case preparing to throw a hand grenade. Daley fired at least five shots in rapid succession, and the man dropped to the ground before he could throw. Time seemed to be moving very slowly, and Daley had just decided the man had failed to arm the grenade when there was a muffled explosion and the man's body was lifted into the air a couple feet by the blast beneath him. Whether through self-sacrifice or happenstance, the man had fallen on the grenade and suffered the consequences.

Someone on the back wall—Ortiz or Most—popped a star shell that briefly illuminated the south size of the fort. With the added light, in front and in back, the firing increased in intensity. The men could now see their attackers, and responded accordingly. Daley could hear the men shouting to each other as they identified targets, their words largely unintelligible over the noise of the battle. Daley pulled the trigger again and again, aiming at figures that popped up and then disappeared before he could be sure he really had them in his sights. The gooks seemed to be everywhere, like ants from a disturbed anthill, jigging left and right, up and down, their rifles sparking and barking all the while. Worse, they seemed to be closing in on the fort. Daley had no idea how effective his shooting was; NVA soldiers dropped out of sight when he fired, but whether he had shot them, or someone else had shot them, or the soldier was simply ducking out of sight, he had no way of knowing. But he kept firing, hoping that by sheer luck alone, if nothing else, the bullets might strike home with deadly effect.

"Shit!" a voice screamed from behind him, and Daley turned his head to see a parachute flare hung up in a tree just outside the east wall, and Benkowski throwing the launcher angrily at the side of the building. Benkowski had misjudged the angle when launching the flare, and now the men on the east wall were brightly outlined by the dazzling white light, the glare of which also mostly blinded them to the approaching enemy. Daley had to tilt his head forward so the front of his helmet shielded his eyes from the brilliance. He could see Tanner doing the same with his left hand, trying to see beyond the bright illumination. Tanner jerked his rifle around to the right and fired off several rapid shots.

"They're up against the building!" Tanner screamed. "Blow the bangalore, Art. Now!" Benkowski ducked down in the corner where the wall met the building and searched for the firing device. He found the wire and followed it to the block of plastic, trying to squeeze the lever. It slipped out of his sweaty hands, and he picked it up to try again. Daley, crouched down as he fumbled to replace the empty magazine in his rifle, watched with tense fascination. Benkowski finally managed to press the lever with enough force to send the electrical charge through the wire to the blasting cap at the end of the bangalore torpedo. A huge blast shook the ground as the flash and smoke erupted from along the outer wall of the building. In that brief blaze Daley saw a body fly through the air—or at least the upper half of a body.

A moment later there was another explosion, even greater than the last, somewhere on the other side of the headquarters building. Gardner, Daley surmised, had blown the other bangalore. Meanwhile the parachute flare in the trees had burned through the shrouds or limbs and dropped to the ground where it sputtered and went out. Benkowski and Tanner resumed firing over the wall, and Daley, now reloaded, again rose and fired at the flitting shadows. There were forty or fifty guns in action, and the noise was far louder than on the rifle range back in training—and far more threatening. Someone on the west side of the fort launched another star shell, and the volume of fire over there increased for the few seconds the blazing fireworks lit up the sky.

"I'm hit!" Gonzalez yelled just to Daley's right. He looked over to see Gonzalez ducked down in the corner of the wall, his left hand pressed to the side of his head.

"How bad?" Lieutenant Jones demanded, while still firing out into the woods.

"Not bad," Gonzalez admitted. "Nicked my ear."

"Keep firing," Jones ordered. "We'll fix it later."

"Roger." Gonzalez wiped his bloody hands on his pants and stood back to continue shooting over the wall.

Daley pulled the trigger again, aiming at a suspicious-looking bush. He was here amongst the noise and confusion, yet somehow separate from it, like he was in a bubble of unreality. It was a weird feeling, like being in two places at the same time. Here he was in an old French fort, at night, shooting at men who were shooting back, trying to kill him, but he was also somehow standing back observing the action with mild interest from an ephemeral position of safety. It was as if he were watching himself in a movie, and critically examining his every action and thought. He mentally struggled to reunite his mind and his body, and had almost succeeded when he heard the shouting.

"Blow the Claymores!" Kessler, up on the roof of the barracks, was panicked. "Blow the fuckin' Claymores right now!"

A bright flash signaled the detonation of the Claymore placed along the front wall, meaning it had sprayed its hundreds of metal ball bearings across the outer face of the barracks, sweeping up any gooks unfortunate enough to be sheltering there. Romano, his wounded arm keeping him from the firing line, had held the firing device constantly ready, and responded instantly to Kessler's anxious demand. It took Cassidy a few moments longer to locate the detonator at the south side of the barracks and blow that mine as well. Daley couldn't see the explosion on the far side of the building, but he heard and felt it.

The blasts of the bangalores and claymores had caused a brief diminishment of the gunfire, as both sides were stunned and deafened, but quickly resumed at it previous hectic level. Daley kept firing, replacing empty magazines from his rapidly dwindling supply of full ones. He noticed that the pounding of the RPD machine gun had stopped, and heard Griffin cursing loudly. "Goddamn commie piece of shit! Mother fucker!" The gun was thrown out into the center of the courtyard, clattering up against the big tree trunk there. Then another M-16 burst into life, this one on full auto, firing three-to-five-round bursts. Obviously Griffin wasn't concerned about conserving ammo.

In the back of his mind, Daley was feeling the seeds of fear and despair growing. The claymores and bangalores had been last-ditch weapons, and now they were gone. The mortar was gone. All they had left were small arms and maybe a few hand grenades, and at this rate they would soon run out of ammunition. Someone yelled "RPG!" a split second before an explosion rocked the west side of the fort.

"Doc!" Daley head Cassidy yell. "Jimmerson's hit!" They were all in the southwest corner of the fort, far from Daley's position, so he couldn't really see what was happening there. Another parachute flare rose from the roof of the barracks and arced to the southwest; Kessler was trying to help that corner of the fort better see how to defend themselves. Jones pushed away from the gatepost and ran across the courtyard to the far corner.

"Keep firing!" Stagakis yelled to those still along the north wall. Daley did so, firing at every movement and shadow he thought he detected. He felt someone come up beside him, and glanced to his left to see Captain Taylor, his crutch in one hand and the pistol in his other. He propped himself up against the gatepost and fired the pistol once down the narrow lane that led out to the main trail.

"Can't let you Yanks have all the fun," he told Daley, before firing again.

From somewhere to the northwest, far outside the walls of the fort, a police whistle was blown. There were three shrill blasts of noise. Daley wondered what that meant.

"Either some poor sheila's getting raped," Taylor commented, "or those fuckers are getting ready to do something different."

"Yeah, but what?" Daley replied, firing off another round as he saw a dark figure jump up and move to his left.

"Probably nothing good," Taylor answered pessimistically. He didn't fire his pistol again, just kept it pointed down the path. Daley wondered how many rounds the Australian had left. To his left Daley heard a ratcheting sound and then a loud boom. Griffin was firing his shotgun. More cocking and firing of the pump-action riot gun followed, and then that ceased.

SEVENTEEN

Daley noticed that there didn't seem to be any more incoming fire. He was very thankful, and hoped it meant they were going to be left alone for a while.

Sergeant Stagakis ran over to Daley and told him in a low voice, "Keep firing, but at a very slow pace. Like once or twice a minute." The sergeant then went over to Gonzalez and gave the same instructions, before continuing to Tanner and Benkowski. Daley didn't understand the logic, but he complied anyway.

"I think they're pulling back," Taylor commented listlessly.

"Then why keep shooting?" Daley asked him. Taylor shrugged.

"Make sure they know we're still here, I guess."

Lieutenant Jones jogged up and stood by Taylor, fidgeting with excitement. "We're getting out of here," he announced breathlessly. "I just spoke to Sergeant Stagakis. We believe the gooks have withdrawn, at least for the moment, and it'll start getting light in another hour or so. Captain Taylor, how mobile are you?"

"I can manage," the Australian said, shaking his crutch.

"Romano should be able to keep up, since it's his arm that's wounded," Jones said, talking more to himself than to Taylor. "Don't know about Jimmerson yet."

Stagakis ran up, calling quietly to the men on the north and east walls, "Get your gear on and be ready to move, but keep up a slow rate of fire." Daley reached for his ruck sack, which Ky helped him put on his back. Ky already had his canteen and kit bag slung over his shoulders.

"Al Most is dead," Stagakis informed Jones.

"What? How? I just saw him." The lieutenant was suddenly frantic.

"He was standing at the wall with a bullet in his head. Everyone was looking at Jimmerson and never noticed he wasn't moving. When I went to tell him to gear up, he just collapsed."

"Now what do we do?" Jones's voice was trembling.

"Just like we planned," Stagakis answered. "We get out of here before they come back, try to make it back across the border."

"What about Most's body?"

"We'll have to leave it. I told Doc to get his dog tags, and give his gear to Sung. We've got to get a move on."

Jones shook his head in disbelief. "What about Jimmerson?"

"He got his bell rung pretty bad," Stagakis told him. "Doc thinks it's a concussion. The bullet just grazed his forehead, and it bled pretty bad, but he'll live. The problem is, he can't think straight."

"But can he walk?"

"Yeah, but we can't count on him in a firefight. He's mostly out in la-la land."

"And there's no way we can take Most with us?"

"No, sir, that'd slow us down too much. We don't have a stretcher, so someone would have to carry him on their back. The gooks will bury him."

There was a thump from the far corner, and then a painful groan. Kessler had jumped down from the roof of the barracks.

"Shit, I think I broke my ankle," Kessler moaned. Daley couldn't see him, as he was hidden by the corner of the small building, but his voice carried clearly.

"Are you fucking with me?" Cassidy barked. "You better not be fucking with me! That ain't funny, man!"

"Hey, I'm serious," Kessler whined. "Doc!"

Aw, Jesus!" Stagakis complained. "That's all we fuckin' need." He ran over to the scene of the accident.

"Okay," Jones said loud enough for all to hear, "let's get ready to move out. We'll file out through that breach in the east wall. Benkowski, you've got point. Don't forget about that booby trap. Tanner, alert Battalion."

Daley fired a shot over the wall, and prepared himself for the upcoming march. Once they were outside the wall, they would be fully exposed, so if the gooks had anticipated this move, it could fuck up their whole day. Everyone waited, the silent anticipation disturbed only by the occasional shots that rang out around the fort. Griffin went over and picked up the fallen RPD, taking it back to the wall. He jammed the barrel into a crevice in the concrete wall and pushed at the buttstock with both hands. Somehow he managed to bend the barrel enough to render the weapon useless. "Cheap commie steel," he commented, leaving the gun hanging by its barrel.

Stagakis ran up, with an M-16 in each hand. "Just sprained, Doc thinks," he told Jones. "Cassidy will have to help him walk." He turned to Daley, holding out one of the rifles. "Can Ky carry this one? It's Al's."

Daley took the rifle and offered it to Ky, explaining in Vietnamese. "You need to carry this. You do not have to use it, just carry it. Okay?" Reluctantly Ky took the weapon by the carrying handle, with the barrel pointed behind him. Even in the moonlight, Daley could see Ky's look of aversion and concern. And then the moonlight went away. Glancing up, Daley saw that clouds were scudding across the sky, quickly blocking out the moon and stars.

"Now's the time, sir," Stagakis told Jones. "You lead out, I'll bring up the rear."

"Okay, Benkowski," Jones said, "show us the way home."

With the arrival of the overcast, the men in the fort were reduced to barely visible lumps of darkness only slightly denser than their surroundings. Benkowski climbed through the crumbled 'V' of the broken wall and moved out quietly. Jones followed him, with Tanner close behind. Daley gestured for Taylor to follow Tanner, and then he and Ky fell in behind. It took a minute for the

Australian to clamber through the collapsed section of wall, maneuvering his wounded leg and the make-shift crutch, but once outside the walls he hobbled quickly to catch up. As Ky deftly stepped through the hole in the wall behind him, Daley felt the first drops of rain on his shoulders.

He had never felt so exposed and vulnerable before. As he emerged from the trees that surrounded the fort and waded out into the high weeds, it felt like there were hundreds of eyes watching him, despite the darkness that totally obscured anything more than a few feet from him. And those hundred eyes belonged to fifty men who all held AK-47s cocked and locked and aimed straight at him. An unreasoning fear gripped his guts, and his teeth were clenched like a vise. He fought to quell his emotions, but his legs kept propelling him forward faster than he should go, causing him to repeatedly bump into Captain Taylor ahead of him.

"Easy, boy," Taylor whispered over his shoulder, not unkindly.

"Sorry, sir," Daley mumbled, breathing deeply to calm himself. Then, as quickly as it had come, the terror subsided and disappeared. He began to tread more carefully, his gaze darting from left to right attempting to pierce the darkness. More through sounds rather than sight he sensed that Sung was right behind Ky, and Cassidy and Kessler were side-by-side farther back. The rest of the platoon was strung out in line behind, he supposed, with Sergeant Stagakis bringing up the rear.

From what Daley could make out, Benkowski was avoiding the main trail and leading them in the grass parallel to it, probably so they could avoid the hand grenade booby trap that still stretched across the trail to the east. Ahead of him the Australian officer was using his crutch as best he could, mostly hopping on his good leg and leaning on the branch while holding the other foot just above the ground. Daley heard muffled groans as the wounded leg was caught and whipped by the stalks of grass. The rain was now coming down steadily; although not truly a downpour, it was enough to soak his uniform and drip from his helmet. Fortunately, Daley thought, the noise of the rain would muffle their departure from the fort and slow any response by the gooks.

Suddenly Captain Taylor was sprawling forward and grunting in surprise. Daley rushed forward to help him, and nearly tripped as well. They had come upon an old rice paddy dike that was hidden in the thick weeds. Daley was annoyed that Tanner had not warned Taylor about the obstruction. He helped Taylor back to his feet, and then told Ky what to watch for. He had Ky go around him to clear the dike, and grabbed Sung's arm to warn him as well. He fell in behind Sung, whispering back to Cassidy and Kessler and telling them to pass it back. Kessler had his arm around Cassidy's shoulder as he favored the sprained ankle, so Daley grabbed his free arm and helped Cassidy boost him over the dike. With everyone now warned, Daley scurried ahead to retake his position behind Taylor. The activity had taken his mind off the danger almost completely, he was relieved to notice.

Daley had just gotten back in the rhythm of the march, parting the weeds, carefully testing each step for hidden obstacles, when behind him he heard Jimmerson's voice.

"Where are we?" Jimmerson was talking very loudly, as if he was in a noisy room, and the question held the emotional content of a curious ten-year-old. Stagakis had said the young man was a little out of it after being shot in the head, and the problem was now obvious. Someone hushed Jimmerson and whispered entreaties to keep quiet, only to have Jimmerson ask "Why?" in the same strident tone.

"Hold up!" Captain Taylor said anxiously, and Daley stopped while passing the word back along the column, talking loudly enough to bypass Ky and Sung. Lieutenant Jones brushed past Daley cursing under his breath, as he wended his way back to Jimmerson. Hoarse whispers and muffled threats could be heard, and then Jones rushed past Daley again to the head of the column, which began moving a moment later. Daley wondered how Jones had handled the problem, and hoped they hadn't had to physically restrain Jimmerson.

The rain made a soft patter on Daley's helmet cover and dripped down the back of his neck. His trousers were soaked by the beads of water collecting on the thin leaves of the grass they were plowing through, and the clean dry socks he had found time to put on the previous evening were now sodden and bunching up around his toes. With effort he climbed over the occasional dikes and across a narrow irrigation channel, simply following the lurching figure of Captain Taylor and checking to make sure Ky was still behind him. His surroundings were virtually invisible, appearing only as undulating waves of grass and distant clumps of blackness that he assumed were trees and bushes. Other than helping Taylor across some of the terrain features, he could only plod ahead and hope the gooks weren't following.

Suddenly the going got tremendously easier. Daley broke out of the clinging weeds onto a trail, with relatively solid footing and nothing to impede his walking. Benkowski had led them around the booby-trap, and now they were on the path that would take them to safety. Daley had never thought a narrow footpath could seem so welcoming. The men ahead of him picked up their pace, and Daley gladly did the same. The sooner they were far from the fort, the better. In the dark and the constant rain, the trail was unrecognizable from the day before, and Daley had to keep reminding himself that Benkowski and Jones knew what they were doing, and therefore they were definitely on the right track.

They continued for what seemed like half an hour before Jones called for a halt. While Daley knelt down to rest, he heard Jones say something, and then Tanner spoke in low tones on the radio. Jones came around Tanner and asked Taylor how he was doing.

"My armpit's getting sore," Taylor told him, "but I'll make it."

"Good." Jones then moved to Daley. "You doing okay?" he asked. "You keeping up?"

"Yes, sir," Daley answered, his voice a little weaker than he had expected. Trying to sound more confident, he continued, "Ky and Sung are doing fine, too. When do you. . ." His question trailed off as Jones moved past him and went on down the line, checking on all the men in the column. Daley took a deep breath and then retrieved his canteen to take a drink of the metallic water.

"Any problems?" he asked Ky in Vietnamese when he remembered his own responsibilities.

"No, Sergeant. We are going back to the base camp now?"

"Yes, Ky. We must get out of Cambodia, and then the Army can send us some help."

"Good. Those Northerners will chase us, I think." Daley had feared the same thing, and was discouraged that Ky felt the same way, since Ky knew the enemy better than anyone.

A thump came from far behind the column, followed by more thumps and a distant flash. More explosions followed, now sounding sharper and more violent, and they were interspersed with crackling like a string of firecrackers.

"The ammunition room," Ky said knowingly, nodding with approval. "The old sergeant set a trap."

"How?" Daley asked, envisioning the chaos that must now be permeating the fort.

Ky shrugged. "I do not know, but it worked."

However it was done, it proved the gooks had reoccupied the fort and knew the Americans were on the run. Daley sincerely hoped that the destruction of the arms room would discourage any pursuit, but feared that was a forlorn hope. Lieutenant Jones ran past him toward the front of the column, telling everyone they were moving out again. Daley rose to his feet and followed Taylor as they continued down the trail, the fading sound of rifle ammunition popping behind them.

It was a slow trek through drizzling darkness, the rain muffling all sounds other than Daley's heavy breathing and the painful grunts from Captain Taylor ahead of him. It was stop and start movement, caused mostly by Taylor's crutch sometimes sinking into the soggy earth and having to be pulled free. The luminescence on Daley's watch had long ago faded to invisibility, but he guessed it was getting close to five. Sunrise wasn't far away, although the heavy clouds would hide it and true daylight would be delayed.

It suddenly seemed even darker, and Daley belatedly realized the trail was passing through the middle of one of the intermittent patches of jungle that dotted the plain of grass. Ahead of him Taylor stumbled again and then fell forward, heavily crashing to the sodden ground and cursing quietly. His crutch, however, remained standing, apparently caught in a tree root.

"LT!" Daley called out to Jones. "Captain Taylor's down."

Kneeling down next to the prone officer, Daley reached out his hand to Taylor's shoulder and asked, "You all right, sir?"

"No," he answered angrily, "but I'm no worse than before. Bloody leg!"

Lieutenant Jones arrived and asked worriedly, "Are you hurt, sir?"

"I just tripped," Taylor answered, obviously frustrated at his own inability to keep up. He struggled to get up, and Daley helped him into a sitting position.

"Maybe we ought to take a break and let him catch his breath," Daley suggested to Jones.

After a moment of hesitation, Jones agreed, and word was passed along the column to move up and spread out in the grove to rest and take a water break. Daley sat down on a pile of wet leaves and pulled out a canteen. The water tasted awful, but made him feel better nonetheless. Sergeant Stagakis nearly tripped over Daley's foot as he entered the grove and sought out the lieutenant. The two men consulted in hushed tones while the rest of the men found trees to lean against or logs to sit on.

"Why are we stopping?" Jimmerson asked. He was no longer yelling, but his words were spoken at a volume more suitable for a crowded barracks than for their current situation. Ortiz patiently explained to Jimmerson in quiet but insistent terms, and Jimmerson plopped to the ground without further questions. A few feet away Cassidy helped Kessler ease down onto a log and stretch his bad leg out straight. Aside from the pattering of raindrops on the leaves overhead, the only sounds in the grove were those of canteens sliding in and out of their carriers. Then a bang was heard, distant and softened by the rain.

"They found the other booby-trap," Benkowski commented from somewhere in the dark.

"Stupid fuckers don't learn," Tanner remarked sardonically.

For Daley, the brief gratification that the gooks had set off the grenade and had perhaps taken some casualties was tempered by the confirmation that they were indeed pursuing the Americans. The enemy was far behind, but would be able to move much faster than this patrol, the members of which were slowed by their injured comrades.

"Let's keep moving," Jones ordered. He helped Daley lift Taylor to a standing position, and while Daley handed the captain his crutch, Jones bustled off to lead the column again. Taylor repositioned the padding on the fork of the limb before stuffing it under his arm, gasping with pain undoubtedly caused by the chafing there.

"I will help him," Ky declared, edging past Daley and moving to Taylor's side, the one not gripping the crutch. Ky took Taylor's arm and draped it across his own shoulders for support. The column began moving, and after a few steps to develop a rhythm, Taylor and Ky hobbled forward with more speed than Taylor had been making alone. Daley was pleased at Ky's offer of help, even though it made him feel a little guilty that he hadn't tried to help Taylor himself. As they emerged from the grove, Daley noticed that his range of vision was improving. The blackness of night was now shading to a dark charcoal gray, and he could just barely make out the figures of Tanner, Jones, and Benkowski ahead of him. They were only jiggling lumps of darkness silhouetted against the barely lighter fields of grass, but at least he could see something; dawn was finally on its way.

EIGHTEEN

The knowledge that the gooks were in pursuit increased everyone's sense of urgency, and with Ky helping Taylor, the pace of the men increased noticeably. They all knew that they had to get out of Cambodia before the gooks caught up with them, for only then could they hope for any support from the rest of the Army. They didn't know how many NVA soldiers were after them, but had to assume it was a force greater than their own, and one that wasn't hindered by casualties. If the Americans—and their three allies—were caught out in the open, it could be disastrous.

Around 0700 hours Jones called for another break and led the patrol off the trail to a nearby stand of three trees surrounded by thick-leaved plants. The men clustered together in this minimal concealment to sit and drink water, and some even opened C-rations to wolf down the meager contents. There was now plenty of ambient light, although the low clouds and perpetual rain kept it muted and gray. Daley squatted, not wanting to sit directly on the wet soil, and opened a can containing a "cinnamon nut roll," a thick chewy bread-like substance that required lots of water to choke down. Sergeant Stagakis and Lieutenant Jones stood together a few feet away, while nearby Doc Ortiz inspected Captain Taylor's bandaged leg as the Australian sprawled on his back, oblivious to the puddles under him.

"How far, sir?" Stagakis asked wearily. Jones reached inside his shirt and pulled out the Vietnamese map, which was now limp with dampness. He unfolded and refolded it, then studied it in the dim light, tracing their route with his finger.

"We should be near the border by now," Jones finally said with little certainty.

"Aren't we there yet?" Jimmerson whined stridently, like an unruly ten-year-old on a family vacation road trip. Sergeant Gardner went over and put his arm around Jimmerson's shoulder, calming him. Jones and Stagakis ignored the interruption.

"I been thinking," Stagakis said. "What if the gooks know a short-cut, or radioed some other unit, and are waiting to ambush us up ahead somewhere."

"That's all we need," Jones sighed. "But what can we do about it?"

"Let's put some guys on the flanks, sweeping out about a hundred yards. If there is an ambush, they'll hopefully see it, or can attack it from the rear."

Jones nodded at Stagakis' suggestion, his eyes sweeping over the men gathered in the small grove. "We're limited in manpower," Jones noted. Daley knew what Jones meant: they had several casualties, and while none were very serious, those men couldn't be detached from the column.

"Me and Sung can do it," Daley volunteered impulsively. The two leaders, somewhat surprised by the outburst, looked Daley over appraisingly.

"Okay," Jones said finally. "Anyone else?" he asked the rest of the group.

When no one said anything or raised their hands, Stagakis took charge without any anger at the lack of volunteers. "Gonzalez, Griff, you guys take the left flank. Daley, you and Sung take the right. Go out about a hundred meters, and try to stay just ahead of the column, but always stay in sight. Got it?"

"Roger that, Sarge," Griffin replied for all of them, apparently neither surprised nor disgruntled by his selection. Daley stood up, repositioned his gear, and gestured for Sung to follow him.

"Stay with the Australian," he told Ky in Vietnamese. "He needs your help."

"Yes, Sergeant," Ky answered dutifully.

"Okay," Jones announced, "the rest of you saddle up, we're moving out again."

With Benkowski and Jones leading the depleted main column back to the trail, Daley and Sung hustled past them and waded through the high grass to take a position on the right flank. Sung seemed to instinctively understand what their mission was and stayed close behind Daley. Once they had distanced themselves from the others, at what Daley hoped was about a hundred meters, they turned and began pushing forward parallel to the patrol that was following the trail. Parting the tall stalks of grass with his boots and his rifle, Daley found the going much tougher than on the trail, but he felt freer because he didn't have to match the pace of the wounded captain.

After following Daley for a while, Sung swung out to take a position a few feet to Daley's right. With hand and eye gestures Sung conveyed the idea that he would search to the front and right, while Daley searched to the front and left. Daley nodded his agreement that this was the best plan, as it also gave him more opportunity to watch the progress of the column. Most of the time Daley could see only their helmets over the sea of grass, and occasionally lost sight of them completely when bushes or trees intervened. He knew that Griffin and Gonzalez were performing the same function on the far side of the trail, but he was never able to catch even a glimpse of them. Daley noted with little satisfaction that the rain had eased up, and was now just a steady drizzle. He was so soaked now, it made little difference.

After an hour the terrain hadn't changed, the pace of the column was slowing slightly, and Daley was nearly exhausted by the exertion required to wend his way through the tall grass. He hadn't seen anything unusual, and was beginning to wonder if the flank guards were such a good idea after all. Then Sung stopped, holding out his left hand to signal Daley to stop as well. Sung lifted his head and sniffed the humid air. Daley imitated him, and detected faint traces of a foul odor, not unlike that of an outdoor latrine. He looked back to his left and waved his hand to get the attention of someone on the trail. When he caught Benkowski's eye, he held up a fist to signal they should stop, and then a single finger indicate they should wait a minute. While Benkowski passed the message back along the line, Daley and Sung spread apart some more and eased forward.

Sung grunted in disgust and pointed toward the ground in front of him. Daley shoved his way through the grass to join Sung, who was staring at the crumpled heap in the middle of a small bare spot. It took Daley only a second to recognize the tiger-stripe fatigues and kepi of Dodie, their missing Kit Carson scout. He was lying on his side, his pants down around his ankles, his face permanently contorted with pain. His eyes were open and glassy, sightlessly staring at his right hand, which was swollen and almost black. He was clearly dead, and the odor came from the feces and urine that appeared to have been expelled after he fell.

Daley turned and waved at Lieutenant Jones, signaling for him to come have a look. Jones signaled the others to stay put and trotted through the grass over to Daley and Sung. When he stopped and saw the dead scout, he winced and said, "What the hell happened to him?"

Sung made a serpentine motion with his hand, then a striking motion with two curved fingers. "Snakebite," Daley translated unnecessarily. "While he was taking a dump."

"Serves him right," Jones said casually. "Has he got our maps?"

Jones looked at Daley expectantly, and Daley steeled himself to the task. He handed his rifle to Sung and squatted down beside the body, tentatively reaching for the man's rucksack. When he found nothing of use inside the pack, he rolled the stiff body onto its back, the legs sticking up in the air and the right hand now raised in a deadly salute. Hesitantly patting down the body, he felt something inside the man's fatigue shirt, so he unbuttoned it, trying to avoid any contact with the man's arm or face. Sure enough, he found the maps, still encased in plastic and still marked with grease pencil. He pulled them out and handed them up to Jones, then backed away and jumped to his feet. The sight and smell of the body was repulsive, and Daley wanted to get as far away from it as possible, but for now he had to wait.

"This is good," Jones said, inspecting the two maps. "Much better than that other map. Good thing you found him." Jones turned and jogged back to the trail, waving the maps at Stagakis. Daley edged away from the body, seeking to find cleaner air to breathe, and Sung followed him after giving him his rifle back. Back at the column, Daley saw Jones confer with Stagakis and give him one of the maps, and then resume his position at the head of the line, waving everyone forward again. Daley and Sung followed suit, anxious to leave the foul odor and ugly sight of the body far behind.

The morning wore on, the thick overcast continued to leak, and Daley was worn out. The constant battle with the grass, the uneven terrain, and the limited visibility all pushed him to his limits, so much so that he sometimes lost focus on his main objective. He would have to figuratively shake his head to clear his mind and concentrate on the job at hand—providing flank protection for the main column and watching for potential enemy ambushes. Thus it was a complete surprise when he suddenly found himself crossing a wide stretch of ground with no high grass. He and Sung both stopped in befuddled amazement, but quickly Daley recognized the road they had crossed on the way to the fort yesterday. Stretching off to his right and left, the road ran almost perfectly straight, like a lawn-mower swath. But unlike yesterday, the road now had visible tire tracks, still fresh and muddy. The tracks appeared to be from a big truck of some sort, and maybe more than one.

A couple hundred yards to his left Daley saw Gonzalez and Griffin pop out into the roadway. They exchanged looks and exaggerated shrugs with Daley, and stopped as well. A few minutes later Benkowski and Jones appeared where the trail crossed the road, halfway between Daley and Griffin. Daley made a sweeping underhand gesture to indicate the road, and then raised his arms slightly as a question. Jones looked up and down the road, nodded, and gave an overhand wave to continue forward.

Daley and Sung plunged into the grass again, stumbling through the hidden water-filled ditch that lined the road, and pushed forward with renewed energy. Daley felt sure the road marked the border between Cambodia and Viet Nam, and now they were in relatively friendly territory. In theory, at least, they could now receive support from the Army and Air Force, and possibly even extraction. Realistically, however, Daley was aware that the cloud cover prevented air support, and that even with the recovered maps, their location was difficult to pinpoint. There were no prominent terrain features in this area, and one clump of jungle amidst a sea of weeds looked pretty much like any other clump of jungle. Without accurate coordinates, calling in artillery was a very risky proposition, and sending additional ground troops might just put additional men in danger with no guarantee of success.

He pushed these thoughts aside and kept scanning from left to center as he plowed through the grass and reeds, seeking any sign of the enemy. After an hour or so since crossing the road, his strength was ebbing again, the brief elation about returning to Viet Nam territory exhausted by the continued slogging along. As he glanced back to his left to locate the main party, he saw Benkowski waving at him, beckoning him to rejoin the column. Daley pointed at Sung and raised his hand in question, and Benkowski nodded, holding up two fingers with a summoning gesture. Daley gestured for Sung to follow him, and the two men jogged over to the trail. They gathered around Lieutenant Jones along with Griffin and Gonzalez, who had arrived seconds before Daley and Sung.

"We need to make better time," Jones told them. "Sergeant Stagakis believes they are still behind us, and may be catching up." Jones looked worried, and that made Daley anxious. "Specialist Griffin, we want you to fall behind Sergeant Stagakis about a hundred meters to give us some advanced warning if the gooks are trailing us. Gonzalez, why don't you help Cassidy with Kessler, and Specialist Daley, you and Sung need to assist Captain Taylor. We have to speed up, so do whatever necessary to help those guys along. Battalion says they are sending someone to help us, but when and where are still unknown. Any questions?"

All of them shook their heads and hurried back along the line to their designated jobs. Daley found Taylor slumped in fatigue, his crutch propping up one side and Ky holding up the other. "How can we help?" Daley asked the Australian, who just shook his head wearily. Several possible solutions came to mind, but most were quickly dismissed as impractical. Using Taylor's crutch as a seat, with Daley and Sung holding up each end, might have worked if the limb that formed the crutch were thicker and stronger, but Daley knew it would bend and probably break under the weight. Having Taylor put his arms on the shoulders of both Daley and Sung for support might have worked if the trail were wider, but as it was, Daley and Sung would have been stumbling through the weeds and been even slower than before.

Once he understood the problem, Sung provided the only viable solution. First handing his rifle to Daley to hold, he took off the backpack he was wearing, the one that had previously belonged to Al Most, and helped Ky put it on. Turning his back to Taylor, he bent his legs and held his arms out at his side, cupping his hands inward, and waited for Taylor to mount him piggy-back. After a moment's hesitation, Taylor climbed on, holding his crutch across Sung's chest. Sung jiggled and hunched until Taylor was in a secure position, before indicating to Daley he was ready to proceed. Daley, meanwhile, had two rifles, one in each hand, and was wondering how to manage that when Ky told him to bend down. Ky took Sung's M-16 and slid it under the straps at the top of Daley's rucksack, tightening them until it was secure. Daley thanked Ky and signaled to Jones they were ready. With Sung and Taylor following Tanner, and Daley and Ky behind, the patrol moved off.

Daley was amazed at Sung's strength. He seemed to have no trouble carrying Captain Taylor and maintaining a steady pace, a pace now much faster than before. Glancing behind him, Daley saw Gonzalez supporting Kessler while Cassidy carried Kessler's pack and rifle. Behind them Jimmerson was keeping up, his eyes somewhat clearer now. Daley hoped the effects of his concussion were wearing off.

Without the high grass to impede him, Daley found the longer strides and speedier travel less strenuous and somehow liberating. The faster they moved, he reasoned, the sooner they would reach safety and the comforts of the base camp. Never before had mess hall food and a dry cot seemed so attractive. In front of him Taylor's back bounced up and down, his legs dangling on either side of Sung, who was marching like a man possessed. According to Daley's watch, it was almost eleven when Jones called for a brief rest stop.

Sung gently lowered Taylor to the ground and helped him sit on the grass beside the trail, then stood and stretched his back and arms. Daley took a drink of water, not trusting himself to actually sit down, then helped Ky put the rifle he was carrying on the rucksack Sung had given him. Ahead of them Jones was talking to Stagakis on the radio, confirming that everyone had been able to keep up. Daley was still trying to calm his heavy breathing when a loud boom shattered the still air from somewhere behind them.

"Sounded like Griff's shotgun," Gonzalez said, jumping to his feet. Like everyone else, Daley tensed and brought his rifle up, gazing through the rain at the surrounding area. Behind him Daley heard Jones anxiously whispering into the radio, asking Stagakis what was going on. Apparently the platoon sergeant asked him to wait, so Jones gestured to Sung and Stagakis to mount up again, while he held the handset to his ear with a worried frown.

Jones eyebrows went up as he received a reply. "Yes. . . What?. . . How far?. . .All right, we're moving out." Jones handed the handset to Tanner and looked at Taylor, who was once more on Sung's back. "Griffin shot a single gook, might have been a scout for the larger unit," Jones explained rapidly. "We've gotta move." With that he turned and signaled to Benkowski, who took off up the trail at almost a jog. The patrol followed with a renewed sense of purpose.

Daley felt a tingle down his back and anxiety growing in his gut. It wasn't fear, he told himself, it was anticipation and concern. He noticed, almost in passing, that the rain had stopped, although the clouds were very low and a mist swirled through the grass and around the occasional bushes and groves of trees. And regardless of what the ambient temperature was, the high humidity and constant exertion made him feel like he was in a steam bath, sweat running down his nose and into his eyes. The sweat was a good thing, he told himself, because it meant he wasn't yet going into heat exhaustion.

"Flare!" Cassidy yelled, and Daley turned just in time to see a green ball of flame disappear into the clouds, about a half mile behind them.

"They're comin'," Gonzalez warned.

Tanner, the handset pressed to his ear, told Jones, "Sarge says they're gainin' on us."

"We need to find cover," Jones said, more to himself than to anyone else.

"Roger that," Benkowski affirmed, his voice going up an octave as he stepped up the pace.

"Over there!" Ky said in Vietnamese, pointing to a large grove of trees to their front right. "That is where we stayed the first night." It looked like any other clump of jungle to Daley, but he trusted Ky's instincts.

"Ky says that's where we camped the first night out," Daley excitedly told the lieutenant, pointing to the grove. "It's got bunkers," he added, knowing Jones already knew that, but saying it to reassure himself as much as anyone.

"Benkowski, check it out," Jones ordered without slowing down. Benkowski sprinted ahead and veered off the trail to dart through the grass and enter the dark clump of trees. He popped back into view a moment later, bobbing his helmet up and down and beckoning to them with his hand.

"Let's go!" Jones ordered, following Benkowski's route to the grove. The rest of the patrol did the same.

NINETEEN

"Okay, men, here's the plan," Jones intoned as soon as everyone had gathered just inside the northwest corner of the grove. "We'll take up defensive positions here, but keep out of sight. Maybe the gooks will go on by and run into our relief column."

"Fat chance," Tanner muttered, drawing a warning scowl from Jones.

"If they do find us," Jones continued, "we'll have a pretty good perimeter to fight from. We can use the bunkers and hold them off until that other unit reaches us."

"Who's still got Claymores?" Stagakis asked. Three hands went up. "Okay, set them up on the west, north, and east sides. Griff, you, Cassidy, and Kessler set up along the west side. Daley, Ortiz, Ky, and Sung will take the east side. Sergeant Gardner, you take Jimmerson and Gonzalez to the south side. Jimmerson, are you all right now?"

"I think so, Sarge," Jimmerson replied dubiously, still speaking a little louder than necessary.

"Me and Benkowski will be on the north side," Stagakis said.

Jones jumped back in: "Captain Taylor, you, Romano, and Tanner will be with me in the center, where we can act to plug any gaps that might occur. Okay, guys, let's hustle and get ready. We don't know how far behind us they are, but they'll probably be here pretty soon. Get set up and then get down and stay quiet."

As Stagakis and Jones had been speaking, Benkowski had wandered over to the entrance of the old bunker on the north side and looked down in. "Bunker's full of water," he announced.

"No shit, Sherlock," Tanner teased. "It's the fucking rainy season. Afraid you'll melt?"

204

"Fuck off, Tanner," Benkowski replied acidly. "I'm more worried about snakes."

Daley hadn't thought about that, but now it seemed obvious. He had hoped to seek shelter in the bunker, but realizing it was filled with water and possibly poisonous snakes or other creatures put a whole new spin on the idea.

"Check 'em out before you go in," Stagakis suggested reasonably. "If you see a snake, call for Tanner here. I heard he used to wrestle alligators down in Florida, so he should be able to handle a little snake." The men chuckled, and after a moment, Tanner joined in.

"It's all in the wrist," Tanner explained jokingly, shooting his hand out in a quick grabbing motion.

"You'd know about that," Griffin said, cupping his hand and moving it up and down in front of his crotch.

"Eat shit and die, Griff," Tanner said, smiling.

"Get to work," Stagakis told them. "Now!"

The men all scattered to their designated positions. Daley signaled for Sung to follow him and explained the situation to Ky as they walked across the grove. He noticed for the first time that there was a collapsed bunker in the center of the grove where Lieutenant Jones was leading Taylor, Romano, and Tanner. It was now just a shallow depression surrounded by bushes, but it would provide them at least minimal cover. Romano, his arm in a sling, looked pale and weak. Taylor just looked exhausted. As Daley reached the old bunker on the east end of the grove, Ortiz came up behind him and dumped his pack.

"I gotta check on Taylor and Romano," Ortiz hastily explained. Holding his aid bag, he ran back to the center of the grove. Daley dropped his own pack and squatted down at the entrance to the bunker. All he could see inside was the glint of standing water which appeared to have filled the bunker half way up. Ky came over and squatted beside him on his right.

"Snakes?" Daley asked in Vietnamese.

"Maybe," Ky allowed. "I do not like snakes."

Sung came up to stand on Daley's left and joined them in staring down the hole, although he seemed puzzled by their reactions. Daley made the serpentine motion with his left hand that Sung had used when he found Dodie, and then pointed down in the hole. Sung grunted something in Korean, then pushed by Daley and jumped down into the bunker where he began splashing around. A moment later he crawled out, mud dripping from his boots, and shook his head while making the snake motion with his hand. Daley and Ky just looked at him with amazement. Sung smiled and shrugged.

"I guess that settles that," Daley said in English. Leading by example, Daley repositioned his pack behind a tree with the straps facing out so it could be put back on quickly, and made sure Sung and Ky did likewise. Sung had reclaimed Al Most's rucksack and ammo, and Romano's rifle. Daley explained to Ky in Vietnamese that they should find good positions around the edge of the grove, but be prepared to fall back to the bunker if necessary. He tried to convey the same plan to Sung with gestures, and Sung seemed to understand. Sung found a tree near the northeast edge of the grove and knelt down behind its thick trunk.

Ortiz returned, looking worried. "Romano's arm is still bleeding," he said with a slow shake of his head. "And the captain's totally worn out. His leg isn't any worse, though. Neither one of them can keep going for much longer without a good rest."

"How about Kessler?" Daley asked.

"He's okay. It hurts, but he can walk if he has to. That's what he gets for jumping off buildings. So what's the deal here?"

"Sung checked out the bunker," Daley told him. "It's full of water, but no snakes. I'm thinking we stay up here and only go in the bunker if we have to."

"Sounds like a plan," Ortiz agreed. "Where are you going to be?"

"I guess I'll stay here at the bunker with Ky. Sung's over there to the left. You want to set up over to the right?"

"Works for me," Ortiz nodded. He grabbed his backpack and found a suitable spot behind a bush. Daley lay down on the side of the bunker, just to the left of the entrance, and Ky copied him on the right side. Daley reflected that Ky's refusal to fire a weapon really limited his usefulness in a firefight, but respected the young man's position. Ky had shown he was ready and willing to help out in any way he could, as long as it didn't involve shooting someone. It was actually a form of bravery that Daley had never seen before.

Sergeant Stagakis came up behind them and asked, "Where's your Claymore, Daley?"

Rolling over to face the sergeant, Daley guiltily admitted, "I don't have one, Sarge."

"I know," Stagakis said, and handed Daley a heavy green canvas bag. "This is Romano's. You know how to set it up?"

"I think so," Daley stammered. He had received very brief instructions in Basic, but that had been a long time ago.

"I'll help him," Ortiz said, coming over from the position he had chosen.

"Make it quick," Stagakis told them, then turned and left.

Together Ortiz and Daley waded out into the heavy grass beyond the edge of the grove and found a slight mound of dirt. Daley pulled the mine out of the bag and fumbled with the folded metal legs until they formed two inverted V's under the curved edge. Shaped like a book that had been bent by the sun, the upper edge had a square peep sight and two plugs. Ortiz helped Daley push the metal legs into the ground, ensuring the convex side was facing away from the grove. Daley actually tried to crouch down and look through the sight, but Ortiz waved him off.

"Don't worry about it," Ortiz told him. "Take out the shipping plug." While Daley unscrewed one of plugs, Ortiz pulled out a coil of brown wire resembling an extension cord, with a black rubber plug on one end and a bright aluminum tube on the other. Ortiz took the plug from Daley and threaded the wire near the blasting cap through the slotted side of the plug. He handed the assembly to Daley and told him to screw it in. Daley cautiously inserted the blasting cap into the hole on the mine until only the wire showed, then slid the plug down the wire and screwed it into the hole, securing the detonator.

"Just a second," Ortiz said, and ran back into the grove, returning a moment later with a short stick broken from a limb. He jammed it deep into the soggy soil and then looped the wire around it a couple times. "Come on," he told Daley, and together they backed away, uncoiling the wire as they went. When they reached the back side of the bunker, Ortiz handed the rubber plug to Daley and let the rest of the wire drop to the ground. Reaching into the Claymore bag, he pulled out the firing device pulled the dust cover off the receptacle on the side.

"Just plug that into here," he told Daley, "and you're ready to go."

"Aren't we supposed to test it first?" Daley asked tentatively.

"Fuck that," Ortiz said. "I don't have a testing device, and these things always work anyway. Just remember to undo the safety bail when you're ready to use it, and squeeze that handle hard and quick." Daley took a minute to familiarize himself with the firing device. It was a block of green plastic a little larger than a pack of cigarettes, with a lever angling up on one side. A wire loop kept the lever from moving accidentally, but the loop could be rotated out of the way when necessary. Daley removed the dust cover from the plug at the end of the wire and inserted the plug into the firing device.

"Okay, you're all set." Ortiz turned and walked back to where he had left his pack. Daley lay back down on the side of the bunker, placing the firing device directly in front of him where it would be in easy reach if the time came. He took a deep breath and tried to get comfortable. Behind him the muffled noises of the other men getting into position faded away to silence. Now all they could do was wait.

They didn't have to wait long. Daley had been scanning the high grass outside the grove for only a few minutes, looking mostly straight east, and seeing nothing but the thin green leaves, the low gray sky, and a few flying insects in between. Then Sung hissed at him. At first Daley thought Sung was warning him of a snake, and prepared to jump up and run, but when he looked over he saw that Sung was pointing out toward the trail to the north. Daley couldn't see anything, but his view of the trail in that direction was mostly blocked by shrubs and trees. He looked to his right and hissed at Ortiz, passing on the warning.

Now concentrating his visual search to the left, Daley tried to discern where the trail was as it threaded through the grass. Perhaps he detected a gap in the gently waving stalks, or maybe it was his imagination. From his low position lying on the side of the bunker, it was too hard to tell. A minute later a blip in his peripheral vision alerted him, and then he saw the rounded green shape of an NVA pith helmet bobbing in and out of sight as it moved from left to right. A single soldier, apparently, probably an advance scout. Daley held his breath and tried not to move. Beside him Ky seemed to melt into the sloping earth.

When the soldier moved out of sight farther down the trail, Daley resumed breathing and resumed scanning all the areas to the east as intently as he could. There were no sounds from within the grove, and Daley could almost feel the tension emanating from Sung, Ky, and Ortiz, all of whom were as motionless as Daley. Sung lowered his helmet a little, his body seeming to shrink behind the tree trunk, and a moment later Daley saw why. A line of pith helmets was snaking down the trail, and metal objects occasionally popped in and out of view; Daley wasn't sure if they were AK barrels, RPG launchers, or something else. He tried counting the helmets, but gave up at twenty.

So far the gooks were passing them by, for which Daley was immensely glad. He wanted them to keep moving, to disappear from sight and leave them alone to wait for their relief column. He prayed for that, and after the head of the column went out of sight to the east, he began to believe his prayers were answered. More helmets were passing by, but Daley was sure the end was in sight. Until it wasn't.

A commanding voice from the trail ordered someone to go investigate the grove, and Daley felt his stomach sink and his heart begin thudding in his chest. A helmet detached itself from the still-moving line and headed toward the grove at a walking pace, obviously not expecting to find anything. Maybe he'll just glance between the trees, not see anything, and leave, Daley hoped fervently. Through the trees Daley could now see the soldier from the waist up, his AK-47 carried loosely in one hand, his face expressing boredom, as he came to the edge of the grove. Then the man looked down, looked back up in panic, and turned to run. Two shots rang out, both fromM-16s, and the man took two steps before collapsing.

Out at the trail all the helmets disappeared as the enemy soldiers flopped to the ground.

"That tore it," Ortiz said just loud enough for Daley to hear.

Out on the trail one of the soldiers fired off a short burst of AK rounds that went high, one thudding into a tree near Daley at about ten feet off the ground. The shots were quickly followed by shouted Vietnamese commands to cease fire. Inside the grove everyone stayed hunkered down and quiet. The Americans couldn't see the NVA, and the enemy couldn't see them, so for the time being, it was a stalemate. Daley knew it wouldn't last. Now that the gooks knew where they were, the Americans presented a specific and definable target. Daley supposed the enemy commander was already formulating plans for the attack on the grove, and he would soon send the soldiers in some sort of pincer movement and attack from all sides. Daley reached out and fingered the Claymore firing device. It was time, he decided, and flipped down the safety bail. He would blow the mine at the first sign of anyone approaching from the east. He felt doomed, but fatalistically resigned. There was no fear, he was gratified to note, just a determination to go down fighting.

And nothing happened. Here he was, all ready to die for his country and his buddies, and there was no gunfire, no bloodthirsty screams, no movement at all. The minutes dragged on, and still no attack. Gradually Daley let his muscles relax a little while he started to feel a glimmer of hope that the gooks had just packed up and gone home. It was possible, he told himself. The enemy couldn't be sure how many men the Americans had, or what armaments or support they might have acquired since the departure from the fort. The

NVA's usual tactics didn't include assaulting a presumably strong defensive position in daylight. Maybe the NVA commander suspected he was walking into a trap. And maybe, Daley thought joyfully, maybe the gooks know about the American unit coming to their rescue, and even know how close it is. That was more than Daley knew, of course. The lieutenant hadn't seemed sure such a relief effort was even under way.

"Have they left?" he asked Ky quietly.

"They are out there," Ky assured him. "They are moving into position."

Daley's spirits sank. He trusted Ky's assessment of the situation more than his own.

"There!" Ky whispered, pointing toward a small patch of jungle a couple hundred meters to the southeast. Daley shifted his gaze in that direction, but saw nothing unusual.

"What?" he whispered urgently.

"Gone now. Two men. They are surrounding us."

Daley's tension ratcheted up a notch or two. His head swiveled left to right, seeking any sign of an enemy approach. The humid air was still, there were no sounds that he could detect, but in his head was the clicking music-box sound of a jack-in-the-box being cranked while he waited for the inevitable but startling revelation. Glances to either side showed Ortiz and Sung equally tense and ready, all waiting for the drop of the flag, the starting gun, the signal that all hell was breaking loose. And then it came.

An AK-47 fired off a short burst to Daley's left, the sharp blasts shattering the calm. Another, different, AK was fired, from about the same location. There was no return fire from Sergeant Stagakis and Benkowski, who faced that direction. Daley hoped that meant the two men simply didn't have visible targets, and not that they had been killed by the first shots fired. Then more shots rang out, this time from Daley's right. It was more than just a couple guns, too. It sounded like the entire North Vietnamese Army was charging the south side of the grove. The men over there—Gardner, Jimmerson, and Gonzalez—began firing back, single rounds fired on semi to conserve their dwindling supplies of ammo. Ortiz scrambled up into a kneeling position behind a tree and began firing as well.

Daley couldn't see what they were firing at, but assumed they could. His attention was drawn to the sound of battle, and he was distantly aware of bullets splitting the air above him, but his main concern was the possibility that the gooks would break out of the grass and into the grove, leaving him exposed to their fire from the rear. He thought about ducking down into the flooded bunker, but before he could act, Ky grabbed his forearm in a panic. His head swiveled to see a handful of pith helmets floating across the sea of grass to the east, approaching him like flotsam on an incoming wave.

Dropping the Claymore firing device, he gripped the handguards of his M-16 and began firing at his attackers, forcing himself to aim below the helmets, not directly at them. He pulled off several rounds, and the helmets disappeared. Like at the fort, he couldn't tell if he had hit someone, or they had simply ducked down out of sight. He reached for the firing device again, intending to detonate the mine immediately, but Ky grabbed his arm again and said, "Wait!" He looked over and saw the grimace of determination on Ky's face. Ky was estimating the speed of the enemy's approach and figuring the best time to detonate. Again, Daley trusted Ky's instincts. He repositioned the device in his left hand, finding the ideal grip that would allow his sweaty fingers to squeeze the firing lever at the right moment.

"Now!" Ky hissed, and Daley dropped his head so the front of his helmet touched the ground and squeezed. A tremendous explosion ripped the air, and his back was peppered with small bits of grass and dirt. A second explosion to his right rear startled him, but he quickly realized that Gardner and his men had blown their own Claymore. A third Claymore went off on the west side of the grove. Daley gripped his M-16 and began firing into the dissipating cloud of smoke where the mine in front of him had been. He heard cries of pain in front of him, and knew the mine had caused at least one casualty. As the air cleared, he saw that it had also blasted a triangular swath through the grass, and he could see at least two bodies on the ground, one perfectly still, the other slightly squirming and moaning. That presented a dilemma. Should he shoot the wounded man and finish him off, or should he let the man bleed out? There were both moral and practical arguments for either action. Before he could reach a decision, other events distracted him.

"RPG!" someone yelled behind him, and the rocket somehow zoomed through the grove without hitting anything, exploding out in front of Gardner's team. The smoke trail from the north side drifted away, and Daley heard a grenade explode somewhere on the north side. He couldn't tell if it was an American grenade or a gook potato-masher. He put in a fresh magazine and resumed firing into the stalks of grass beyond the grove, aiming low in the hopes of hitting any gooks law-crawling toward him. To his left, Sung was now standing up behind a tree trunk and firing around it, methodically putting rounds into any clump of grass he saw. To his right Ortiz was no longer there, and Daley felt a moment of panic, thinking Ortiz must be dead, until he remembered hearing someone call for a medic just before the RPG round had gone through.

That left the southeast corner of the grove undefended, so Daley shift his fire to his right, hoping Sung could guard his left flank. Through the trees behind him he caught a brief glimpse of Gonzalez moving left to fill in where Ortiz had been. The roar of the gunfire, muffled only slightly by the heavy air and the trees, continued unabated. Daley felt his bolt lock to the rear as another magazine had emptied, and reached down to feel along his bandolier for another one. He was dismayed to discover he had only two magazines left. As his trembling fingers pulled at the cloth covering one of the magazines, he felt a nudge and saw that Ky was handing him a full magazine, the one from Al Most's rifle that Ky had been reluctantly carrying since they left the fort.

Daley had just seated the magazine in his rifle when he heard Lieutenant Jones call out, "Cease fire!" Like the others, Daley repeated the order, and the firing quickly tapered off. Only then did Daley notice there was no incoming fire, no rattle of AK-47s. The silence was almost deafening. Maintaining a watch on his field of fire, Daley kept glancing back to see what was happening with the rest of the men. He saw Lieutenant Jones run over to Gardner's position for a minute, then run back to the center of the grove. Then Doc Ortiz returned and plopped down near his gear just to Daley's right.

"What's going on?" Daley asked him. Ortiz just shook his head slowly.

"Jimmerson bought it," he said mournfully. "Just stood up and started marching toward them. Cassidy got shot in the ass, but he'll live."

"What are the gooks doing?" Daley asked, depending on Ortiz's greater experience to provide an answer.

"Fuck if I know. But LT says there's somebody coming to help us. Don't know who or when. Hope they get here pretty soon, though, or we are totally fucked."

Sergeant Stagakis came running up, a Claymore bag in his hand, and asked "How many mags you got?"

"Four," Ortiz answered.

"Three," Daley told him. Stagakis reached in the bag and handed Daley one more full magazine.

"Conserve your ammo," Stagakis told him. "Don't shoot unless you have a good target." He hurried over to Sung and using gestures and pidgin English asked him about ammo as well. After Sung showed him two fingers, Stagakis handed him two more magazines and scurried off.

"That's not good," Ortiz said. Daley nodded.

"Maybe we should get in the bunker," Daley suggested hesitantly.

"Not me," Ortiz asserted. "Might get trapped in there. And you can't see out for shit."

Daley had to agree with him. Crouching in that muddy water, only able to see a few feet in front through the narrow gun ports, didn't really sound appealing. If the gooks were using mortars or grenades, the bunker might make sense, but in a fluid battle based mainly on small arms, Daley wanted the opportunity to quickly maneuver. He gazed out beyond the edge of the grove, and with clinical detachment noted that the wounded gook was no longer moving or moaning. Good, he thought, that solved one problem. He looked over at Ky, who was studying the area intently.

"What do you think they are doing?" Daley asked.

Ky shrugged. "They will try something different. But they will try again."

Daley had reached the same conclusion, but it was no comfort. He was again starting to feel doomed. They had been attacked twice at the fort, and were now awaiting the second attack here. It just wasn't fair. Why didn't the gooks just leave them alone? They weren't trying to hurt the gooks, they were just trying to get away. Couldn't the gooks see that letting the Americans leave would avoid casualties on their part? It just didn't make sense to keep attacking the Americans without any potential gain, other than increasing the American casualties. And that, Daley realized, was probably the reason. The Americans had taken their fort, freed their prisoners, and embarrassed them in their sanctuary. Therefore, the Americans had to die.

Gunfire erupted to his left and quickly increased in intensity. Daley looked over and saw that some gooks had somehow reached the northern edge of the grove and were pushing forward, while Stagakis, Benkowski, and Sung tried to pick them off. There was still no movement to the east, and Daley felt terribly exposed to the enemy fire on his flank. Ky scrambled into the entrance of the bunker and tugged at Daley's shirt to follow him. Daley jumped into the wide muddy hole, but kept his shoulders above ground as he turned to fire at the gooks who appeared between Sung and Stagakis. If anyone attacked from the east he was screwed, but he had to direct his fire to the most immediate threat, which was from the north.

There were shots to his left rear, and he glanced back to see that Ortiz had moved to the south side of a tree and was firing around it, aiming at the area in front of Sung and Stagakis, also trying to stem the assault on the north side of the grove, which seemed to be the only action at the moment. Daley saw an uncovered head appear just beyond a bush a few feet to Sung's right, and he swung his M-16 around to fire at the bush. The head disappeared. From the corner of his eye Daley saw Stagakis and Benkowski crawling backwards, falling back to Lieutenant Jones' position in the center, firing as they went. Somewhere past them Griffin's shotgun rang out, boom, boom, boom, easily heard over the rattle of the rifles. A grenade exploded where Stagakis and Benkowski had been before. Gardner had moved to a tree near Ortiz, and the two of them were pouring rounds toward the center of the north side. Sung was now firing almost straight west, as enemy soldiers flitted from tree to tree, invading the northern side of the grove.

Incongruously, yellow smoke began spewing out of a grenade in front of the center position, where Jones, Taylor, Tanner, and Romero lay flat in the depression, with Stagakis and Benkowski on either side. Daley at first assumed they were hoping to blind the enemy, but then his heart leaped as he decided it was a signal, marking their location for somebody coming to their rescue. And sure enough, over the roar of the gunfire, he heard a mechanical rumble.

TWENTY

There was a gradual lessening of gunfire that coincided with the increasing noise from the east, a metallic clattering and diesel roar approaching with the sound of some medieval monster. At first Daley could not see anything, but then the box-like shape of an armored personnel carrier appeared, steaming around a far clump of jungle like a warship rounding the cape. Due to the high grass, Daley could only see the upper half of the vehicle, its side covered by some muddy panel, it's angular machine gun cupola poking up menacingly, and a couple rows of metal ammo cans and wooden crates strapped to the roof. He could see three helmeted heads—one in the driver's compartment, one behind the fifty-caliber machine gun, and one peeking around the cupola, the man's body hidden inside the troop compartment behind the fifty.

The tracked vehicle had just cleared the far grove when another appeared behind it. On the first APC the fifty gunner swung the barrel slowly back and forth, seeking targets, and the second track swerved to its right and roared as it swung out to take a position fifty yards to the side of the first. The gunner on the lead track opened fire, and the distinctive "budda-budda-budda" thump of the fifty overpowered the rattle of small arms from the grove. The gunner on the second track began firing as well, while a third APC hove into view, this one swerving left to cross the field of grass in front of Daley at an angle.

Daley had never been so glad to see anyone before. He broke into a delighted grin, shouting with glee over the noise of the tracks and gunfire. "Take that you cocksuckers!" he yelled with joy, firing one more round at the unseen enemy just ahead of the advancing APCs.

From seemingly out of nowhere an NVA soldier stood up near the northeast corner of the grove, a loaded RPG launcher on his shoulder, and aimed the weapon at the third APC which was now broadside to the man. Without thinking, Daley swung his rifle to take hasty aim and began firing as rapidly as possible. To his left front, Sung was doing the same. The soldier's pith helmet flew off and pink spray jetted from his head as he collapsed back into the grass. Immediately there was smoke and a whooshing sound as the man's death grip launched the missile. The rocket skittered along the ground like a Fourth of July whistling chaser, leaving a trail of smoke as it zoomed through the weeds, passing just in front of the third track. Just past the APC it hit a bump and shot up into the air, sparks trailing behind it as it arced through the sky and came down again, exploding harmlessly far to the southeast.

The loader in the back of the APC waved his thanks as the track continued on around the grove, turning west to parallel the two vehicles that were sweeping the north side. The gunner fired random bursts of suppressive fire into the grass, in case any enemy soldiers were hiding there.

"Don't shoot! We're coming in!" Someone was shouting over the noise, and Daley saw the camouflage helmets of American GIs bobbing toward him through the grass. A soldier stepped into the area cleared by the Claymore, glancing down at the two bodies that lay there, and then kept coming, one hand in the air. "Mickey Mantle, Joe Dimaggio," the man shouted facetiously. "We're the good guys."

"Thank God," Daley shouted back, climbing out of the bunker entrance to face the soldier, who was now joined by three others who were popping out of the grass and filtering into the grove through the underbrush. The gunfire within and outside the grove was diminishing. Daley could hear the pounding of the fifties, the rapid chatter of an M-60, and an occasional M-16, but no AK-47s. The four new arrivals gathered around the bunker, and Daley could see they included a Spec-four, a PFC, a buck sergeant, and a Sergeant First Class. The E-7, a wiry guy with sharp blue eyes and a nametag that said "Samples," spoke up first.

"Sorry we're late," he apologized. "Lots of traffic on the freeway."

"Fuckin' mud," the E-5, named Jamison, complained.

"Where's your platoon sergeant?" Samples asked abruptly. Daley looked around behind him, and spotted Stagakis through the trees. He pointed him out to Samples, who trotted off in that direction. Ky, holding his cowboy hat in his hand, poked his head up out of the bunker. The Spec-four, named Sweet, immediately brought his rifle to bear on Ky, a menacing look clouding his face.

"Don't shoot," Ortiz said, joining the group. "He's with us."

Sweet lowered his rifle slowly, still eyeing Ky suspiciously. Ky crawled up from the bunker, dripping water, and stood as close as possible to Daley. Sung also came over and took a protective stance next to Ky.

"Who's this?" Jamison asked, noticing Sung's different uniform.

"His name's Sung," Daley explained. "He's Korean. The gooks were holding him captive, along with an Australian captain."

"No shit?" Sweet chuckled. "This is like the fuckin' United Nations, then, huh?"

"Can it, Sweet," Jamison ordered. "Crosby, go over to the track, provide flank security." The PFC, with the new uniform and bewildered look of an FNG, nodded and hurried off.

A huge explosion on the far side of the grove made Daley duck, and he noted that Ky, Sung, and Ortiz did likewise. Jamison and Sweet, however, barely noticed. More explosions ripped the air, and Daley turned to see smoke rising from somewhere down the trail.

"One-oh-fives," Jamison said casually. "We brought an FO with us. It's only one battery, but you take what you can get." It took Daley a moment, but he remembered that FO stood for Forward Observer, a specialist in calling in artillery strikes. "How come you guys didn't call in any arty?" Jamison asked.

"Well," Daley disingenuously explained, "we don't have an FO, and our Kit Carson scout stole our maps. We just got the maps back this morning."

"Huh." Jamison seemed to accept that explanation.

"So we heard you guys took a gook fort," Sweet said.

"Yeah," Ortiz said with humble pride. "Held it all night, then 'exfiltrated' to here this morning."

"And rescued the two POWs," Daley added, acting like it was something they did every day.

"Far out," Sweet said, nodding and trying to not look impressed.

"How'd you guys get here, anyway?" Ortiz asked. "How'd you get across the river?"

Sweet scoffed, and Jamison explained with disgust. "Some numbnuts at Division thought it would be a good idea to see if the squids could take us across on their landing craft. We sank into the mud just trying to go down the bank to the loading ramp. So they brought us a bunch of PSP to use."

"PSP?" Daley asked. That was an Army abbreviation he hadn't heard before.

"Pierced Steel Planking," Jamison said. "Like they use to make temporary airplane runways with. You can hook them together like an Erector set. We laid it out over the mud and managed to get the tracks on the landing craft to cross one at a time. We had to do the same thing on the other side, and use the tow cables to pull the tracks up the bank. Took us all afternoon yesterday. Last night we laagered there on the shore, and with all that rain last night, we were bogged down this morning."

"Tracks sunk right up to the floorboards," Sweet interjected. "Took us three hours to get them all unstuck."

"Hung the PSP on the side of the tracks and headed out for here," Jamison continued. "Got stuck at least four times on the way. This terrain just isn't meant for Papa Charlies."

"Glad you made it," Daley told them. "We were running out of ammo."

"Any casualties?"

Ortiz nodded. "One kilo at the fort, and one here. A bunch of walking wounded."

"Well, you can ride home with us," Jamison said. "For a nominal fee, of course," he joked.

"Whatever the price," Daley said, "it'd be worth it."

Daley absently noted that the artillery explosions, which had been walking away from them, had now ceased.

"Why'd they stop?" he asked, almost rhetorically.

"I heard a couple of your companies are in contact south of Tay Ninh," Jamison said. "We were lucky to even get one battery. I guess they've been diverted."

"Looks like the gooks are gone anyway," Sweet commented.

Behind him Daley heard Sergeant Stagakis bellow, "All right CRIP, get your gear and load up."

Daley relayed the order to Ky in Vietnamese, generating a look of surprise on both Jamison's and Sweet's face.

"You speak gook?" Sweet asked with a raised eyebrow.

"Yep," Daley told him. "Learned Vietnamese at the Army language school."

"Damn," Sweet said. "Well, you guys gonna ride with us on one-one?" He motioned toward the APC south of the grove.

"I guess," Daley said.

"You got room for a body?" Ortiz asked. He tilted his head over to where Gardner and Gonzalez were just finishing wrapping Jimmerson in a couple ponchos.

"Sure," Jamison said, albeit a little reluctantly. "You can put it inside." He looked at Sweet. "Go tell Gunn to check with the lieutenant first, and then move the track around over there by the body. Be sure he swings wide so he doesn't dig in."

Sergeant Stagakis, with his radio and pack already on his back, walked over, with Samples right beside him. "Daley," he announced, "you, Ky, Sung, Gardner, and Gonzalez go with

Sergeant Samples. Ortiz, get with their medic and help the wounded guys onto whatever APC their lieutenant says." He looked over to the still form wrapped in green rubberized fabric.

"They're going to put Jimmerson in that track," Daley told Stagakis, gesturing toward the one-one, as Ortiz jogged away.

"Good." Stagakis turned and walked back toward the center of the grove, where Jones, Tanner, Taylor, and the mech platoon's lieutenant and RTO were talking. The mech RTO listened to his radio, consulted with their lieutenant, and replied into the handset. A moment later the engine on the one-one track roared and it jerked forward, throwing huge globs of mud and grass into the air behind it. It made a wide circular turn to the left and then eased through the brush to stop next to where Gardner and Gonzalez stood watch over the body.

"Let's get it loaded," Samples said, walking off toward the track, which was now lowering its rear ramp. Daley, Ky, Sung, and Sweet followed.

Daley's initial impression was that riding on an APC was better than walking, although it did make you a more obvious target. Since no one wanted to ride inside the troop carriers, the roofs were pretty crowded. Gardner and Gonzalez had taken the only two vacant ammo boxes, at the rear of the track, so Daley, Ky, and Sung sat on the open cargo hatch cover. Daley and Ky faced forward, bracing their legs to the sides of hatch, while Sung dangled his legs off the back of the vehicle, providing a semblance of a rear guard. Crosby, as the new guy on the mech squad, had to ride standing up inside the cargo hatch opening, just behind the machine gun turret. Daley noted that Sergeant Jamison sat right behind the driver, on the driver's compartment hatch cover, and Samples, the platoon sergeant, sat directly behind Jamison. Jamison had on what looked like an olive drab football helmet that connected to the radio, matching one on the driver, and Daley assumed there was also an intercom between them. Samples was monitoring the radio traffic as it blared on the big radio inside the track, and a porkchop mike dangled on a coiled cord coming up through the turret.

The ride was surprisingly smooth, and Daley had little trouble maintaining his seat on the hatch cover. Granted, the terrain was pretty level, but even when they encountered ditches or bumps, the vehicle seemed to glide over them with a motion like a boat on the water. The diesel engine's exhaust was at the top right front corner of the vehicle, and depending on the wind, the sooty fumes would occasionally drift back over Daley with an acrid odor. The track's crew seemed to be oblivious to the smoke, so Daley pretended to be so as well. The three tracks moved across the plain at a pretty good clip in a staggered V formation, and Daley, curious, asked the reason. Crosby, directly in front of Daley and anxious to demonstrate his barely superior knowledge, turned and explained.

"We have to go fast, to keep from sinking into the mud. And we spread out so we don't run in each other's tracks, where the ground is softer and already churned up." Crosby looked left and right, at Sergeant Samples and Sweet, and grinned when they didn't correct him.

"What about mines?" Daley asked. Crosby's expression clouded as he tried to come up with an answer. Samples answered for him.

"We're not on a road," Samples intoned over the engine and track noise, "where they usually lay mines. And big vehicles don't come out here very often, so why lay mines for them?"

"So you've never been out here before?"

"Nope, and hope we never come out here again." Samples shook his head wearily. "I don't know what it's like in the dry season, but right now it's damn near impassable for us. We'll be real lucky if we don't bog down at least twice before we get to the river."

And sure enough, five minutes later the one-two track dipped down into a depression hidden in the grass, and as it tried to crawl out of the hole, the tracks started spinning and digging in, spitting out sod behind the track until the belly pan was resting on the rim of the hole. With minimal radio commands, Samples had the other two tracks move into positions side by side just in front of the one-two. With practiced efficiency, the crews all dismounted, unhooked the

PSP from the sides of the vehicles, and arranged them in front of the trapped vehicle. The corrugated steel panels, with holes regularly spaced along the ridges, could be attached to each other with a sort of hook-and-eye system, and soon there was a wide steel mat laid. Then long steel tow cables were strung between the one-two and the other tracks. While everyone else stood to the side, the three drivers coordinated their efforts according to the hand signals Samples gave them, increasing their revs gradually until the one-two's tracks edged onto the metal planking and began to get a grip.

Once the vehicle was out of the hole and had passed over the PSP to solid ground, the crews quickly went to work unhooking the planks and rehanging them on the sides of the tracks. Daley offered to help, but there were plenty of more capable hands available, so he just stood aside to watch the work with Ky by his side. Sergeant Samples, supervising the activities, came over and stood beside Daley.

"I hear you speak Vietnamese," Samples remarked conversationally.

"Yes, Sergeant."

"So you're not an eleven bush?" Samples asked, using the common euphemism for infantryman, the Military Occupational Specialty of 11B.

"Ninety-Six Bravo," Daley explained, giving his own MOS. "Interrogator."

"And you volunteered to come out here with these guys?" Samples voice was tinged with disbelief.

"Yeah, sorta," Daley admitted. "Ky, here, doesn't speak English, and he was the only one who knew where the fort was."

"Huh. Interesting." Samples started to yell at one of the guys hanging the PSP, but the man corrected his error before Samples could speak. Samples nodded with satisfaction.

"Sergeant Stagakis says you did all right out there. For a base camp warrior."

"Really?" Daley was surprised and greatly pleased. His chest swelled a little with pride.

"Okay, mount up!" Samples yelled, since all the PSP was now back in place, mud and grass slowly dripping down the sides of the vehicles. Like the others, Daley scrambled back up onto the vehicle and held on as they took off again. He still grinned at the second-hand praise he had just received.

TWENTY-ONE

They made it to the river by late afternoon, after only one more time getting stuck in the mud. Two of the Navy river patrol boats were cruising up and down the river as security, and the landing craft was visible across the river. As soon as the three APCs appeared at the top of the bank, the landing craft backed away from the far shore to turn around and chug across to where they waited. The skies, which had been overcast most of the day, began to drip rain again. Everyone on the armored personnel carriers dismounted and milled around until Samples and Stagakis put their heads together and ordered four of the men to go back down the trail about a hundred meters in case any gooks had been following them. The rest were instructed to start unhooking the PSP and laying it out. This time Daley joined in, and so did Ky. It took two men to carry the mud-laden planks down toward the shore. A partial ramp of PSP was already there, left from the earlier crossing, but they needed to extend that ramp with the planks that had been on the APCs.

The landing craft, its bluff square bow pushing brown waves ahead of it, came right toward the base of the ramp at full speed, its painted shark's mouth adding menace to what was otherwise a non-threatening shape. With a lurch and squeal the bow rose over the sloping river bottom and slammed to a stop at the water's edge. Motors hummed and whined, and the huge metal ramp slowly fell forward until the upper edge settled on the lowest sections of PSP. While sailors scurried to secure the craft, a lone Army officer strode forward up the ramp. His uniform was clean and pressed, and he wore a well-made but not Army-issue rain jacket with his gold leaf prominently displayed at the collar. Another gold leaf adorned his helmet, which had an immaculate camouflage cover that had never seen action. In his hand, incongruously, was a brown leather briefcase. At the end of the craft's loading ramp the officer stepped out onto the PSP and promptly slipped and went down on one knee.

The muddy PSP, now dampened by the light rain, was difficult to climb. The enlisted men on shore, watching this peacock approach them, had to stifle their laughs as the major regained his footing, the knee of his uniform now blotted with mud.

Stepping back on the boat ramp where the footing was more secure, the major called out in a non-commanding voice, "Lieutenant Jones, Lieutenant Carr, I need to see you. Right now."

Daley saw Jones and the mech lieutenant, whose name he hadn't known until now, exchange glances and shrug. Staying off the PSP, they dug their heels in to the soft river bank as they descended to near the water's edge, and then climbed laterally onto the boat ramp. The major led them back into the open bay of the landing craft, but Daley could still see them. Though he couldn't hear the conversation due to the engine noise of the landing craft and the patrolling river boats, he tried to interpret the body language. It didn't look like a pleasant conversation. Carr looked disgusted, and Jones looked defiant, while the major presented with bland arrogance. Finally, with obvious resignation, the two lieutenants came back up the ramp and stepped off into the mud, where they waited.

The major had turned to speak to the naval officer in command of the craft, a man Daley recognized as Ensign McMichaels. McMichaels also looked unhappy with what he was being told, and walked away shaking his head. The major then came out to where Jones and Carr waited and allowed them to assist him climb the muddy bank to the top of the bluff. Once on level ground, the major stomped his boots to try and dislodge some of the mud. He looked around for a place to set his briefcase, found nothing to his liking, and kept it in his hand. His eyes swept over the soldiers waiting by their vehicles and settled on Samples, whose Sergeant First Class pin was clearly visible on the front of his helmet.

"Sergeant," the major trumpeted, sounding like a high school debater, "have all your men gather around, please." Daley could see that Jones and Carr were both angered by this command that bypassed their authority.

"We've got four men on rear guard," Samples noted reasonably.

"Bring them in," the major ordered.

"Sir?" Stagakis said, stepping forward and looking at Jones, his tone clearly indicating he thought this was a bad idea.

"Call them in, Sergeant Stagakis," Jones told him gently. Carr nodded his concurrence to Samples. The two sergeants looked at each, and then strolled away from the group to holler at the men down the trail. As those four straggled in, Stagakis and Samples herded the rest of the men, including the track drivers, over to where the major waited impatiently. Once everyone was gathered and the hubbub had settled down, the major began.

"Gentlemen, I am Major Dempsey from Division Headquarters. I am about to brief you on a matter of national importance, so listen up." Daley looked around, and saw that most of the men were paying only minimal attention. They were used to such overblown announcements, and not impressed by the major's credentials.

"You men have just completed a dangerous mission and rescued allied prisoners of war, and for that we commend you. Unfortunately, to complete that mission you had to cross an international border into a country that is nominally neutral, a clear violation of international law. If that were to become widely known, it would present our president and our military with a potential embarrassment and possible condemnation on the world stage. I'm sure you can see the implications."

"What the fuck?" Daley heard Tanner mutter behind him.

"Therefore," Dempsey continued, "you must never discuss the details of this mission with anyone else, under penalty of law."

"What?" someone else blurted out.

"This mission is classified Top Secret. If you reveal what happened, you can and will be court martialed. I'm not kidding, men. This is serious business."

"What border?" Sweet asked quietly, standing a few feet from Daley.

"These guys went into Cambodia to get the POWs," a guy named Hicks explained.

"So?" Sweet remained confused.

"We ain't allowed to do that."

"The gooks do it," Sweet pointed out.

"Yeah, but we ain't gooks." Hicks' explanation was as clear as anything else going on, so Sweet shut up.

Up front Major Dempsey had opened his briefcase, leaning it against the front glacis of the one-three track for support. He pulled out a sheaf of printed forms and handed half to Lieutenant Carr, half to Lieutenant Jones. "These are non-disclosure forms," Dempsey announced loudly. "I'll need every one of you to sign and date the form and return it to me ASAP. Lieutenants, would you pass them out."

"Are you shittin' me?" Griffin mumbled somewhere in the back. Dempsey, if he heard the remark, chose to ignore it. Daley took a form from Lieutenant Jones and quickly perused it. It was boiler-plate, filled with dire warnings about failure to comply. Daley, as a member of Military Intelligence, had signed such forms before, so he wasn't too upset about it. Others, however, were voicing their displeasure as they read the forms, albeit in low voices they hoped Dempsey wouldn't hear.

"You got any pens, sir?" Tanner asked Dempsey with pretended innocence.

"Get your own, Tanner," Stagakis said angrily. "I seen you writing letters, so I know you got one." Some of the mech guys went inside their tracks to rummage around in their personal gear. Daley had a cheap ballpoint in his shirt pocket and pulled it out to sign with. Then he noticed Ky and Sung, each holding a form and looking at him questioningly.

"Ky and Sung don't speak English, sir," Daley informed Dempsey.

"Have them sign it anyway," Dempsey told him imperiously. Daley started to object, but recognized the futility of bucking Army bureaucracy. He explained to Ky what the form was, and gestured to Sung to just sign his name.

"Specialist. . . Daley, is it?" Dempsey said to him. "Would you gather up the forms for me?" It wasn't a request, it was an order, so Daley complied. As he took the forms from the other men, he suppressed a smile when he noticed that several of the forms were signed by Mickey Mouse. He buried those at the bottom of the stack before handing all of them to Dempsey.

Without looking up from his briefcase as he stuffed the damp forms inside and latched it shut, Dempsey said, "Lieutenants, you probably should get your men across now, before it gets dark." Both Jones and Carr quickly turned away, but Daley saw the flash of anger in both men's eyes. "Oh, and have Captain Taylor and that Korean on this first crossing with me. We need to get back to Division Headquarters."

Lieutenant Carr turned back toward Dempsey and asked, while obviously trying to suppress the sarcasm in his voice, "May we send the wounded over on the first trip, also, sir?"

"I suppose."

They didn't offer to help Dempsey back down the bank to the landing craft, and Daley noted with satisfaction that the major slipped a couple times, one time landing hard on his butt in the mud while holding the briefcase high in the air. There was plenty of assistance for Taylor and the other wounded. Sung took off his borrowed pack and gear, and handed the M-16 to Sergeant Stagakis before he, too, made his way down to the landing craft. Kessler, claiming his ankle was much better now, was allowed to wait for the final withdrawal.

With shouted orders, Carr and Samples began the delicate task of bringing the first of the metal monsters down the sloping bank to board the landing craft. The sailors unwound a thick hawser with a metal hook on the end, handing it to the soldiers to pull from a huge motorized winch. The soldiers dragged it up the slope, took it around a stout tree, and secured it to the tow hook on the back of the one-three. Daley watched as the driver eased the behemoth onto the highest PSP and guided it slowly down the ramp while the hawser squealed against the tree, causing the limbs to sway precariously as it slowed the descent. After several tense minutes and anxious shouting of commands, the track made it onto the loading ramp and nosed inside the landing craft. There was only room for a single APC, so the hawser was retrieved, the ramp was raised, and with difficulty the landing craft was backed off the shore and turned around. The same process, in reverse, would have to be completed on the other side. Meanwhile, Jones ordered the CRIP platoon to spread out in a semi-circle around the loading ramp to provide security while they waited for the other two to be transported. Daley, Ky, and several of the mech platoon members joined the hasty defensive perimeter.

Daley found a clump of bushes to provide some concealment, if not cover, and sat down on the wet ground, no longer concerned about such mundane considerations as comfort. He had left his pack in the one-three track, but the mech guys had passed out handfuls of 5.56mm ammo from their wealth of ammo cans, so Daley began pushing the rounds into some empty magazines he pulled from the cargo pockets of his pants. Ky, having happily given up the rifle and pack he had been carrying, squatted down beside him on his left. One of the mech guys, a buck sergeant with a radio on his back, knelt down on his right.

"You're Daley, right?" the man enquired. He looked Hispanic, but had no accent.

Daley nodded, wincing as he jammed his finger on the sharp edge of a magazine.

"I'm Jesse Rael," the guy said. "Arty FO."

"Ah," Daley said in understanding. He had thought Rael was an RTO, but it was unusual that a sergeant would fill that position. An artillery forward observer, however, could easily be a sergeant.

"I heard you speak Vietnamese. Where'd you learn that?"

"Army language school," Daley replied. "Near Ft. Bliss."

"I thought the language school was in California?"

"Everything but Vietnamese, yeah," Daley explained. "The other languages are in Monterey and San Francisco."

"That must be good duty," Rael commented.

"Not bad," Daley admitted. "Better than here."

"Anything's better than here. Hell, Fort Sill sucked big hairy donkey dicks, but it was better than here."

Daley chuckled. "Know what you mean. So you called in the arty back there?"

"Yeah," Rael replied, like it was no big deal. "How come you guys didn't request any?"

"We don't have an FO," Daley explained, knowing that wasn't really a good excuse, "and we weren't exactly sure where we were, either. Our Kit Carson scout had stolen our maps, and we just found them about an hour before you guys got there."

"Lucky for you we showed up. Man, tracks do not belong in this area. I was thinking they'd have to bring in a Skycrane to haul out asses out of here."

"Well, we're sure glad you made it. We were running out of ammo."

"So, what'd you guys do to piss off the gooks so bad? I mean, besides rescuing those two POWs."

"They had this old French fort out in the jungle," Daley told him, sliding a full magazine into his bandolier. "We took the fort, killed one of their officers, and freed Sung and Captain Taylor. Then they attacked the fort last night, and we killed a bunch more of them. We snuck out of the fort early this morning, and left booby traps that blew up in their faces when they retook the fort. I guess they didn't like being fucked with in their own backyard."

"And the fort was in Cambodia?"

"Yeah, but we didn't know that at first. See, Ky, here, told me about the fort, but he can't read a map, so he had to take us there. When Dodie, the Kit Carson scout, stole our maps, we couldn't tell for sure where we were."

"Great story to tell your kids someday, but you can't."

Daley made a face. "That asshole major. Fuck him if he can't take a joke."

"Hey, what'll they do to us if we tell anyone, send us to Viet Nam?"

"Leavenworth, more like it," Daley warned him. "Those fuckers get serious about classified information."

Rael started to say something, but was distracted by a call on his radio. He stood up and strolled in a circle while he apparently gave a situation report. Daley finished loading magazines and looked out across the sea of grass with its scattered islands of trees. He glanced over at Ky, and saw the young man's eyes were closed. With his arms wrapped around his knees, Ky was sleeping in a squat, somehow able to retain his balance at the same time. Daley admired his skill. After Rael finished his radio conversation, he wandered off toward the two remaining APCs. Daley stood up to stretch and try to stay awake. Across the river he could see that the first track had just made it to the top of the bank, and the sailors were reeling in the hawser in preparation for raising the ramp and coming back over. Daley checked his watch, and estimated how long it would take to get the other two tracks across. It would be getting close to dark by then, and that was if everything went smoothly, which it rarely did.

As it happened, the transfer of the second track went more quickly than the first, and the boat quickly returned and prepared to take on the last track and the remaining men. The rain, which had been intermittent all afternoon, swelled to a heavy shower and then stopped entirely. Daley had gotten some C-rations from the mech guys and woke Ky up to share them. While the third track was maneuvered into position and secured with the hawser, Rael came back and knelt down next to them.

"Think I could go to the language school if I re-upped?" he asked.

"I don't know," Daley said. "You have to take a language aptitude test. What language would you want?"

"I already speak a little Spanish, from my folks, you know, but I'd like to learn German. I could see being stationed there, drinking good German beer and eating schnitzel."

"Worth a shot," Daley told him. "If you learned German, they probably wouldn't send you back here. Probably." They both laughed, knowing how the Army often did things that didn't make sense.

Daley saw the track starting the dangerous descent down the slope to the landing craft, and then heard the two hollow "plonk" sounds from somewhere off to the west.

"Mortars!" Rael yelled, and Daley, like everyone else, dived to the ground and lay as flat as he could. After a few seconds, the mortar rounds exploded behind him. One hit the riverbank about fifty yards south of the landing craft, and the other burst in the water on the other side.

"Fire mission! Fire mission!" Rael was yelling into his radio handset. Daley raised his head and heard two more mortar rounds being launched. He closed his eyes and tried to interpret the sounds to determine what direction they had come from, and then pointed. Rael nodded and began giving instructions and coordinates. The second two mortar rounds fell in front of the American perimeter, detonating harmlessly in the wet grass. "Overcompensated," Rael said critically.

A split second later Daley heard a roaring rush overhead just before a sequence of huge explosions shook the ground, ripping up grass and trees a couple hundred yards to his front. Next to him Rael was calling in corrections, and more artillery rounds shattered the air and blasted the ground on either side of the trail they had traveled earlier. The barrage was far heavier and louder than the one Daley had seen back at the bunker complex, and he could feel the earth tremble beneath him as the blasts buffeted his ears. The volcanic eruptions of the artillery rounds stretched from north to south, creating a virtual wall of fire and smoke that pulsated with deadly intensity. One large explosion was rapidly followed by a series of smaller detonations, and Rael noted with great satisfaction,

"Secondaries!" Daley guessed that meant the American round had caused enemy ammo to explode.

The storm of fiery bursts and smoke ravaged the land for several minutes, and then suddenly tapered off and ceased. Daley's ears were ringing. The smoke settled and slowly drifted away. There were no more mortar rounds launched. Daley glanced back and saw that the last track had just made it into the landing craft.

"Let's go!" Sergeant Stagakis bellowed from somewhere.

"Don't have to ask me twice," Rael said as he scrambled to his feet along with Daley and Ky. All the remaining soldiers ran to the bank and stumbled and slid down the muddy slope, hurrying to get into the landing craft and not be left behind. Stagakis and Samples did a quick head count, then signaled to Ensign McMichaels that all were accounted for. As Daley watched the loading ramp rise and lock into place, he felt safe for the first time in days. It was a great feeling.

TWENTY-TWO

"So, back to your day job, huh?" Ortiz asked with a smile. He and Daley were sitting on some sandbags in Fire Support Base Haskell, just soaking up some rays. Ky was sprawled on a nearby cot, lightly snoring.

"Guess so," Daley replied without enthusiasm. They had been brought back to Haskell by truck yesterday evening, arriving just as it started to get dark. They had all been allowed to sleep while other soldiers stood guard, and ate a big, if uninspiring, breakfast at the mess hall. Everyone spent an hour thoroughly cleaning and oiling their weapons, and loading up spare magazines. Daley returned his borrowed equipment, washed and shaved, put on a clean uniform, and repacked the duffle he had brought from the division base camp. Sergeant Stagakis told him a jeep would be coming later to take him and Ky back. After that, it was simply the standard Army "hurry up and wait."

"Must be nice," Ortiz said. "Sleeping in a cot every night, three meals a day at the mess hall, easy access to the PX. I could live with that."

Daley shrugged. "It's okay," he admitted, "but it gets boring. Interrogate prisoners and Chieu Hois every morning, write up reports every afternoon."

"Boring, huh?" Sergeant Stagakis said from right behind him. Daley hadn't heard the platoon sergeant approach. "Not exciting like with us, having gooks shoot at you and living in the mud?" Stagakis sat down beside him, chewing a large wad of gum. Daley noticed the smell of alcohol was not entirely masked by the spearmint.

"Well, it was interesting," Daley told him. "Not fun, for sure, but interesting."

"Think you'd like to do shit like that some more?" Stagakis eyed him curiously.

"I wouldn't mind," Daley told him, surprising even himself with the admission.

"Well," Stagakis said, looking up at the sky, "since we lost Dodie, we ain't got a Kit Carson scout and can't talk to the locals like we usually do. I'm thinkin', maybe you'd be okay with being op-conned to the CRIP for a while, help us out."

Now Daley was really surprised. In a perverse way he had enjoyed working with these hardened infantrymen, but he had felt like an outsider, someone not quite up to their standards of toughness. To be asked to join them meant a lot to him, and gave him a real sense of confidence that he had previously been lacking. He glanced over at Ky, still asleep on the cot, and felt like the young man was a good friend now.

"What about Ky? Could he come, too?"

"Don't see why not?" Stagakis said genially. "We've got a slot for a scout."

"How would that work, though? I mean, I'm a 96B, assigned to MI."

"You'd have to request it, I guess. I heard that your major is coming out to get you two today, you could ask him then. We can even get your MOS changed, if you want. You do ninety days OJT as an eleven bravo, and we can do the paperwork."

On the job training. Daley thought about that. Three months with CRIP and he could officially be an infantryman. Maybe even get a Combat Infantryman's Badge. Of course, he could also get shot. But then, he could also be killed by a rocket or mortar at the base camp. The possibilities and alternatives swirled through his brain. On the one hand, there was the relatively soft life of an interrogator in a major base camp, and on the other hand the hard life of an infantryman in the field, risking that life every day. Boredom versus excitement, possibly deadly excitement. His fellow interrogators were okay, but distant. These guys in the CRIP had already become close friends, people he enjoyed being with.

"We could sure use you," Ortiz added helpfully.

"Hey, Daley." Tanner came jogging up, looking slightly annoyed, as usual. "LT wants to see you over at the company headquarters." He pointed at an above-ground bunker made of ammo boxes topped by a section of sand-bagged corrugated metal culvert about fifty meters away. "He said you need to look presentable, whatever the fuck that means."

Daley stood up, and Stagakis looked him up and down. He tugged Daley's shirt to straighten it. "You look okay," the sergeant said. "Put your boonie hat on, though, and button all your pockets."

Daley did as instructed as he hurried over to the bunker. Some of the dirt-filled wooden ammo boxes that formed the walls had gaps between them to provide light and ventilation, and the amateurishly-constructed wooden door was wide open. Daley stuck his head in the door and saw Lieutenant Jones leaning over a clerk who was typing at a small portable wooden desk. Despite the windows, the air in the hut was stifling, and sweat beaded on the faces of both the men. Jones looked up as Daley blocked some of the light coming in through the door.

"There you are," Jones said in greeting. "Come on, we've got to go see the commander." Daley stepped back to let Jones exit the bunker and then followed him at a resolute pace as they weaved around tents and vehicles toward the center of the fire support base. They stopped at the entrance to a large house-shaped tent with the sides rolled up a couple feet, and PSP laid inside to cover the mud. Jones stuck his head in for a second, then stepped through the flaps and motioned for Daley to follow. A canvas partition created a small anteroom just inside the doorway, occupied by a slight blond lieutenant sitting behind a gray metal desk. The young man, whose name tape said LEWIS, held up the palm of his hand to tell them to wait, then stood up and went to the partition, which was made of two overlapping pieces of dark green canvas. Pushing through the split, Daley heard the guy announce, "They're here."

The lieutenant pulled the canvas back like a curtain and told Daley and Jones, "They're waiting for you." There was a slightly accusatory tone that Daley took personally. Jones pushed by Lewis, and Daley followed, giving the blond lieutenant as wide a berth as possible. Past the curtain was a much larger section of the tent, with a number of folding chairs and an easel. There were also a number of officers, and Daley unconsciously came to attention.

He immediately recognized his own commander, Major Wheeler, who smiled at him and nodded. Wheeler was standing, looking a little uncomfortable. Seated in a semi-circle were three men. On the left was another major, an average-looking guy whose name tape read HOWARD. Next to him was a lieutenant colonel named Thompson. Even though he was seated, Daley could tell that Thompson was tall, with black curly hair and blue eyes. He recognized the name as belonging to the CRIP's battalion commander. Thompson sat ramrod straight, and the hand resting on his knee had a large class ring on it. The third man wore the eagle of a full colonel, and his nametag indicated he was named Granville. He was short and a little pudgy, with thinning brown hair brushed across his head to hide a receding hairline.

Granville stood up and held out his hand to Jones. "Lieutenant Jones, glad to finally meet you." The two men shook hands, and then the colonel held his hand out to Daley. "Specialist Daley, I'm Colonel Granville, the brigade commander here. I've heard a lot about you."

"Sir," Daley acknowledged, shaking the man's hand. Thompson and Howard also stood, out of respect for their superior, but didn't offer their hands. Lieutenant Lewis, who had followed Jones and Daley into this meeting room, edged over to stand beside Major Howard.

"Sit, sit," Granville said, waving his hands toward the chairs. "I want to hear all about this mission you were on." The chairs were quickly rearranged in a circle, and Daley dragged a chair over to sit between Jones and Major Wheeler. Wheeler took a moment during the shuffling to shake Daley's hand and give him an approving wink.

Once everyone was settled, Granville looked at Daley. "So you interrogated a Viet Cong defector, I understand, and he told you about this fort."

"Yes, sir," Daley responded nervously. "He told me about the fort, and thought he had seen a Chinese and a Russian advisor. As it turned out, they were actually a Korean soldier and an Australian captain."

"Yes, yes, so I hear. And you volunteered to escort this defector while he was leading Lieutenant Jones and his men to the fort."

"Yes, sir," Daley said, fudging the truth a little. "Ky, the Chieu Hoi, doesn't speak any English, and can't read a map, so I went along to translate."

Granville turned to Jones. "Tell me how the mission went. What happened?"

Jones gave a detailed report, almost hour by hour, of the patrol crossing the river, missing a turn, bivouacking in the bunker complex, finding and seizing the fort, defending the fort, and then escaping back to the bunker complex. Understandably, he minimized any mistakes that might be attributed to him, and glossed over the fact that they had been in Cambodia in violation of Lieutenant Colonel Thompson's orders. He emphasized the successful rescue of the two allied POWs and praised the bravery and competence of all the men under him, even singling out Daley and Ky.

Granville absorbed the story with interest, occasionally asking pertinent questions and commenting favorably on what had occurred. Finally he directed his attention back to Daley.

"So, Specialist, I take it this was your first experience in the field."

"Yes, sir," Daley confirmed.

"And Lieutenant Jones says you performed admirably, as well as any of his trained infantrymen."

Daley had no response to that and remained silent.

"Major Wheeler," Granville said suddenly, "is Specialist Daley due for promotion?"

Wheeler, caught off guard, hesitated before saying, "Uh, I'm not sure."

"Well, I'd recommend he be made sergeant as soon as possible. Don't you agree?"

"Yes, sir," Wheeler toadied. "I'll look into that."

Turning back to Daley, Granville asked, "Would that be okay with you?"

"Certainly, sir," Daley stammered.

"And is there any other way we can reward you for your exemplary service with CRIP?"

Without thinking about it, Daley found himself saying, "Actually, sir, would it be possible for me to transfer to CRIP, along with Ky?"

Granville was clearly not expecting this, and sat back in astonishment. "You want to join CRIP?"

"Yes, sir, if Lieutenant Jones will have me." He glanced to the side and saw the look of surprise on Jones' face.

"That'd be great," Jones finally managed to say. "We need someone who speaks Vietnamese. And Specialist Daley has demonstrated that he is an excellent infantryman."

"Major Wheeler, would that work for you?" Granville asked.

"Certainly, sir. If he's needed here, then that will be fine." Daley wasn't sure if Wheeler really believed that, or was simply caving in to higher authority. Whatever the reason, he was pleased.

"Do you have any objections, Rance?" Granville asked Thompson in a tone that precluded a positive response.

"Great idea, sir," Thompson said through gritted teeth. "Lieutenant Lewis, will you get with Major Wheeler and work out the details?"

"Right away, sir," Lewis answered.

Colonel Granville stood up abruptly, and the rest of them hastily followed his lead.

"Okay, gentlemen, I'll leave you to it. Lieutenant Jones, Specialist Daly, it was good to meet you. Keep up the good work." And with that he bulled his way out of the tent.

There was an awkward silence. Daley wasn't sure what the protocol was in this kind of situation. Outside they heard a helicopter, presumably Colonel Granville's, spooling up. Lieutenant Colonel Thompson took that sound as his cue.

"Major Wheeler, thank you for coming, and thank you for sending Specialist Daley to us. And Specialist Daley, thanks for your invaluable support over the last few days, and welcome to my battalion. Lieutenant Lewis, why don't you take them over to the orderly room and get the paperwork squared away. Lieutenant Jones, if you'll wait, we need to talk."

Daley followed Lewis and Meyer out of the tent and back to the company headquarters bunker, his mind a turmoil of emotion. He was pleased by the prospect of an early promotion to sergeant, and proud that he had been allowed to join the CRIP platoon. On the other hand, he worried that he had not thought this commitment all the way through, and wondered if he had made a serious mistake just now. Most grunts, he knew, were trying to get out of the field to cushier base camp jobs, while here he was volunteering to leave such a position and go out into the boonies. Was he deluding himself? Oh, well, he thought, what's done is done.

EPILOGUE

Because Thompson and Major Howard remained standing, Lieutenant Jones did as well. He wasn't quite at attention, but he was definitely not at ease. Thompson was giving him a hard stare while he waited for Wheeler, Lewis, and Daley to get out of earshot.

"John," the colonel said without a bit of warmth, "you have put me in an awkward position."

"Sir?" Jones wasn't sure what Thompson meant specifically, but it didn't sound promising.

"Colonel Granville wants me to put you in for a medal, but there are problems with that. First and foremost, you disobeyed my direct orders by continuing to the fort without your maps. Granted, the end result, although unexpected, was more than I had hoped for. But again, it involved crossing the border into a neutral country, potentially involving us in an international incident that would have tarnished the reputation of almost everyone in your chain of command. Frankly, I'm not all that pleased with your leadership skills, and I think you were far more lucky than good. And I don't think you have set a good example for the rest of your people in the Army. I just don't know." Thompson shook his head slowly with a frown.

"Sir, if I could explain. . ." Jones began, but Thompson held his hand up to stop him.

"I don't want to hear it. You'll just make it worse. I'd like to relieve you of command, but because Colonel Granville doesn't know the full story and therefore thinks highly of you, I can't really do that. You'll remain in command of the CRIP platoon, at least for now, but I will be keeping you on a very short leash. Do you understand?"

"Yes, sir," Jones answered.

"To keep Granville happy, I'll put you in for an Arcom, but that's it." Arcom was short for Army Commendation Medal, an award that many soldiers referred to as the Perfect Attendance Award, since it was received by virtually every soldier who completed a tour without being charged with a crime.

"Thank you, sir," Jones said with obvious insincerity.

"You're dismissed." Thompson's eyes were flashing because he recognized the subtle insubordination in Jones' tone, but couldn't pursue it.

Jones snapped to attention and saluted, then did a parade-ground about-face and marched out of the tent.

"Sorry-ass black bastard," Thompson muttered angrily.

Major Howard nodded in agreement. "He'll never make general, that's for sure."

"Damn good thing," Thompson said. "Let's hope none of them do, or the Army's in real trouble."

Made in United States
Orlando, FL
02 September 2024